RED RANGE

A Wild Western Adventure

Drew Ford
PUBLISHER/EDITOR-IN-CHIEF

BOOK DESIGN/EDITORIAL CONSULTANT Jon B. Cooke

PROOFREADER Rob Smentek

IDW®

Ted Adams, CEO & PUBLISHER
Greg Goldstein, PRESIDENT & COO
Robbie Robbins, EVP/SR. GRAPHIC ARTIST
Chris Ryall, CHIEF CREATIVE OFFICER
David Hedgecock, EDITOR-IN-CHIEF
Laurie Windrow, SENIOR VP OF SALES & MARKETING
Matthew Ruzicka, CPA, CHIEF FINANCIAL OFFICER
Lorelei Bunjes, VP OF DIGITAL SERVICES
Jerry Bennington, VP OF NEW PRODUCT DEVELOPMENT

ISBN: 978-1-63140-994-3 | 20 19 18 17   1 2 3 4
June 2017. First Printing. All Rights Reserved.
Red Range: A Wild Western Adventure ©1999-2017 Joe R. Lansdale.
"I Could Eat a Horse" ©2017 Sam J. Glanzman
"When Old is New and New Old" ©2017 Richard Klaw
"Beneath the Valley of the Klan Busters" and "A Brief History of Cowboys & Dinosaurs"
©2017 Stephen R. Bissette

IT'S ALIVE PRESENTS

RED RANGE

JOE R. LANSDALE
Creator & Writer

SAM J. GLANZMAN
Illustrator

JORGE BLANCO & JOK
Colorists

DOUGLAS POTTER
Letterer

RICHARD KLAW
Original Edition Editor

DREW FORD
New Edition Editor

A Wild Western Adventure

RICHARD KLAW
Introduction

STEPHEN R. BISSETTE
(A Sort of) Afterword

PLUS: Sam Glanzman's "I Could Eat a Horse!"

With additional material by Stephen R. Bissette and Jon B. Cooke

RED RANGE

TABLE OF CONTENTS

WHEN OLD IS NEW AND NEW IS OLD

Introduction by Richard Klaw

"You got anger and you got misery. Thing to do is put them to work."
Rufus Range (a.k.a. The Red Mask)

Joe Lansdale and Sam Glanzman get it. The seem-ingly-gratuitous violence, overt racism, and disturbing imagery, all which abound in *Red Range*, are remarkable representations of both post-Civil War and contempo-rary 21st century America. Course, when Joe wrote this in the waning years of the last century, the world seemed to be moving away from the violence and racism of previous times. We were less than a decade from electing our first African-American president and violent crime rates were near all-time lows. The overt racist groups had scurried back into their holes. But, as Joe is apt to do, he revealed a terrible underbelly of society.

Joe was already doing these types of stories across numerous genres and in several mediums for over a decade when, while promoting my wares at the 1993 Aggiecon in College Station, Texas, I asked Joe if he'd like to contribute to my next anthology, *Creature Features*. He agreed and thus began our long creative and personal friendship.

Over the next year, we spent many hours on the phone discussing ideas. When Joe broached the concept of a horror comics anthology featuring prose writers, I, as I'm apt to do, leapt without looking into the fray, readily agree-ing to co-edit the book. *Weird Business*, which grew from a 100-page concept to a 420-page, 23-story, 56-creator behemoth, and included contributions from Neal Barrett, Jr., Robert Bloch, Poppy Z. Brite, Nancy Collins, Charles de Lint, Pia Guerra, Phil Hester, Michael Lark, Michael Moorcock, Ted Nai-feh, Norman Partridge, John Picacio, Howard Waldrop, F. Paul Wilson, and Roger Zelazny, led directly to the creation of Mojo Press with Ben Ostrander

as publisher and me as managing editor. It was during those lengthy talks that the idea of *Red Range* emerged.

Largely thanks to Joe's work with Timothy Truman on titles such as *Jonah Hex* and *The Lone Ranger*, and the Garth Ennis/Steve Dillon *Preacher* series, horror Western comics had become a minor-sensation in the mid-'90s. Joe wanted to elevate what he was doing in the corporate-owned projects into something that combined his loves of Westerns, horror, and pulps, but wouldn't flinch away from the inherent violence and rampant racism of that era. In other words, a dystopic Western, Lansdale-style.

I remember the shock and disgust reading that first page in the script. It was so… visceral. I hadn't seen something like that outside of some amateur comics. But, unlike most of those inferior, crude predecessors, Joe along with Sam used violence that bordered on the absurd as an insightful examination of the horrors of the age.

Above: *Weird Business* and *Creature Features*, two lively comics anthologies from Mojo Press. **Top right:** Cover of the Mojo edition of *Red Range*, from a painting by N.C. Wyeth.

Joe created a masked African-American hero, still a relative-rarity in comics even now, bent on vengeance—definitely not a comic book rarity of any time. Unlike most in any medium, Rufus Range confronts racism directly. Under Joe's expert tutelage, what first appeared as a shallow über-violent, humorous tale actually confronted uncomfortable issues in a refreshingly direct manner.

Red Range TM & © Joe R. Lansdale.
Weird Business and *Creature Features* TM & © the respective copyright holder.

Sam came to the project through Truman, who we had commissioned to produce the cover to my own weird Western anthology, *Wild West Show*. Hearing about the book, Sam reached out to Mojo publisher Ben Ostrander with "I Could Eat a Horse!" We both loved the silent work and decided to include the tale within the anthology. I'm glad to see it reprinted here.

Silence describes my relationship with Sam. I've never spoken with the great artist. All of his interactions regarding *Red Range* went through either Joe or Ben. Thankfully, except for one weird couple of weeks, it all went without a hitch. In the middle of the project, Sam disappeared. For a few weeks, no one knew where he was. Apparently, he decided to ride his Harley from upstate New York to Kansas City with nary a word to anyone. It all worked out just fine. Being a pro, Sam turned everything in on time. His excellent craftsmanship deftly mastered and even elevated the story beyond Joe's initial vision.

As I write this, some two weeks into the Trump Administration, it's become obvious that the messages and lessons from a nearly 20-year-old graphic novel resonate today. The purveyors of racism and the violence that typically accompany it now feel safe to scurry from the darkness of their hidey-holes and into the national spotlight. The threat of ostracization to people of color, non-Christians, LBGTQ, and women is higher now than any point this century.

RED RANGE
A WILD WESTERN ADVENTURE

Red Range TM & © Joe R. Lansdale.

Above: Title panel from the black-&-white edition of *Red Range*, published by Mojo Press in 1999. Art by Sam Glanzman.

WILD WEST
SHOW
MO
JO
PRESS
$5.95

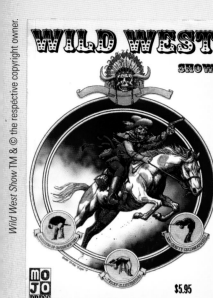

I had forgotten those profound bits before I re-visited *Red Range*. It'd been about 15 years since I looked at the book. All I could really recall was that first page, Glanzman's amazing art, a few of the action sequences, and, of course, that it was pretty damn funny. As I lost myself in the story, the power of Lansdale's message really hit me. Not that it's subtle in any way. Subtlety is not always one of Joe's strengths. And the ending, as it did when I first read it, really shocked me.

This edition gives the under-appreciated Lansdale story a minor work over, replete with color (the original was in black & white), the previously mentioned Glanzman story, and an astute afterword from Stephen R. Bissette. None of the original story or art was changed. After languishing in relative obscurity, I'm glad *Red Range* is finally available once again.

—***Rick Klaw***
Austin, Texas
February 1, 2017

Geek maven and optimistic curmudgeon, Richard Klaw's recent editorial works include The Apes of Wrath *(Tachyon Publications),* Rayguns Over Texas *(FACT), and* Chicken Fried Cthulhu *(Skelos), as well as the three Joe R. Lansdale Hap and Leonard titles from Tachyon. He co-founded the influential Mojo Press, one of the first publishers dedicated to both graphic novels and prose books for the general bookstore market. For the past 20 years, Klaw has provided countless reviews, essays, and fiction for a variety of publications, many of which were collected in* Geek Confidential: Echoes from the 21st Century *(MonkeyBrain). He lives in Austin, Texas with his patient wife, a perpetually confused dog, a pair of befuddled kittens, and an impressive collection of books.*

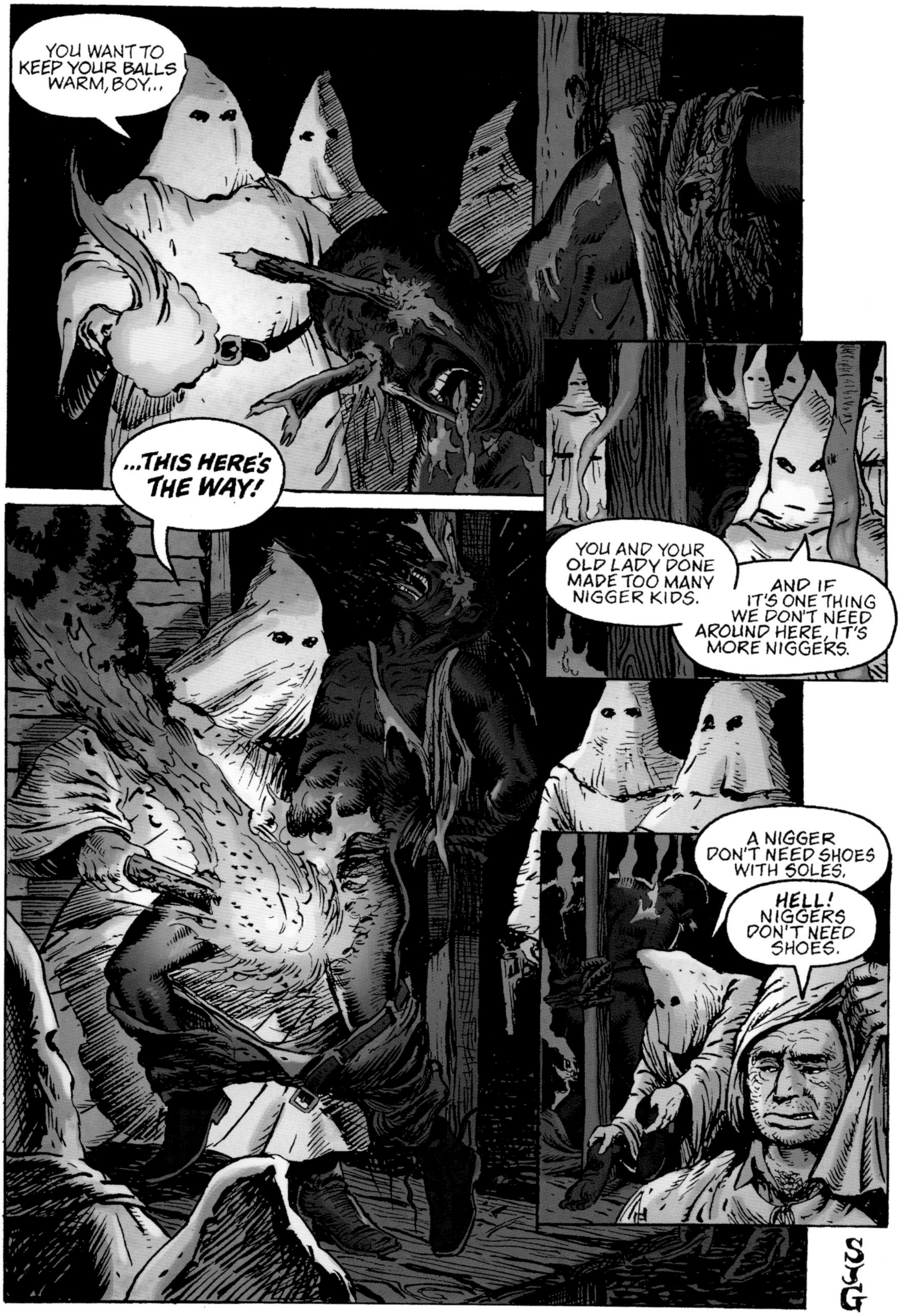
YOU WANT TO KEEP YOUR BALLS WARM, BOY...
...THIS HERE'S THE WAY!
YOU AND YOUR OLD LADY DONE MADE TOO MANY NIGGER KIDS.
AND IF IT'S ONE THING WE DON'T NEED AROUND HERE, IT'S MORE NIGGERS.
A NIGGER DON'T NEED SHOES WITH SOLES.
HELL! NIGGERS DON'T NEED SHOES.
SJG

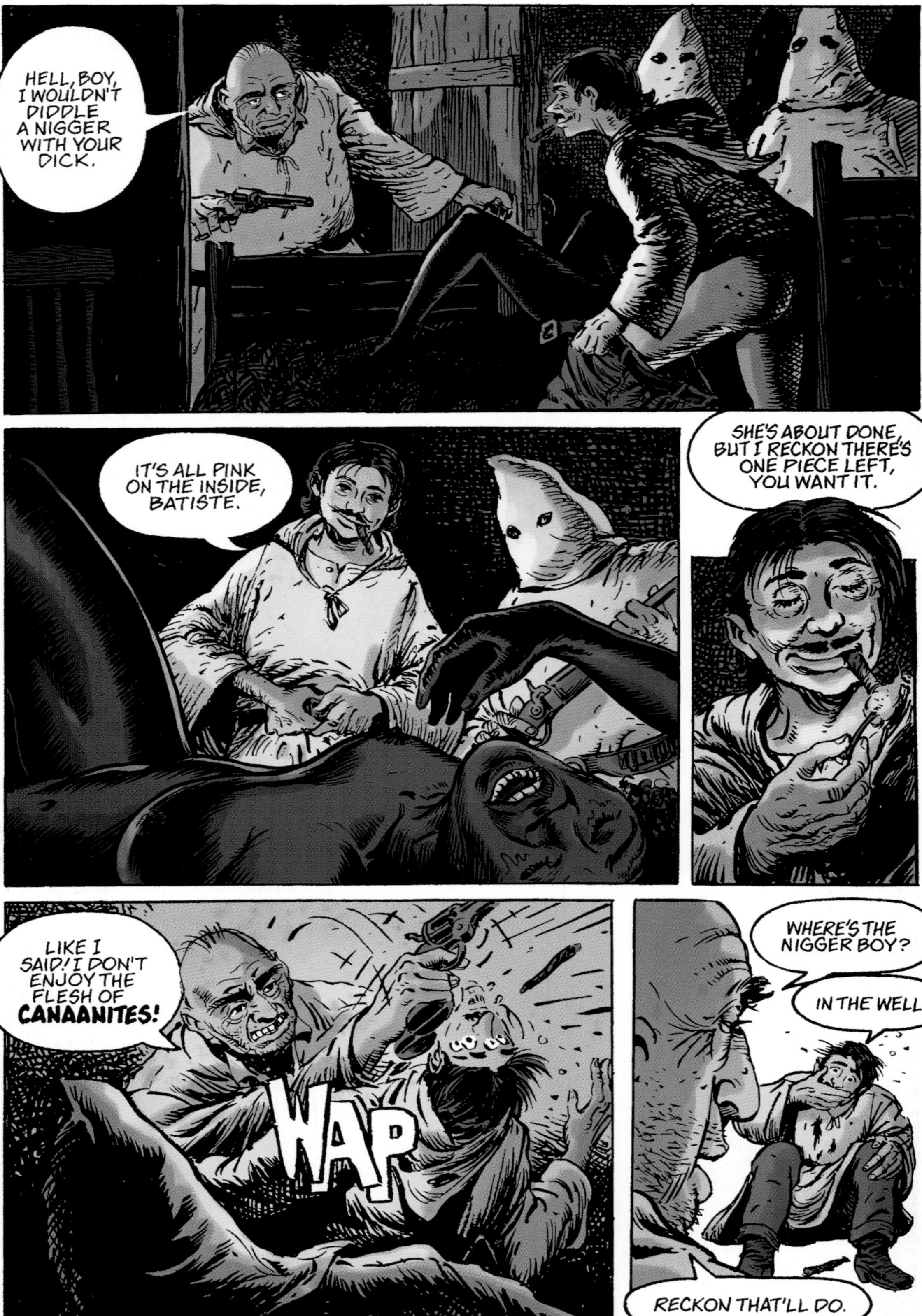
HELL, BOY, I WOULDN'T DIDDLE A NIGGER WITH YOUR DICK.
IT'S ALL PINK ON THE INSIDE, BATISTE.
SHE'S ABOUT DONE, BUT I RECKON THERE'S ONE PIECE LEFT, YOU WANT IT.
LIKE I SAID! I DON'T ENJOY THE FLESH OF **CANAANITES!**
WAP
WHERE'S THE NIGGER BOY?
IN THE WELL.
RECKON THAT'LL DO.

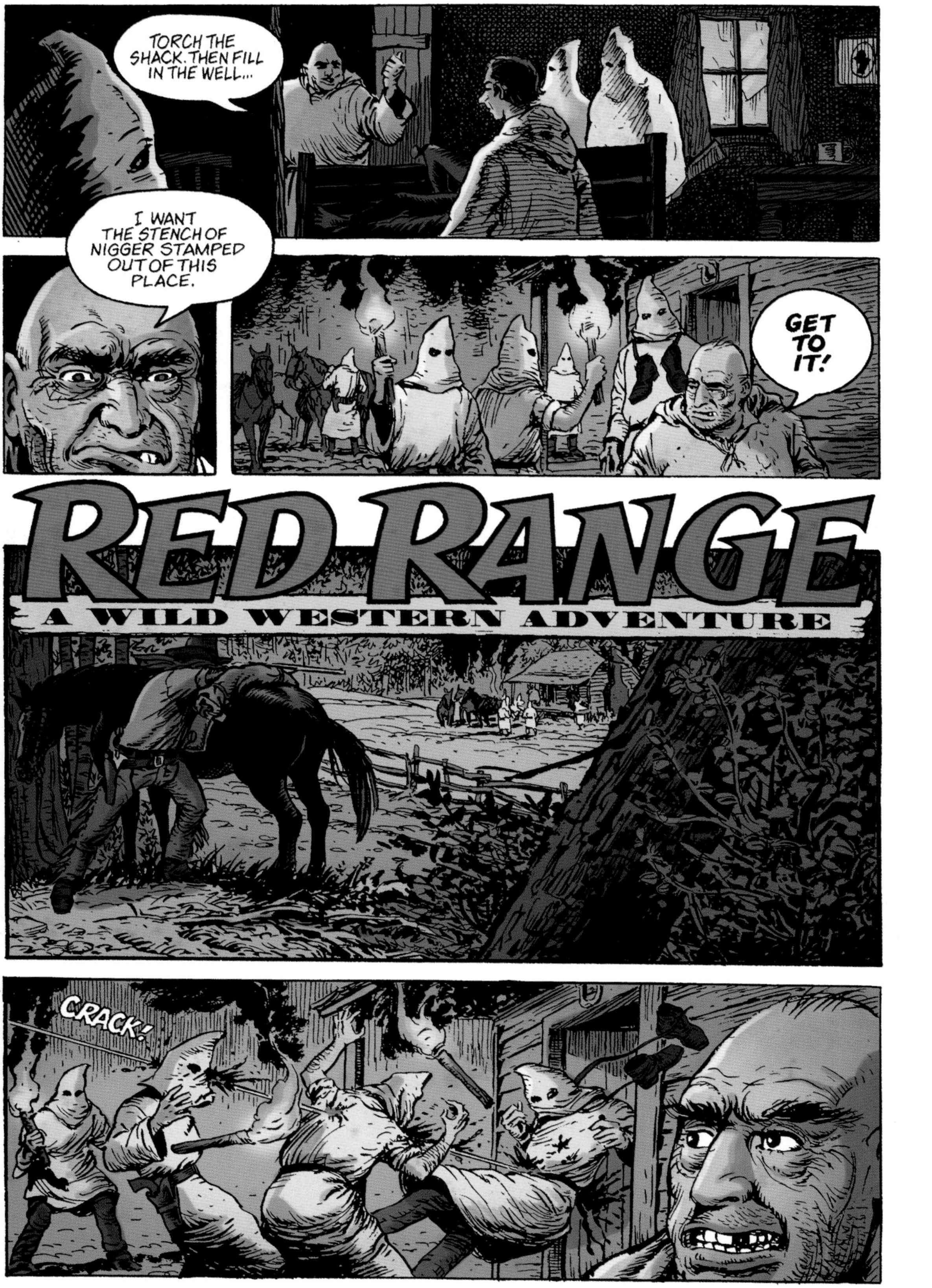
TORCH THE SHACK. THEN FILL IN THE WELL...
I WANT THE STENCH OF NIGGER STAMPED OUT OF THIS PLACE.
GET TO IT!
RED RANGE
A WILD WESTERN ADVENTURE
CRACK!

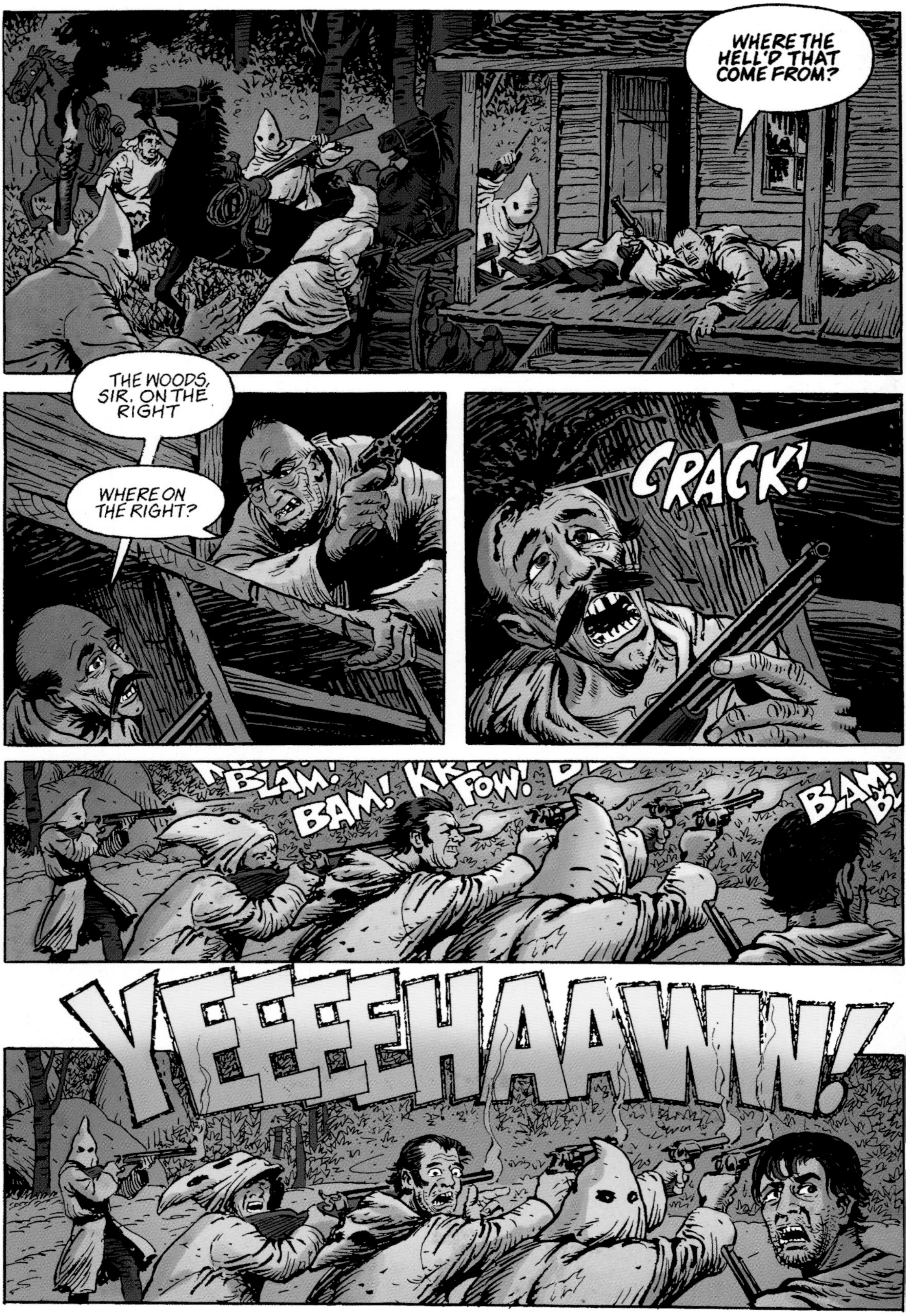
WHERE THE HELL'D THAT COME FROM?
THE WOODS, SIR. ON THE RIGHT
WHERE ON THE RIGHT?
CRACK!
BLAM!
BAM!
POW!
BAM!
YEEEEHAAWW!

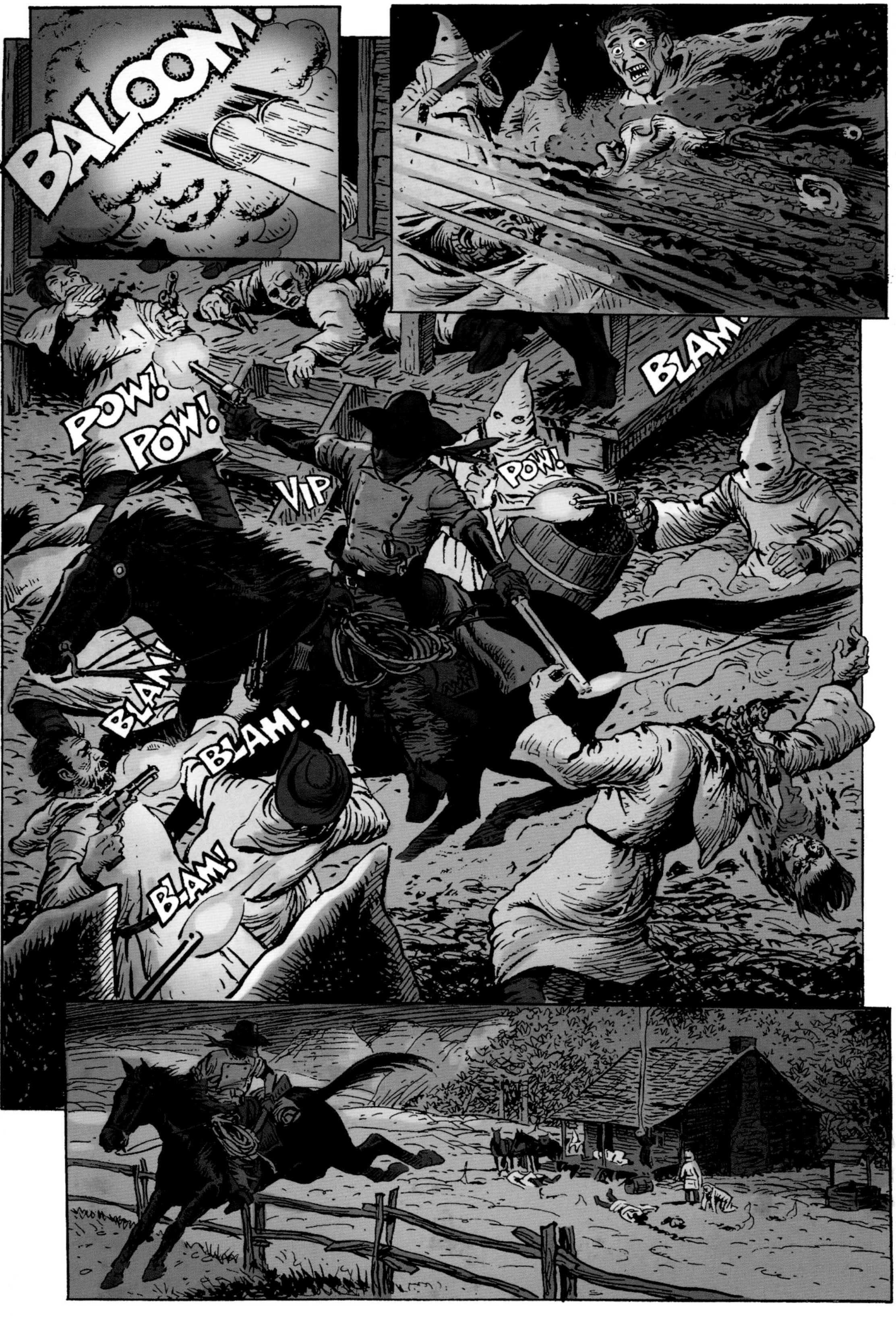
BALOOM!
POW! POW!
VIP
POW!
BLAM!
BLAM!
BLAM!
BLAM!

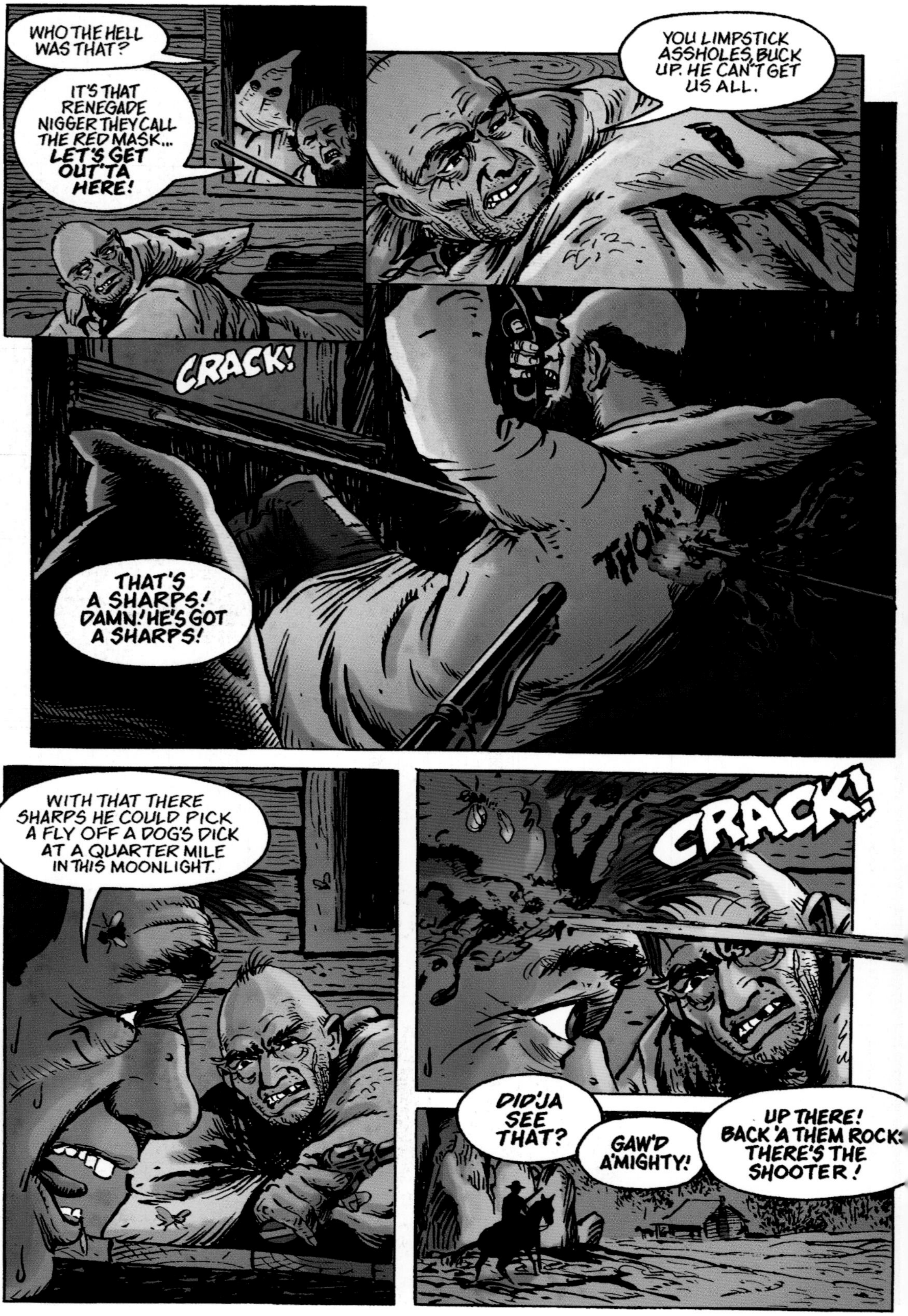
WHO THE HELL WAS THAT?
IT'S THAT RENEGADE NIGGER THEY CALL THE RED MASK... LET'S GET OUT'TA HERE!
YOU LIMPSTICK ASSHOLES, BUCK UP. HE CAN'T GET US ALL.
CRACK!
THOK!
THAT'S A SHARPS! DAMN! HE'S GOT A SHARPS!
WITH THAT THERE SHARPS HE COULD PICK A FLY OFF A DOG'S DICK AT A QUARTER MILE IN THIS MOONLIGHT.
CRACK!
DID'JA SEE THAT?
GAW'D A'MIGHTY!
UP THERE! BACK 'A THEM ROCKS! THERE'S THE SHOOTER!

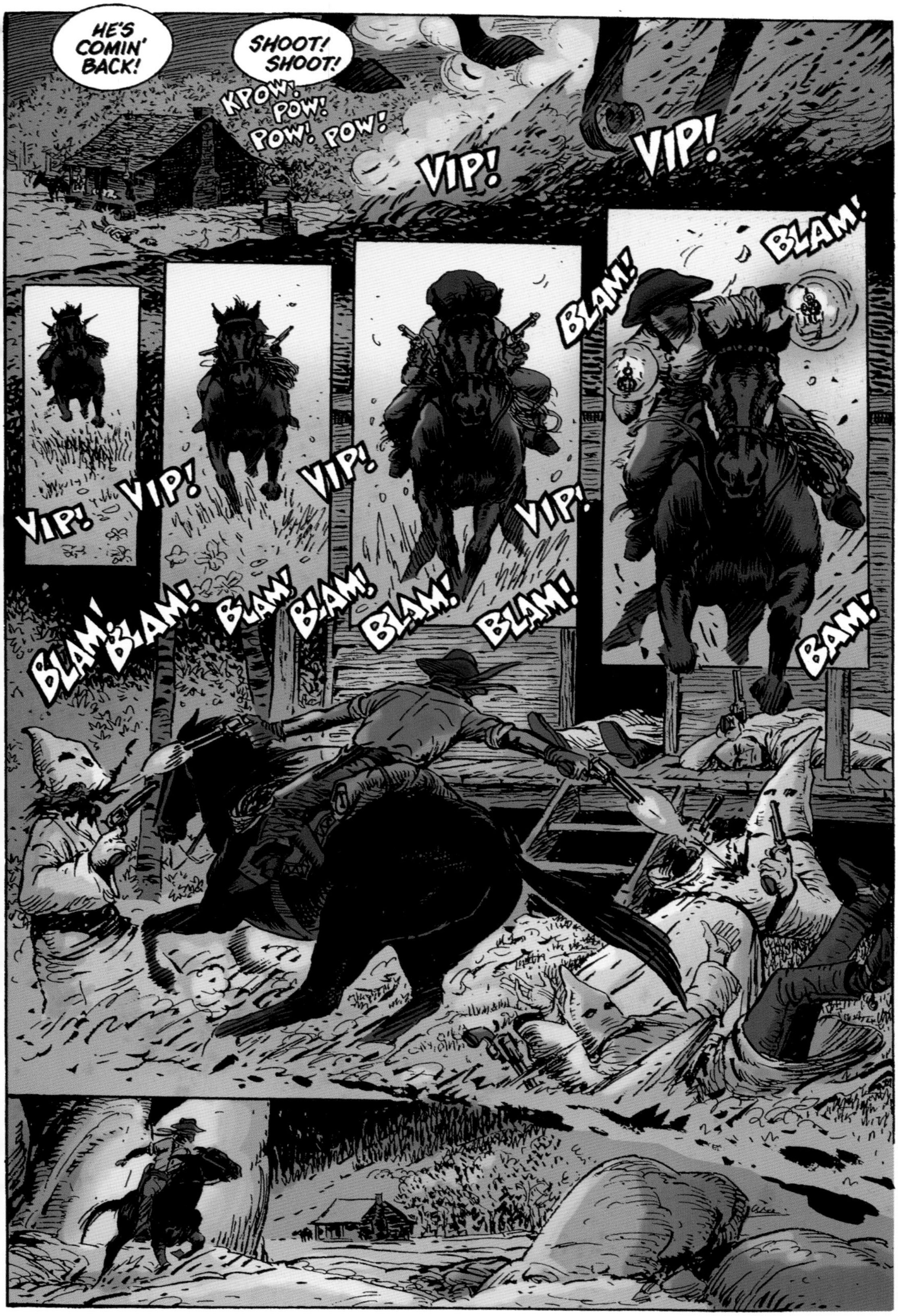
HE'S COMIN' BACK!
SHOOT! SHOOT!
KPOW! POW! POW! POW!
VIP!
VIP!
BLAM!
BLAM!
VIP! VIP!
VIP!
VIP!
BLAM!
BLAM!
BLAM!
BLAM!
BLAM!
BLAM!
BLAM!
BAM!

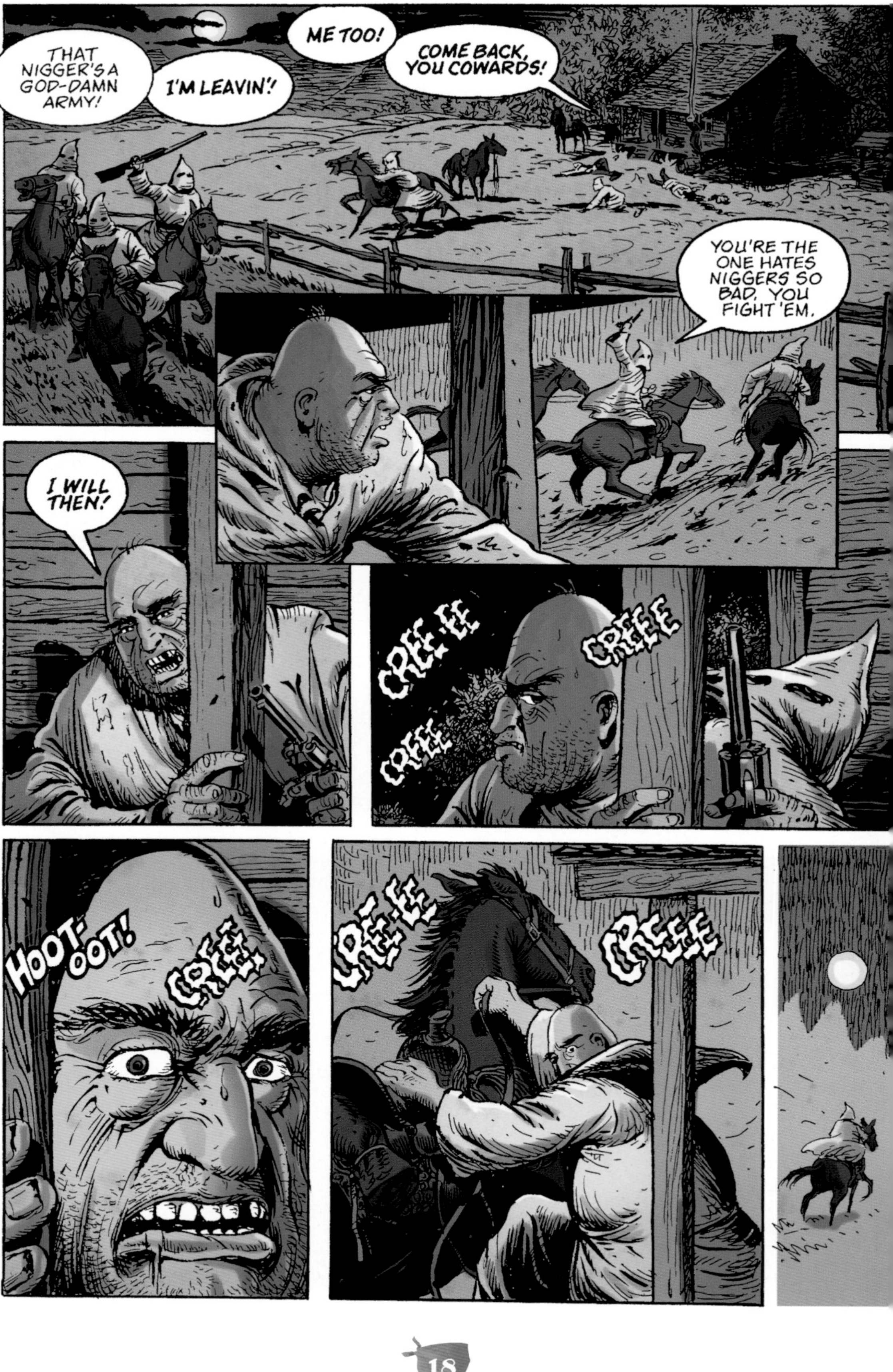
THAT NIGGER'S A GOD-DAMN ARMY!
I'M LEAVIN'!
ME TOO!
COME BACK, YOU COWARDS!
YOU'RE THE ONE HATES NIGGERS SO BAD, YOU FIGHT 'EM.
I WILL THEN!
CREE-EE
CREEE
CREEE
HOOT-OOT!
CREEE
CREE-EE
CREEE

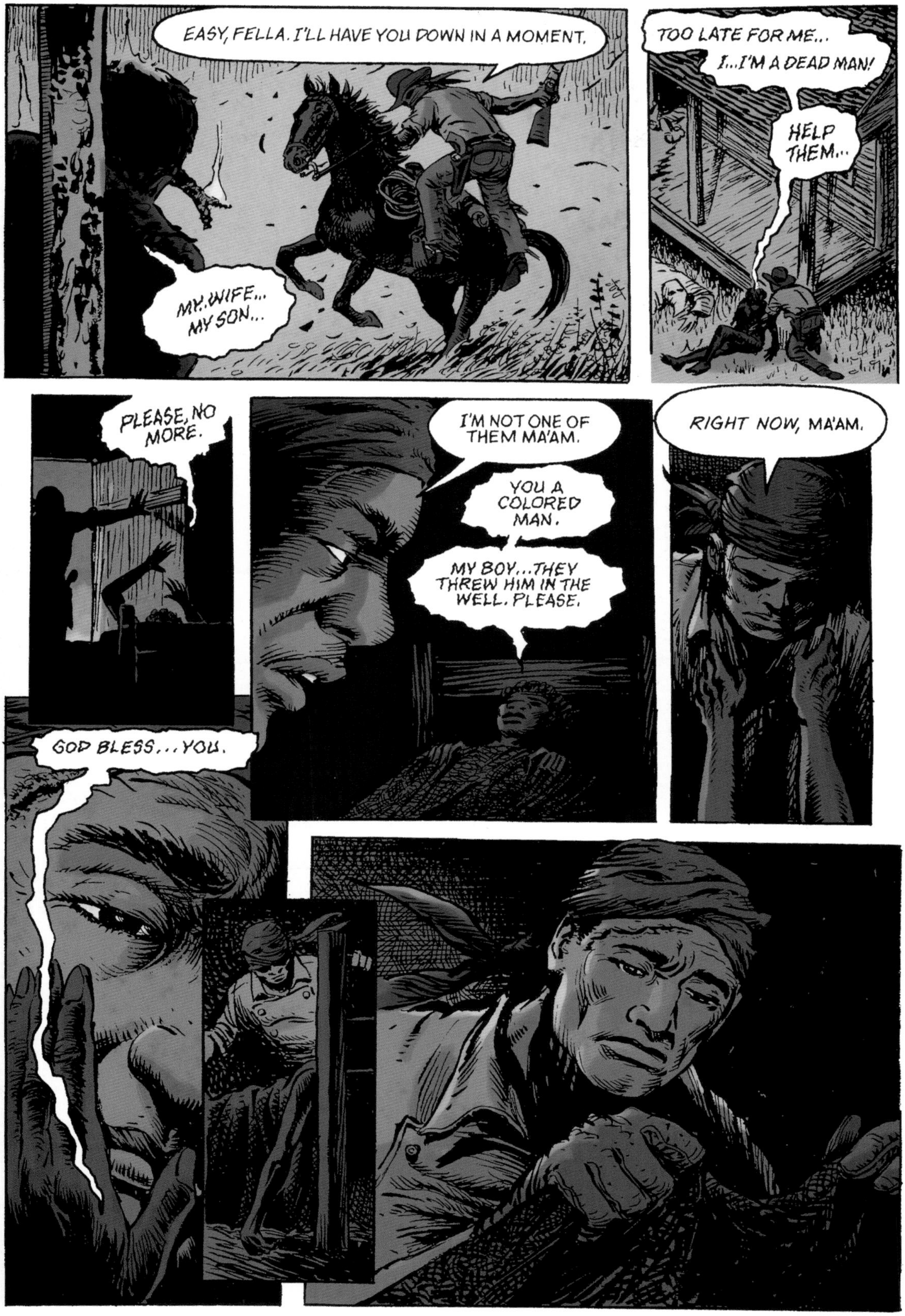
EASY, FELLA. I'LL HAVE YOU DOWN IN A MOMENT.
MY WIFE... MY SON...
TOO LATE FOR ME...
I...I'M A DEAD MAN!
HELP THEM...
PLEASE, NO MORE.
I'M NOT ONE OF THEM MA'AM.
YOU A COLORED MAN.
MY BOY...THEY THREW HIM IN THE WELL. PLEASE.
RIGHT NOW, MA'AM.
GOD BLESS... YOU.

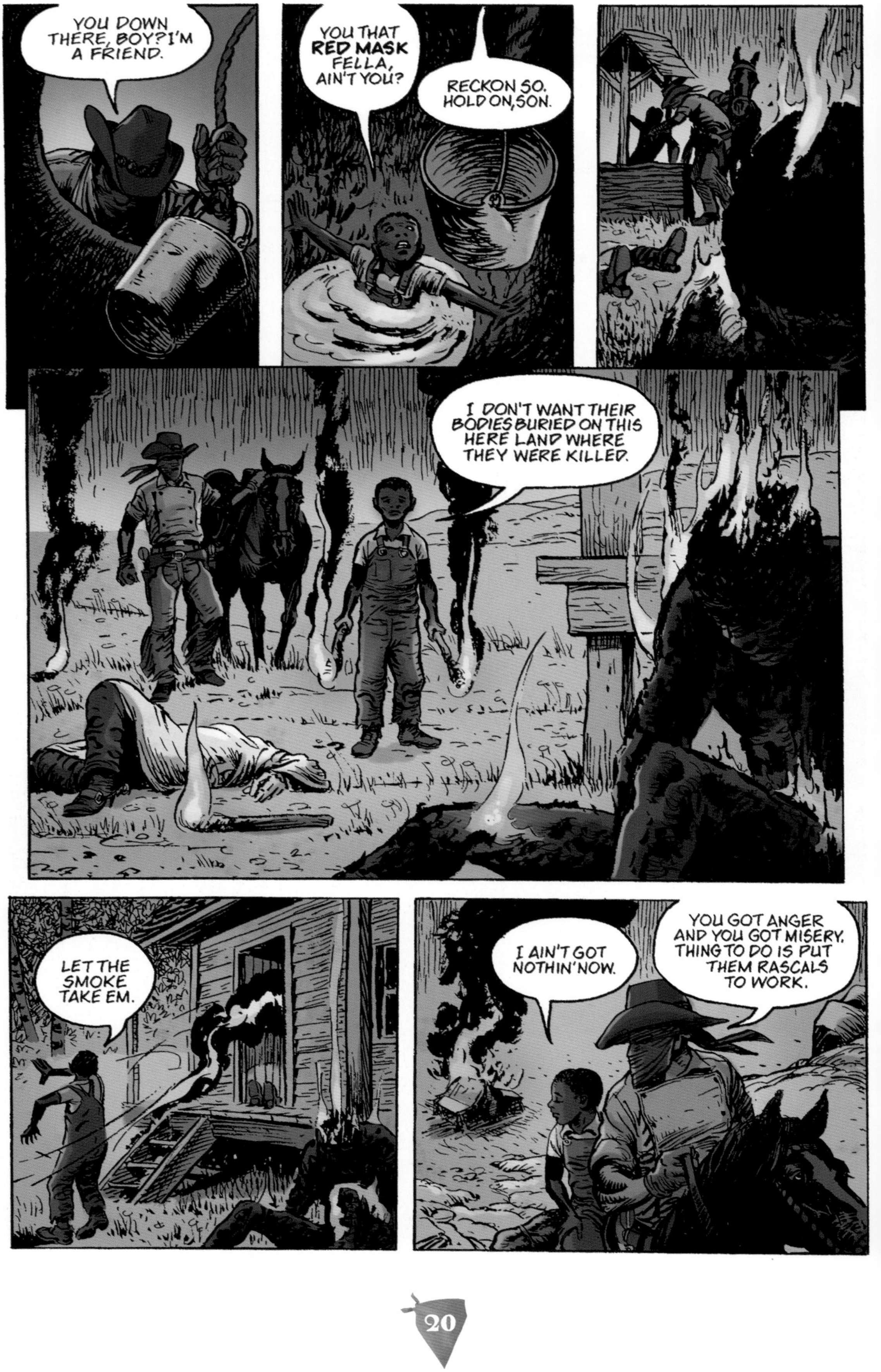
YOU DOWN THERE, BOY? I'M A FRIEND.
YOU THAT **RED MASK** FELLA, AIN'T YOU?
RECKON SO. HOLD ON, SON.
I DON'T WANT THEIR BODIES BURIED ON THIS HERE LAND WHERE THEY WERE KILLED.
LET THE SMOKE TAKE EM.
I AIN'T GOT NOTHIN' NOW.
YOU GOT ANGER AND YOU GOT MISERY. THING TO DO IS PUT THEM RASCALS TO WORK.

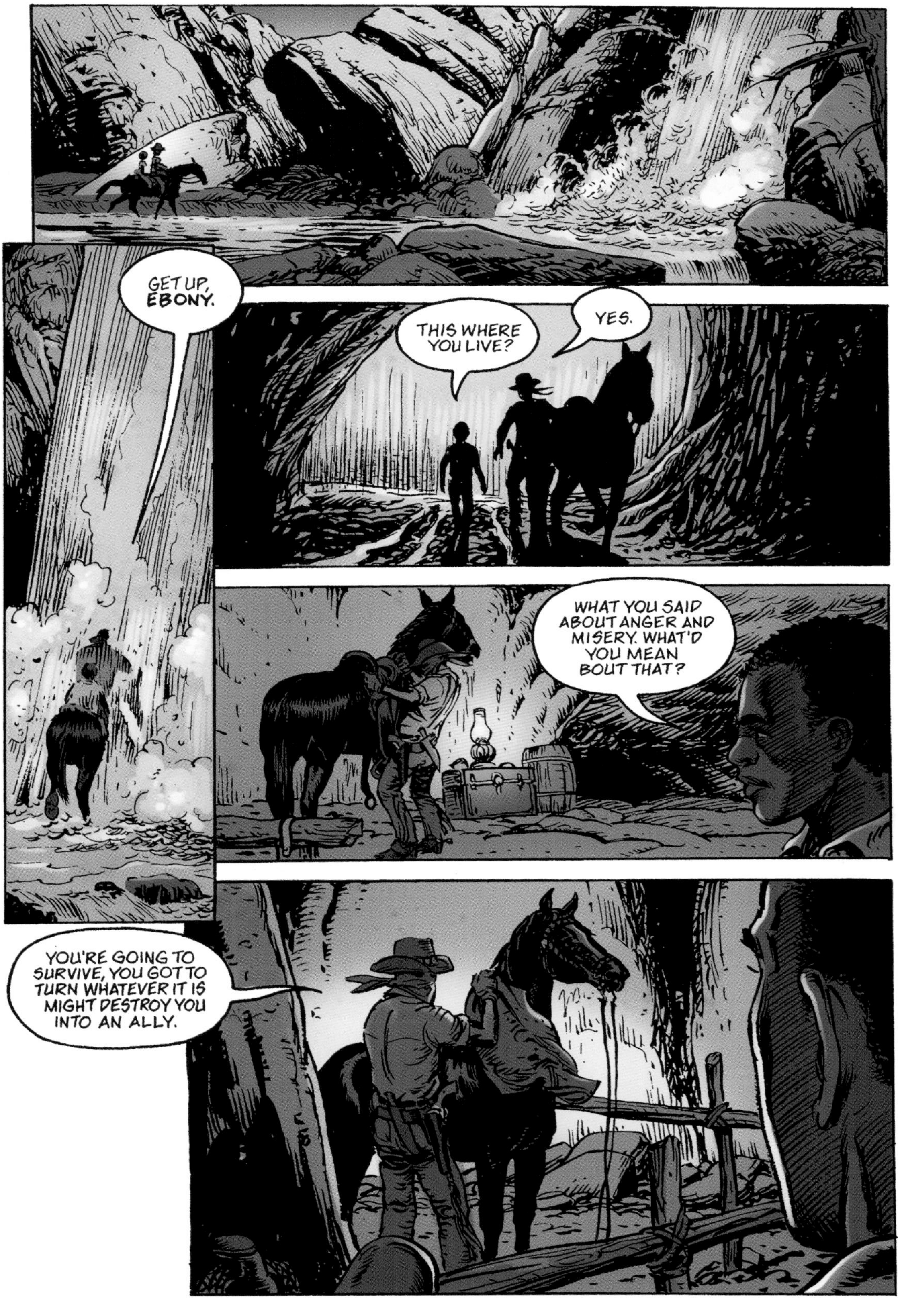
GET UP, EBONY.
THIS WHERE YOU LIVE?
YES.
WHAT YOU SAID ABOUT ANGER AND MISERY. WHAT'D YOU MEAN BOUT THAT?
YOU'RE GOING TO SURVIVE, YOU GOT TO TURN WHATEVER IT IS MIGHT DESTROY YOU INTO AN ALLY.

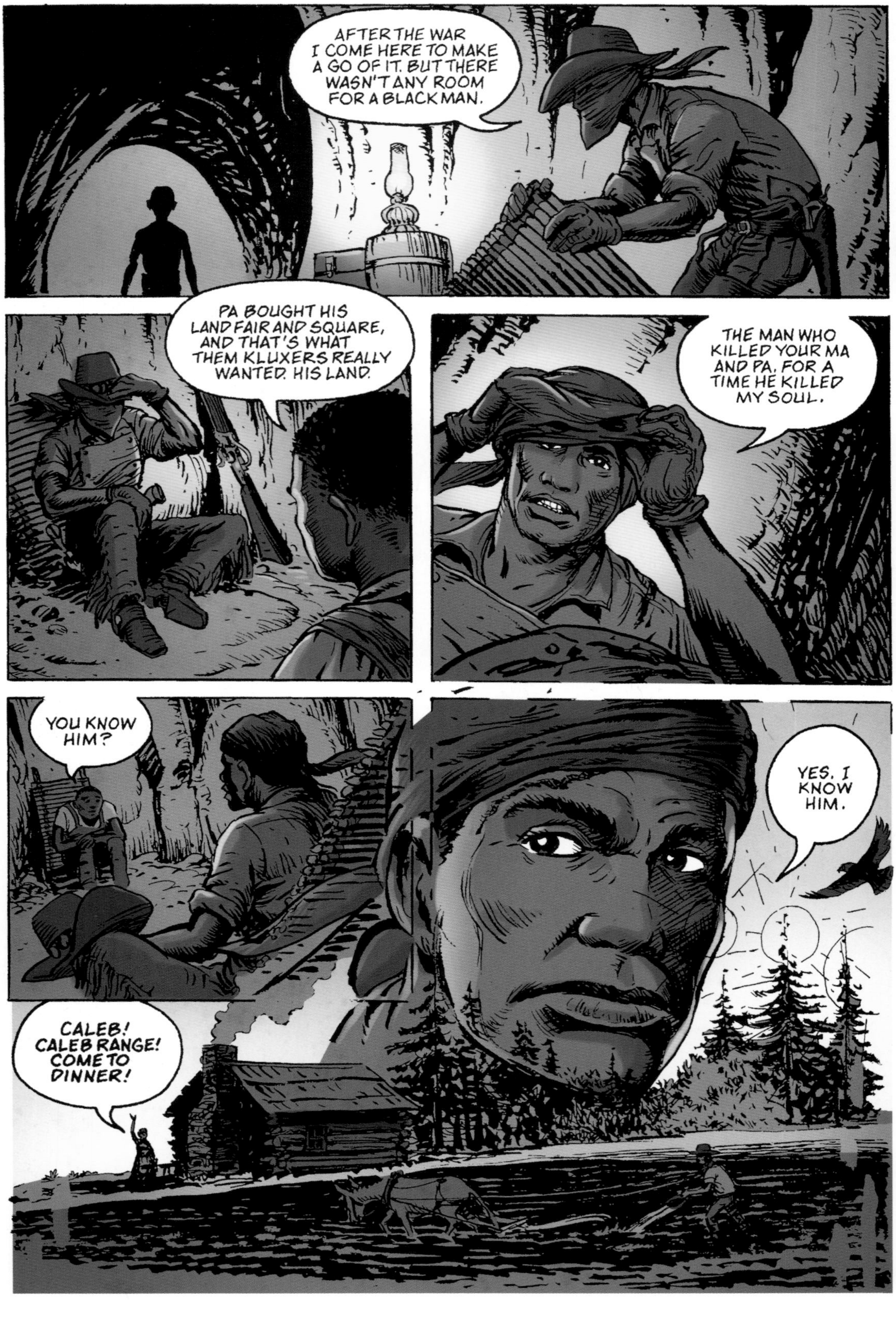
AFTER THE WAR I COME HERE TO MAKE A GO OF IT. BUT THERE WASN'T ANY ROOM FOR A BLACK MAN.
PA BOUGHT HIS LAND FAIR AND SQUARE, AND THAT'S WHAT THEM KLUXERS REALLY WANTED. HIS LAND.
THE MAN WHO KILLED YOUR MA AND PA. FOR A TIME HE KILLED MY SOUL.
YOU KNOW HIM?
YES. I KNOW HIM.
CALEB! CALEB RANGE! COME TO DINNER!

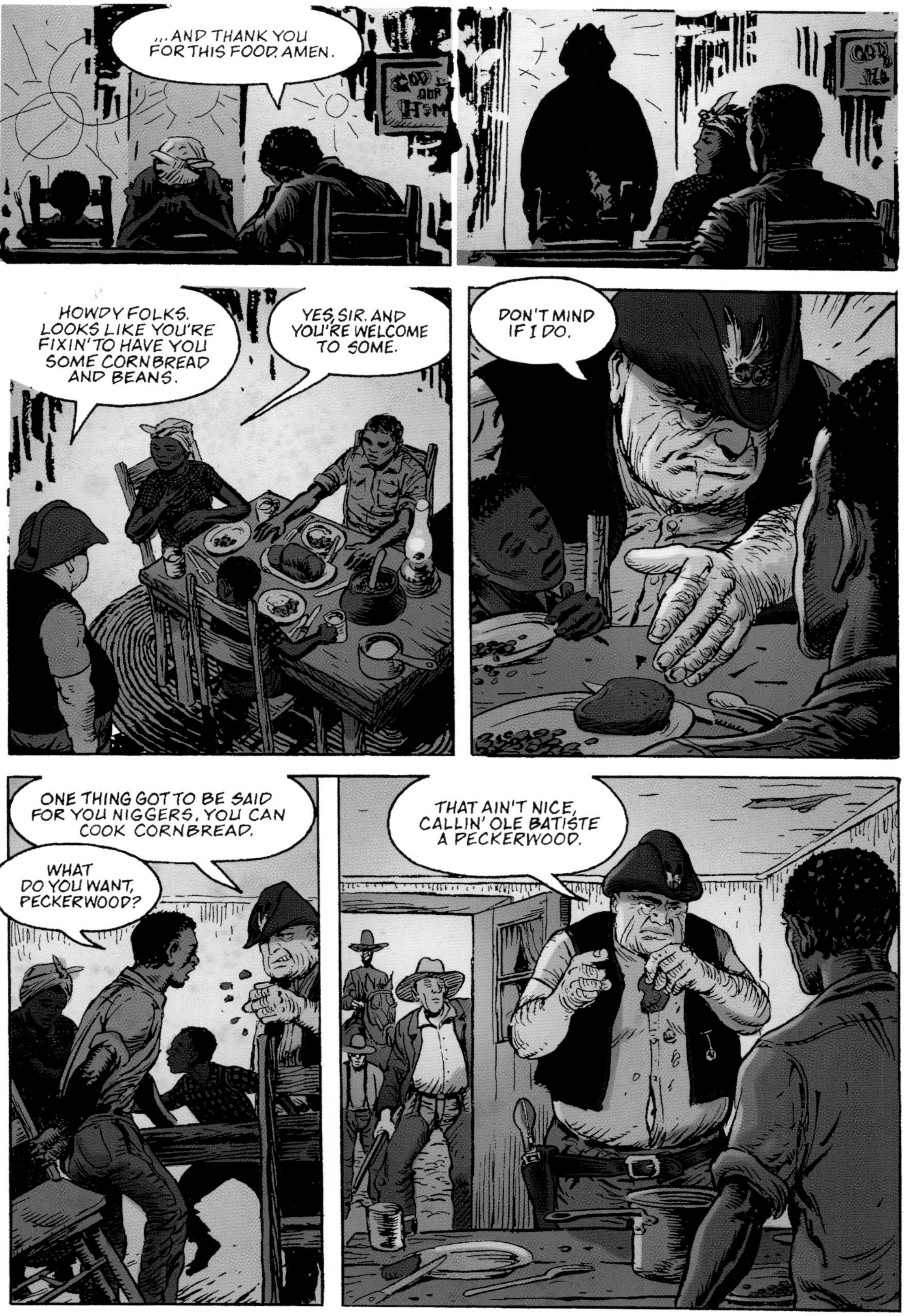
...AND THANK YOU FOR THIS FOOD. AMEN.
HOWDY FOLKS. LOOKS LIKE YOU'RE FIXIN' TO HAVE YOU SOME CORNBREAD AND BEANS.
YES, SIR. AND YOU'RE WELCOME TO SOME.
DON'T MIND IF I DO.
ONE THING GOT TO BE SAID FOR YOU NIGGERS, YOU CAN COOK CORNBREAD.
WHAT DO YOU WANT, PECKERWOOD?
THAT AIN'T NICE, CALLIN' OLE BATISTE A PECKERWOOD.

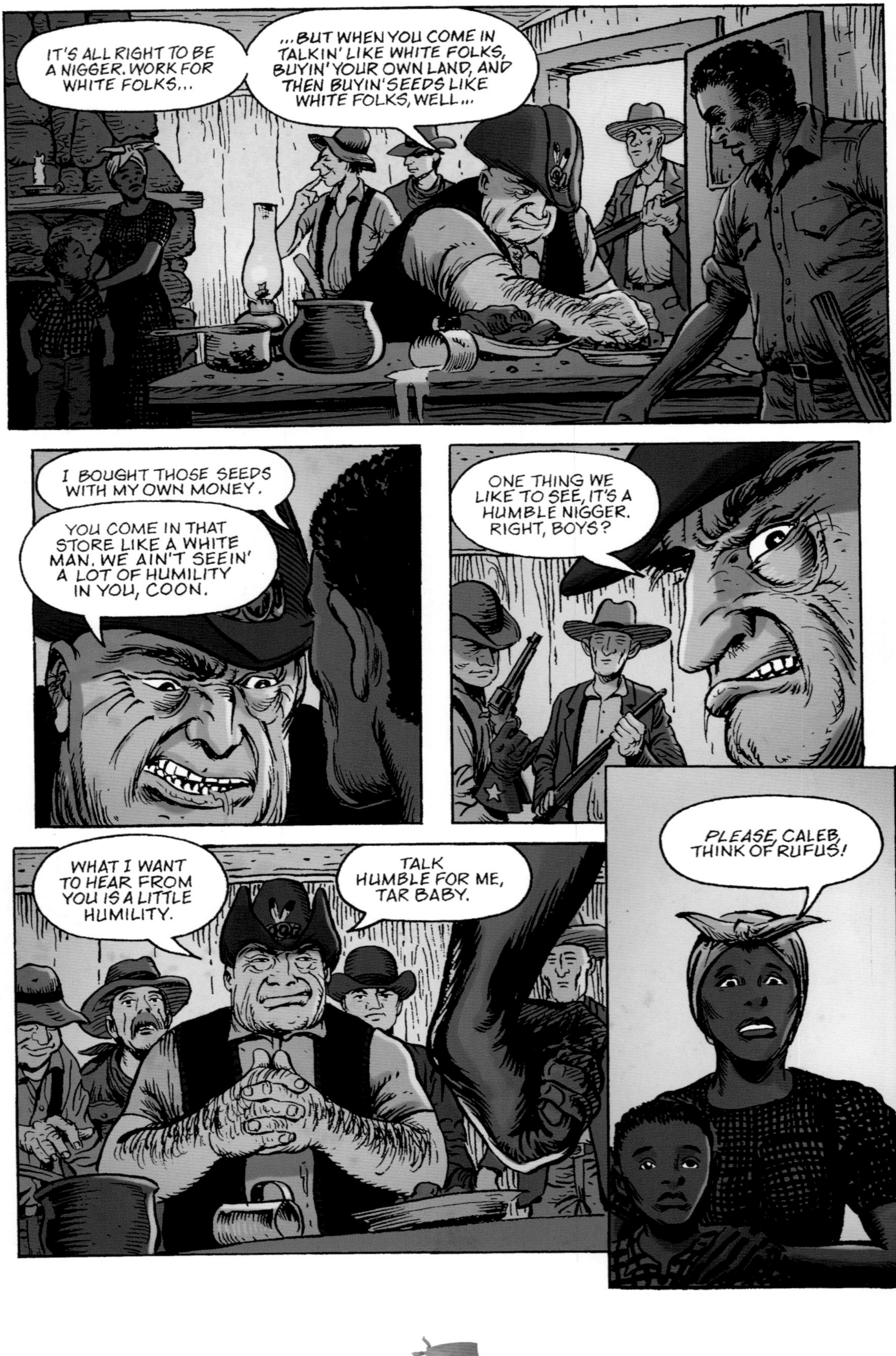
IT'S ALL RIGHT TO BE A NIGGER. WORK FOR WHITE FOLKS...
...BUT WHEN YOU COME IN TALKIN' LIKE WHITE FOLKS, BUYIN' YOUR OWN LAND, AND THEN BUYIN' SEEDS LIKE WHITE FOLKS, WELL...
I BOUGHT THOSE SEEDS WITH MY OWN MONEY.
YOU COME IN THAT STORE LIKE A WHITE MAN. WE AIN'T SEEIN' A LOT OF HUMILITY IN YOU, COON.
ONE THING WE LIKE TO SEE, IT'S A HUMBLE NIGGER. RIGHT, BOYS?
WHAT I WANT TO HEAR FROM YOU IS A LITTLE HUMILITY.
TALK HUMBLE FOR ME, TAR BABY.
PLEASE, CALEB, THINK OF RUFUS!

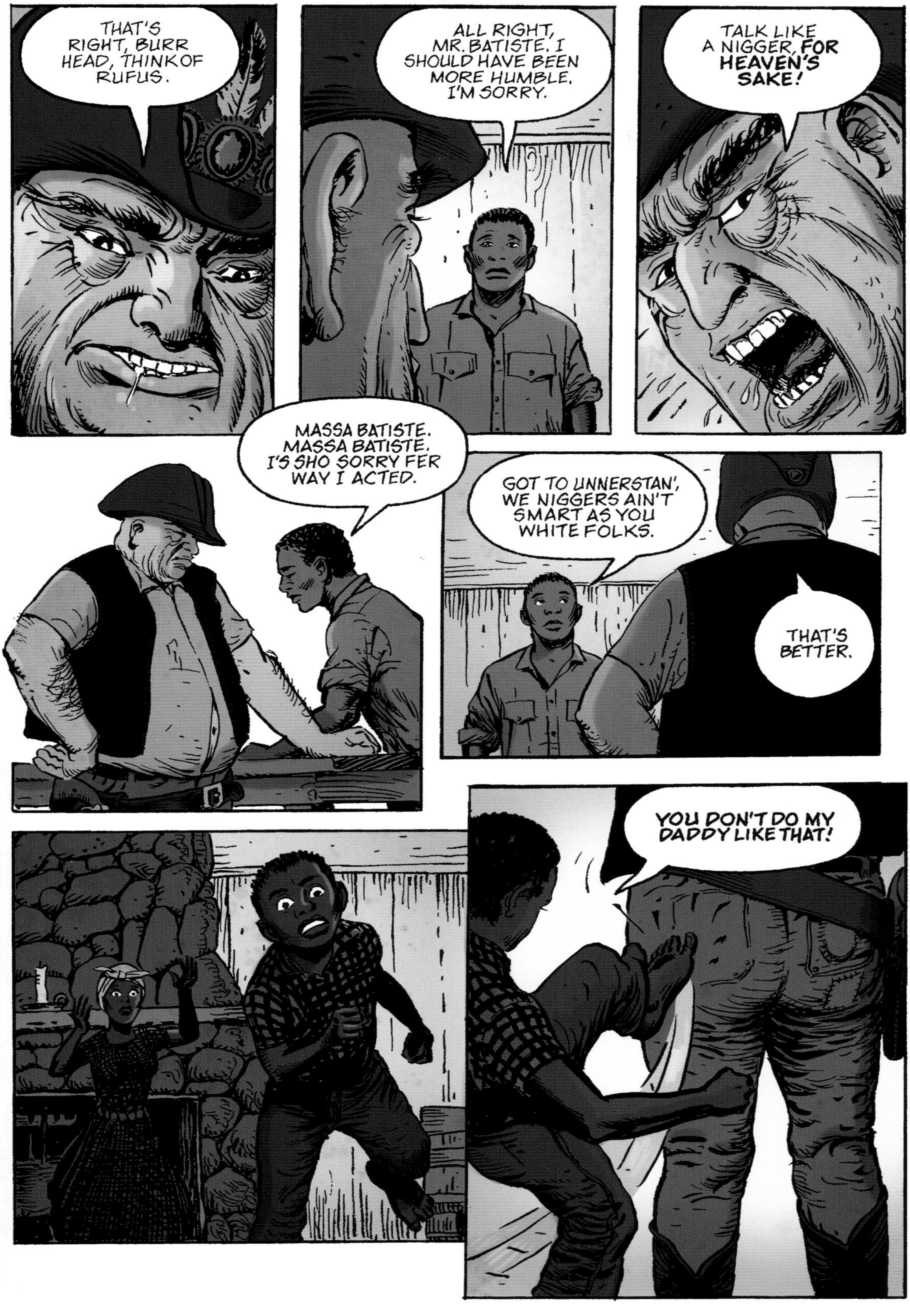
THAT'S RIGHT, BURR HEAD, THINK OF RUFUS.
ALL RIGHT, MR. BATISTE. I SHOULD HAVE BEEN MORE HUMBLE. I'M SORRY.
TALK LIKE A NIGGER, **FOR HEAVEN'S SAKE!**
MASSA BATISTE. MASSA BATISTE. I'S SHO SORRY FER WAY I ACTED.
GOT TO UNNERSTAN', WE NIGGERS AIN'T SMART AS YOU WHITE FOLKS.
THAT'S BETTER.
YOU DON'T DO MY DADDY LIKE THAT!

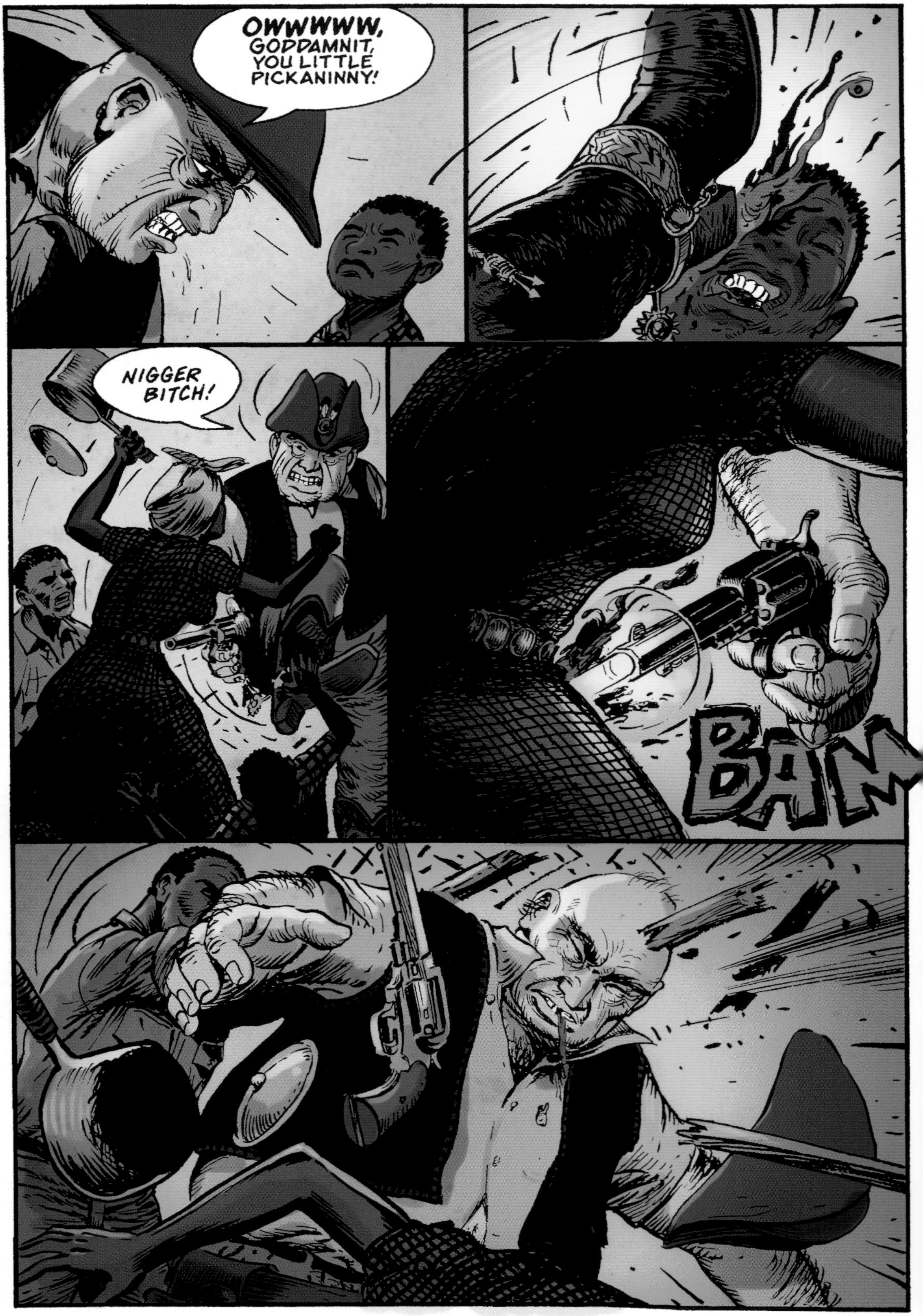
OWWWWW, GODDAMNIT, YOU LITTLE PICKANINNY!
NIGGER BITCH!
BAM

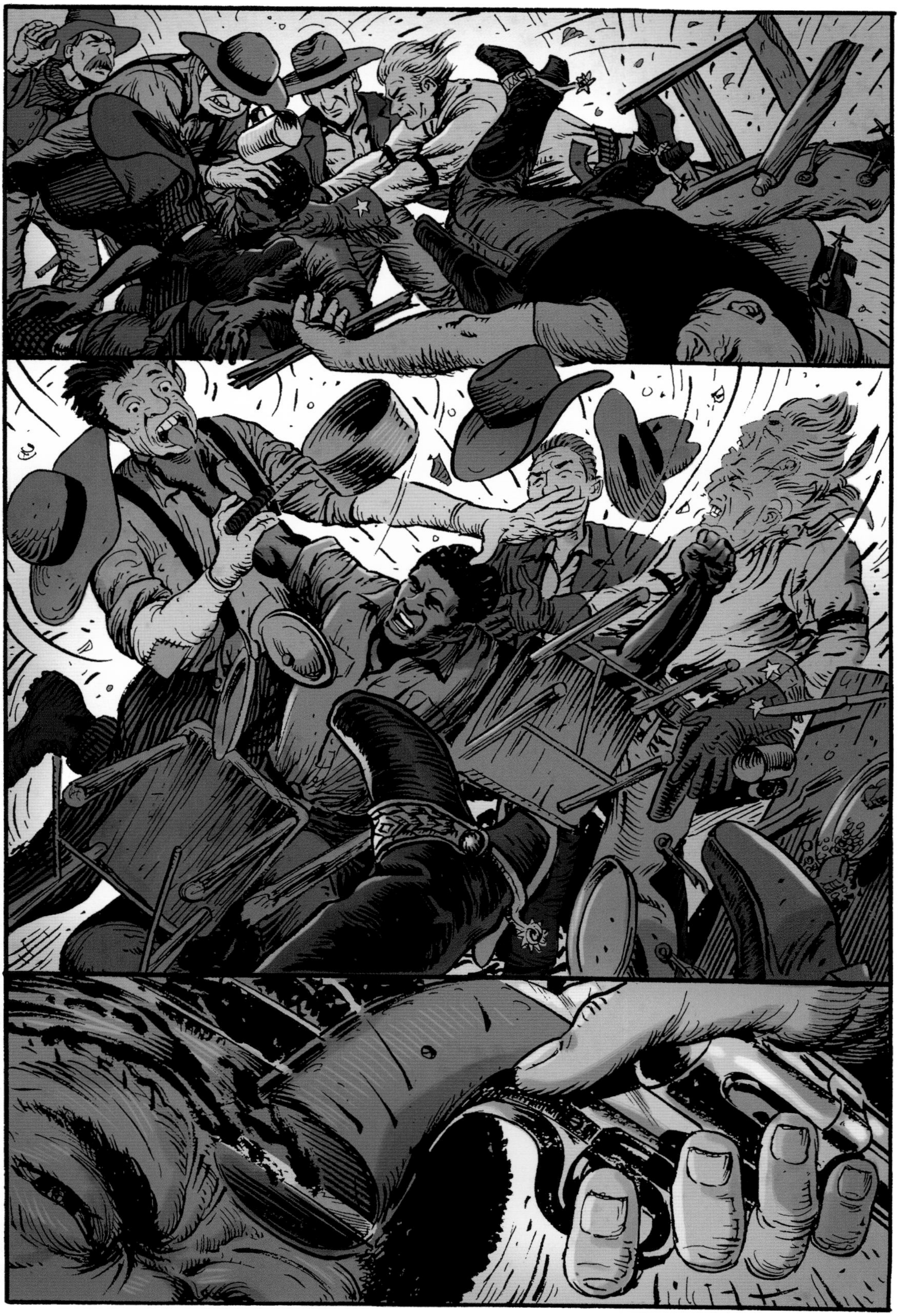

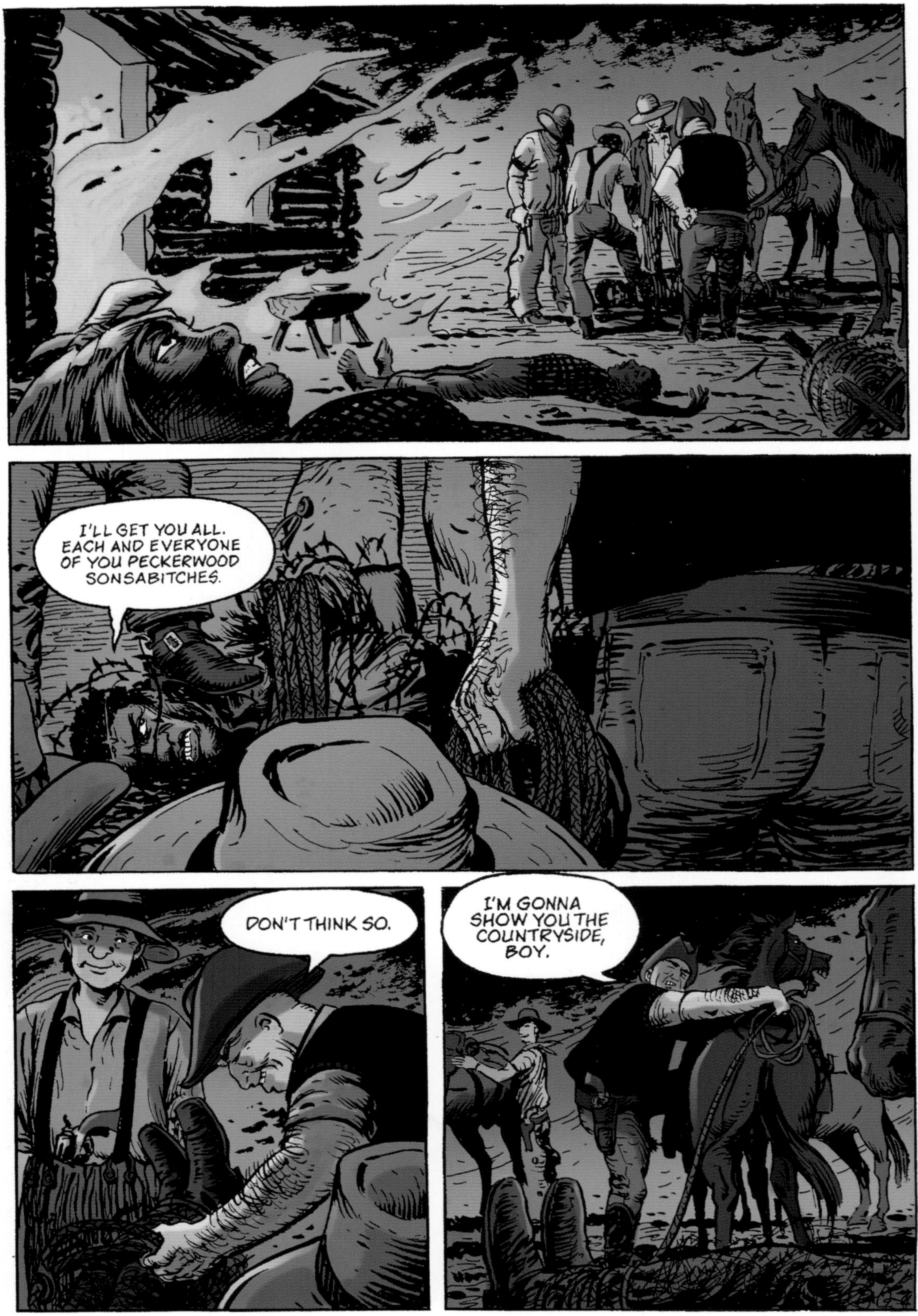
I'LL GET YOU ALL. EACH AND EVERYONE OF YOU PECKERWOOD SONSABITCHES.
DON'T THINK SO.
I'M GONNA SHOW YOU THE COUNTRYSIDE, BOY.

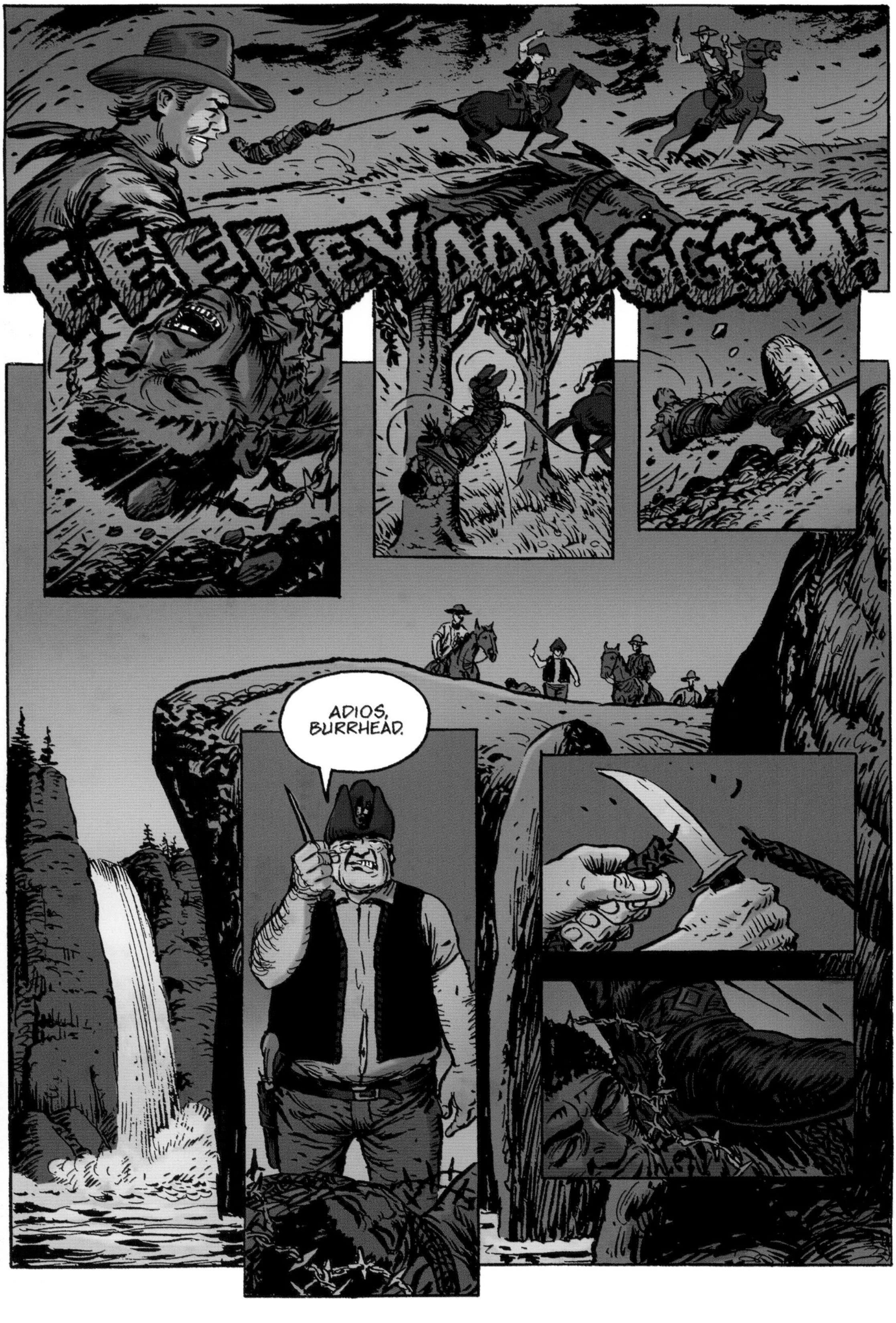
EEEEEYAAAGGGH!
ADIOS, BURRHEAD.

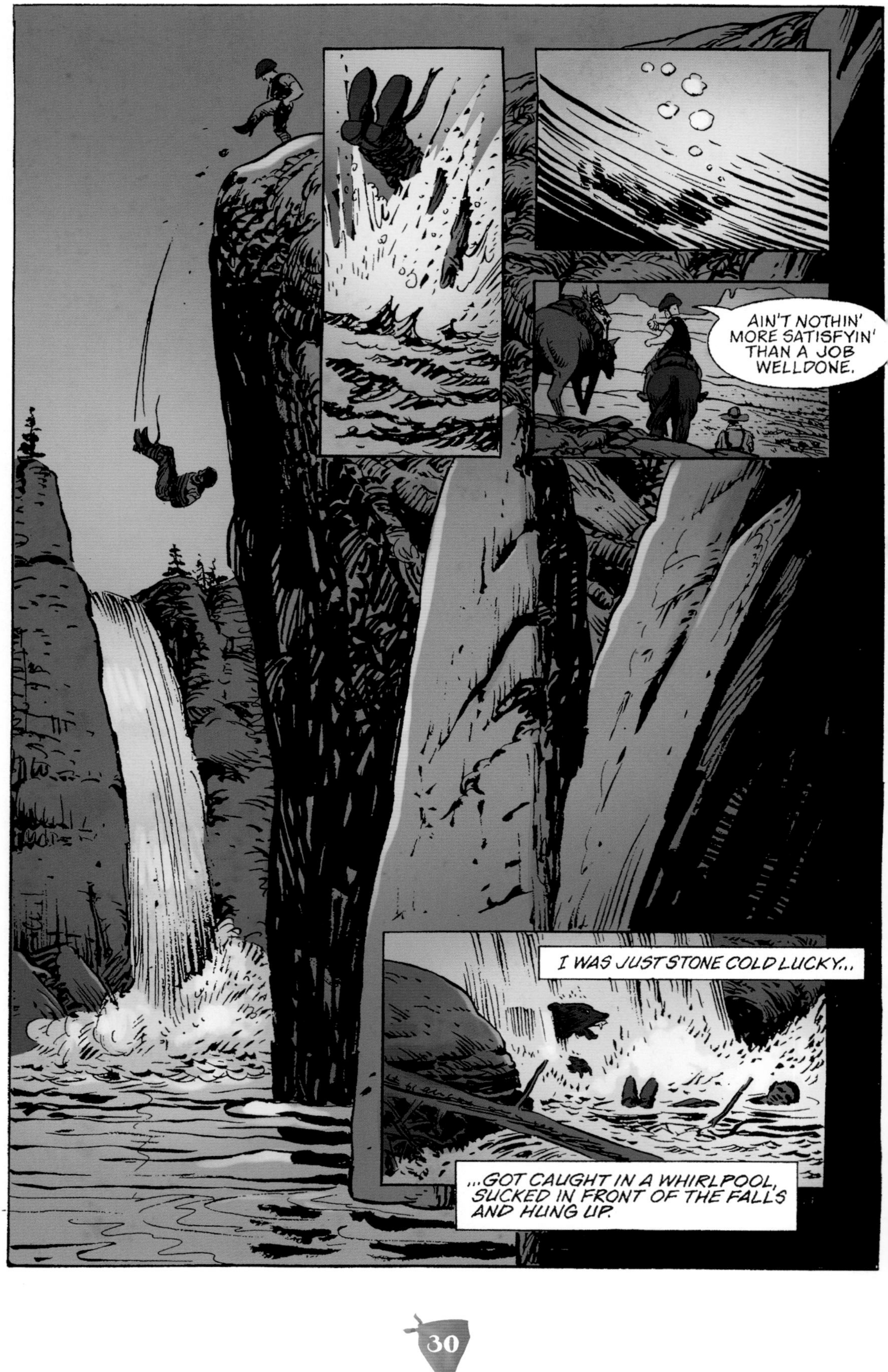
AIN'T NOTHIN' MORE SATISFYIN' THAN A JOB WELLDONE.
I WAS JUST STONE COLD LUCKY...
...GOT CAUGHT IN A WHIRLPOOL, SUCKED IN FRONT OF THE FALLS AND HUNG UP.

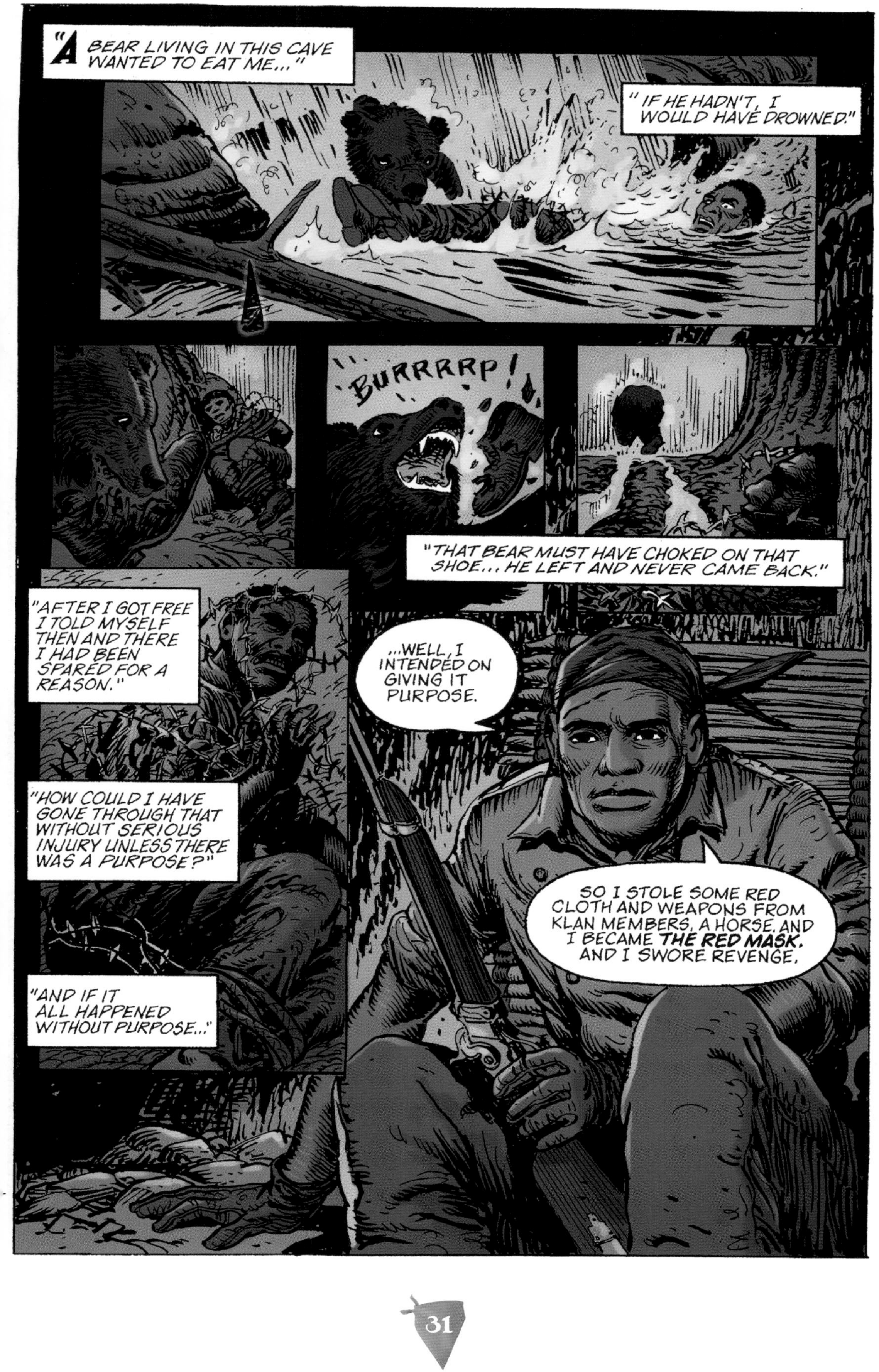
"A BEAR LIVING IN THIS CAVE WANTED TO EAT ME..."
"IF HE HADN'T, I WOULD HAVE DROWNED."
BURRRRP!
"THAT BEAR MUST HAVE CHOKED ON THAT SHOE... HE LEFT AND NEVER CAME BACK."
"AFTER I GOT FREE I TOLD MYSELF THEN AND THERE I HAD BEEN SPARED FOR A REASON."
"HOW COULD I HAVE GONE THROUGH THAT WITHOUT SERIOUS INJURY UNLESS THERE WAS A PURPOSE?"
"AND IF IT ALL HAPPENED WITHOUT PURPOSE..."
...WELL, I INTENDED ON GIVING IT PURPOSE.
SO I STOLE SOME RED CLOTH AND WEAPONS FROM KLAN MEMBERS, A HORSE, AND I BECAME THE RED MASK. AND I SWORE REVENGE.

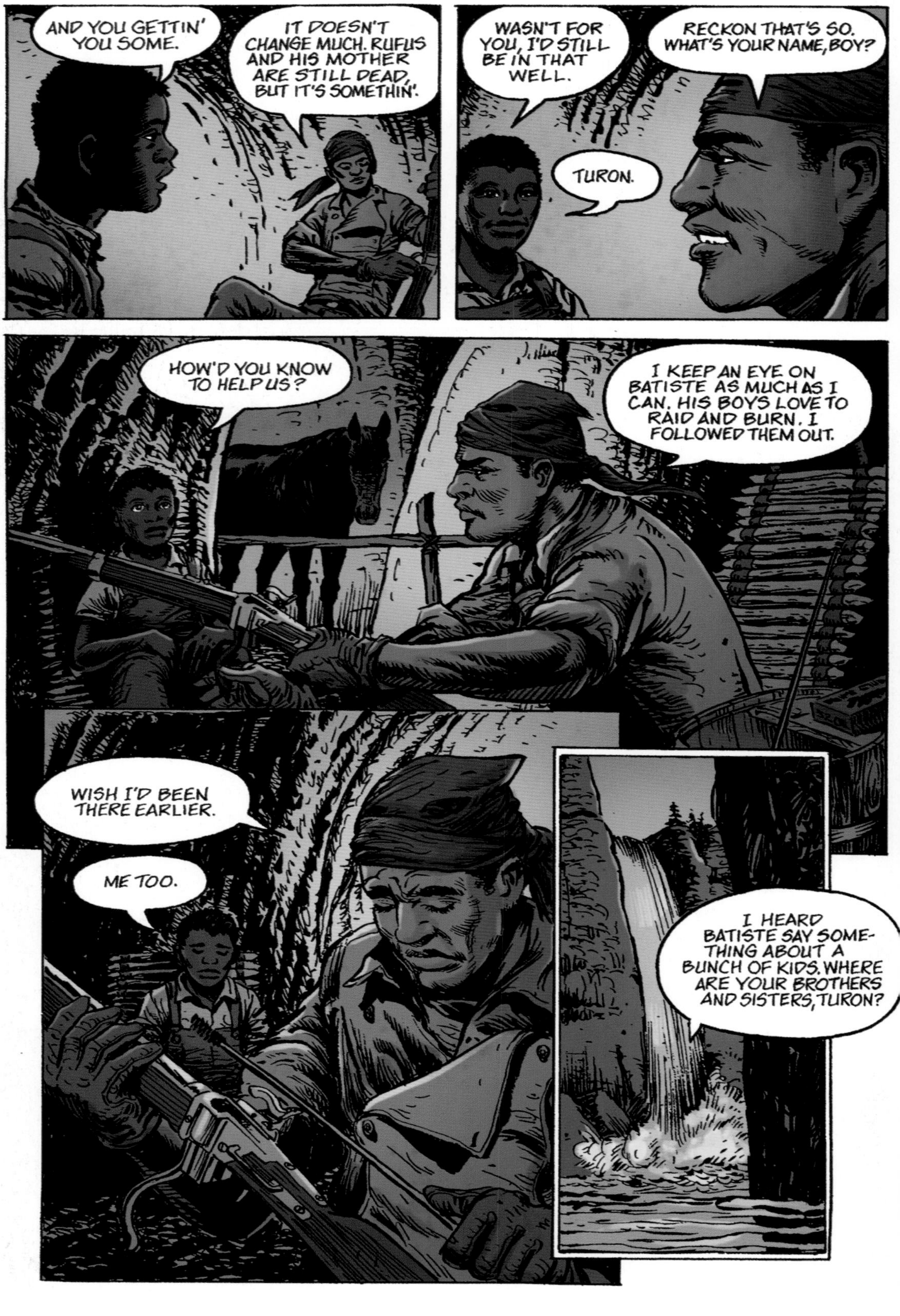
AND YOU GETTIN' YOU SOME.
IT DOESN'T CHANGE MUCH. RUFUS AND HIS MOTHER ARE STILL DEAD, BUT IT'S SOMETHIN'.
WASN'T FOR YOU, I'D STILL BE IN THAT WELL.
RECKON THAT'S SO. WHAT'S YOUR NAME, BOY?
TURON.
HOW'D YOU KNOW TO HELP US?
I KEEP AN EYE ON BATISTE AS MUCH AS I CAN. HIS BOYS LOVE TO RAID AND BURN. I FOLLOWED THEM OUT.
WISH I'D BEEN THERE EARLIER.
ME TOO.
I HEARD BATISTE SAY SOMETHING ABOUT A BUNCH OF KIDS. WHERE ARE YOUR BROTHERS AND SISTERS, TURON?

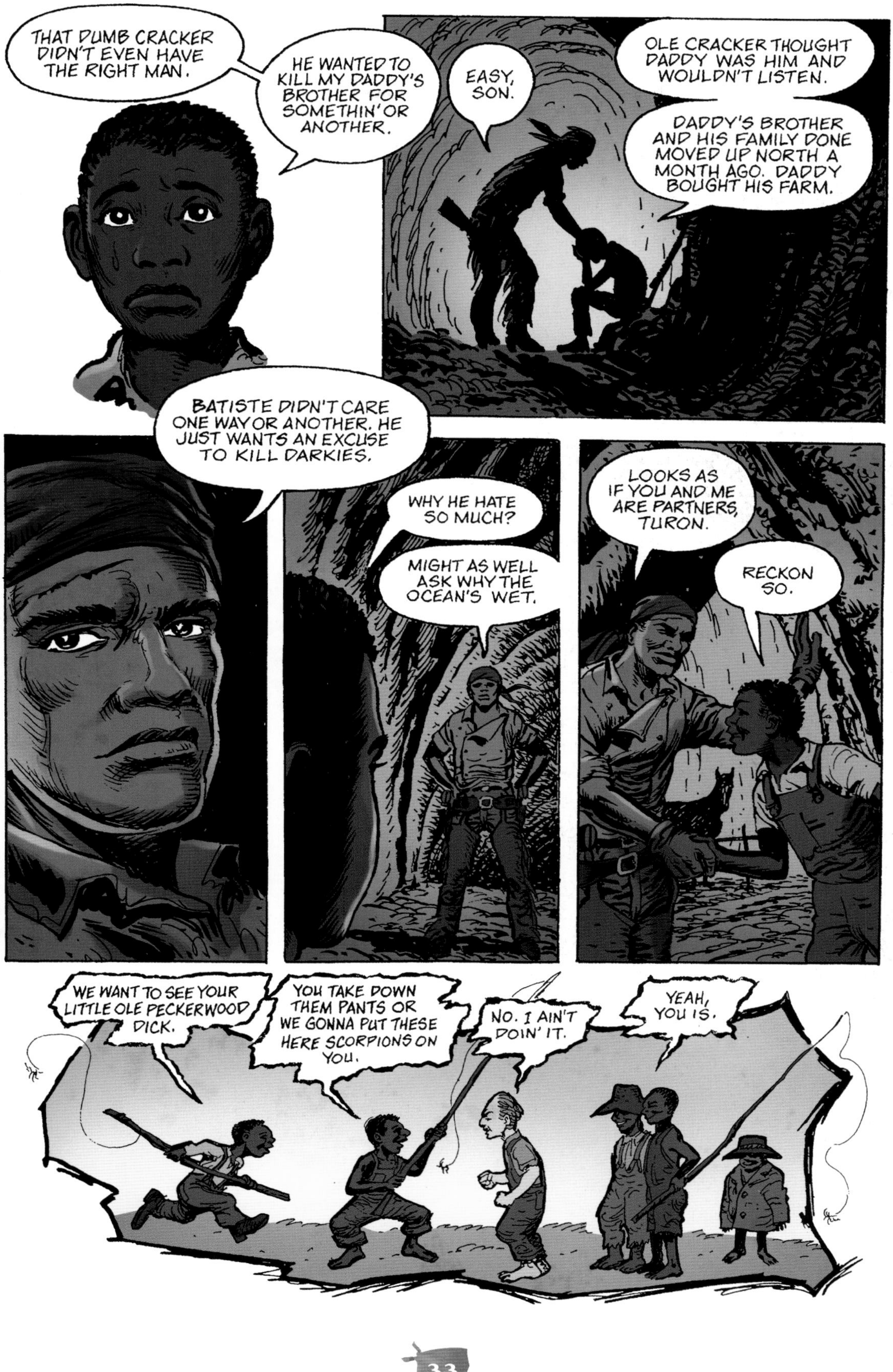
THAT DUMB CRACKER DIDN'T EVEN HAVE THE RIGHT MAN.
HE WANTED TO KILL MY DADDY'S BROTHER FOR SOMETHIN' OR ANOTHER.
EASY, SON.
OLE CRACKER THOUGHT DADDY WAS HIM AND WOULDN'T LISTEN.
DADDY'S BROTHER AND HIS FAMILY DONE MOVED UP NORTH A MONTH AGO. DADDY BOUGHT HIS FARM.
BATISTE DIDN'T CARE ONE WAY OR ANOTHER. HE JUST WANTS AN EXCUSE TO KILL DARKIES.
WHY HE HATE SO MUCH?
MIGHT AS WELL ASK WHY THE OCEAN'S WET.
LOOKS AS IF YOU AND ME ARE PARTNERS, TURON.
RECKON SO.
WE WANT TO SEE YOUR LITTLE OLE PECKERWOOD DICK.
YOU TAKE DOWN THEM PANTS OR WE GONNA PUT THESE HERE SCORPIONS ON YOU.
NO. I AIN'T DOIN' IT.
YEAH, YOU IS.

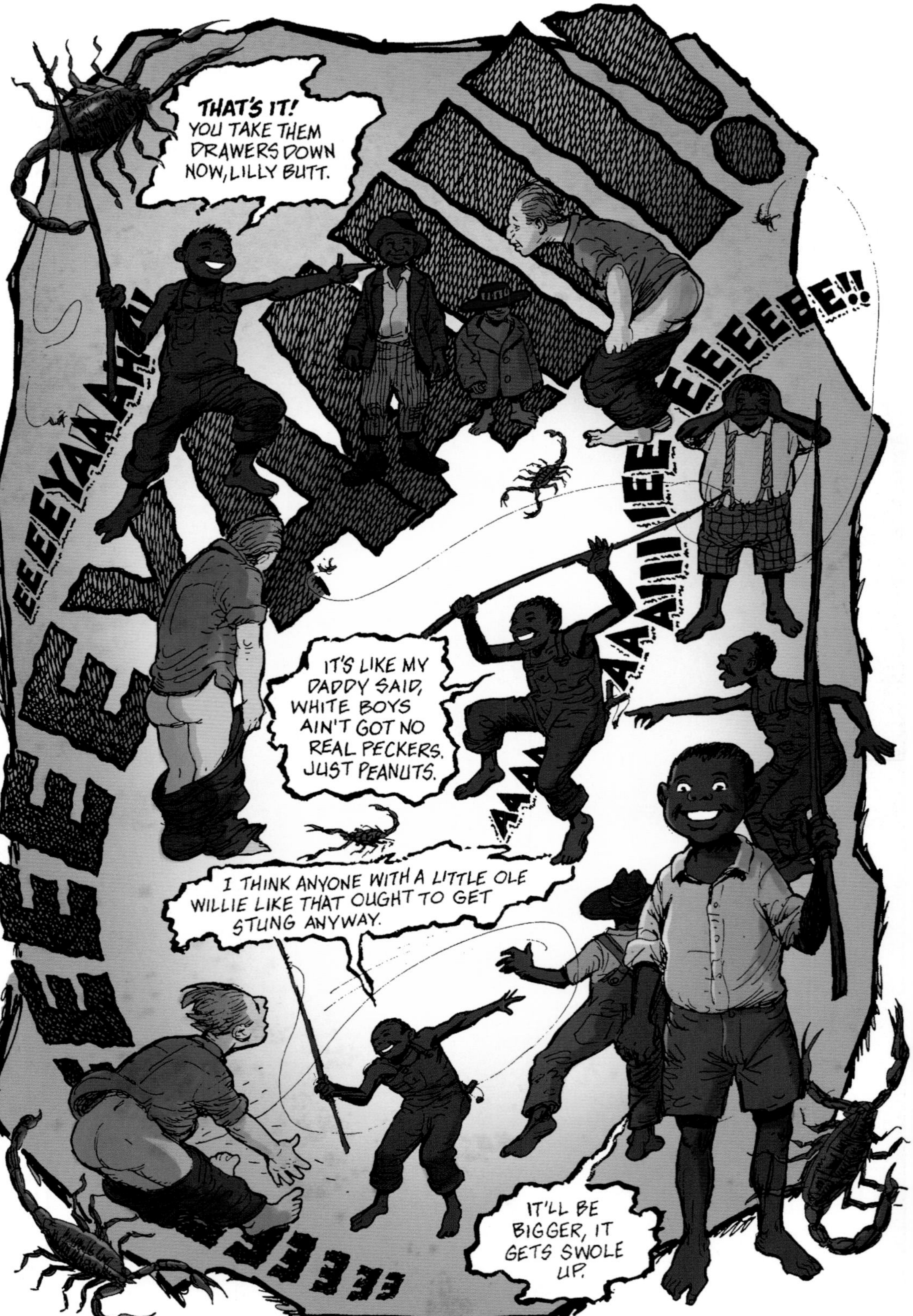
THAT'S IT! YOU TAKE THEM DRAWERS DOWN NOW, LILLY BUTT.
EEEEYAAAHH!!
EEEEEBE!!
IT'S LIKE MY DADDY SAID, WHITE BOYS AIN'T GOT NO REAL PECKERS. JUST PEANUTS.
I THINK ANYONE WITH A LITTLE OLE WILLIE LIKE THAT OUGHT TO GET STUNG ANYWAY.
IT'LL BE BIGGER, IT GETS SWOLE UP.

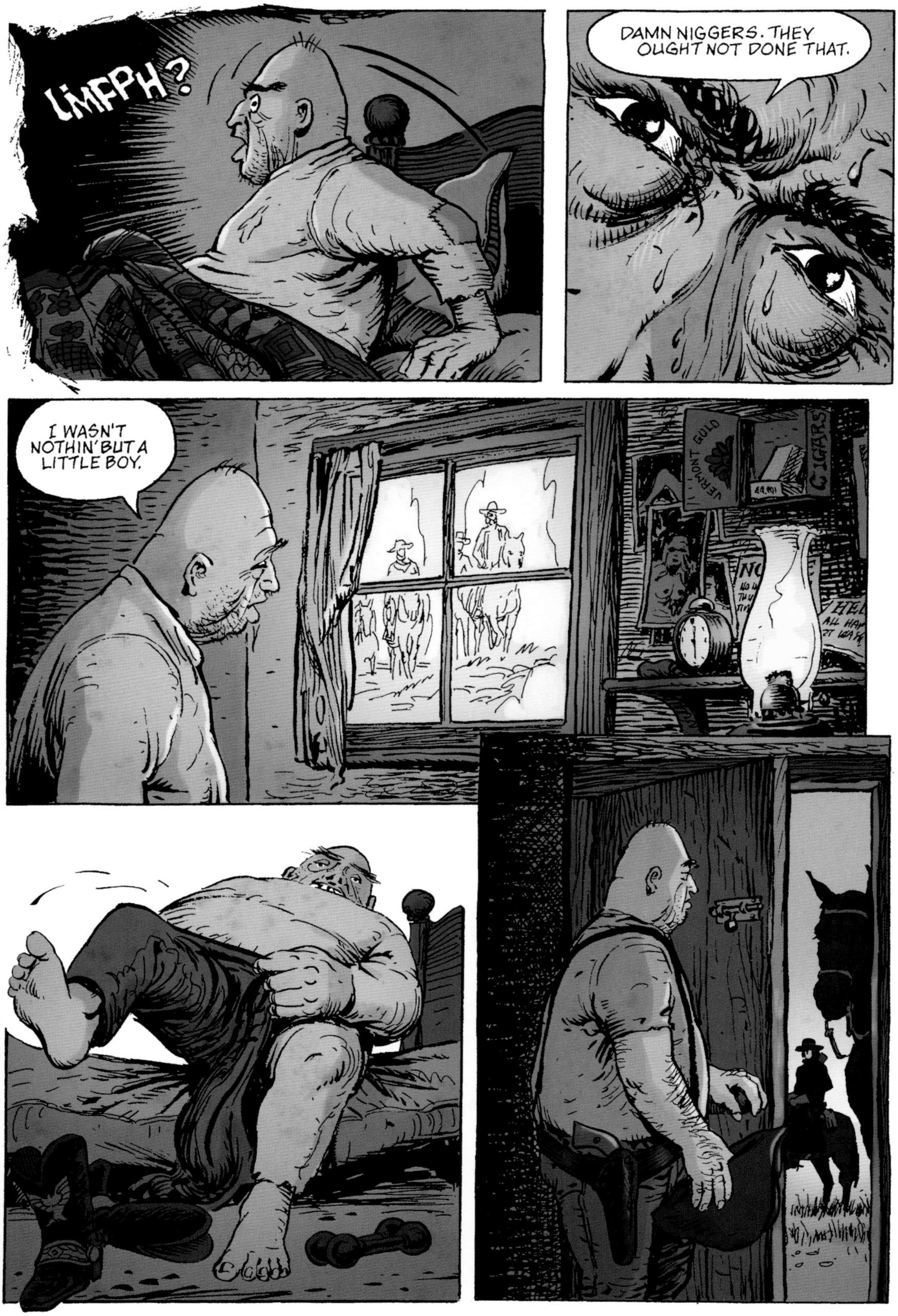
UMFPH?
DAMN NIGGERS. THEY OUGHT NOT DONE THAT.
I WASN'T NOTHIN' BUT A LITTLE BOY.
VERMONT GOLD
CIGARS

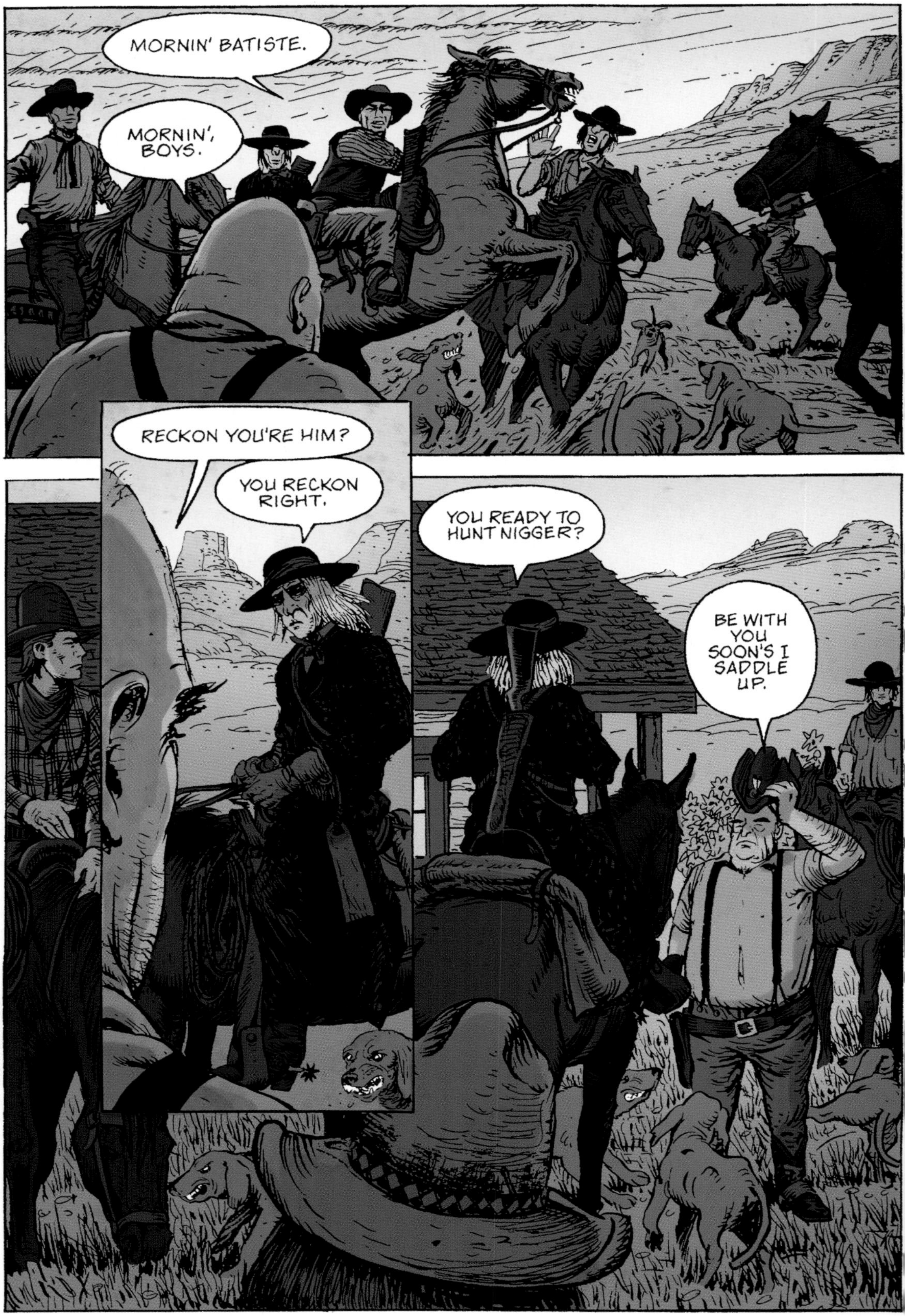
MORNIN' BATISTE.
MORNIN', BOYS.
RECKON YOU'RE HIM?
YOU RECKON RIGHT.
YOU READY TO HUNT NIGGER?
BE WITH YOU SOON'S I SADDLE UP.

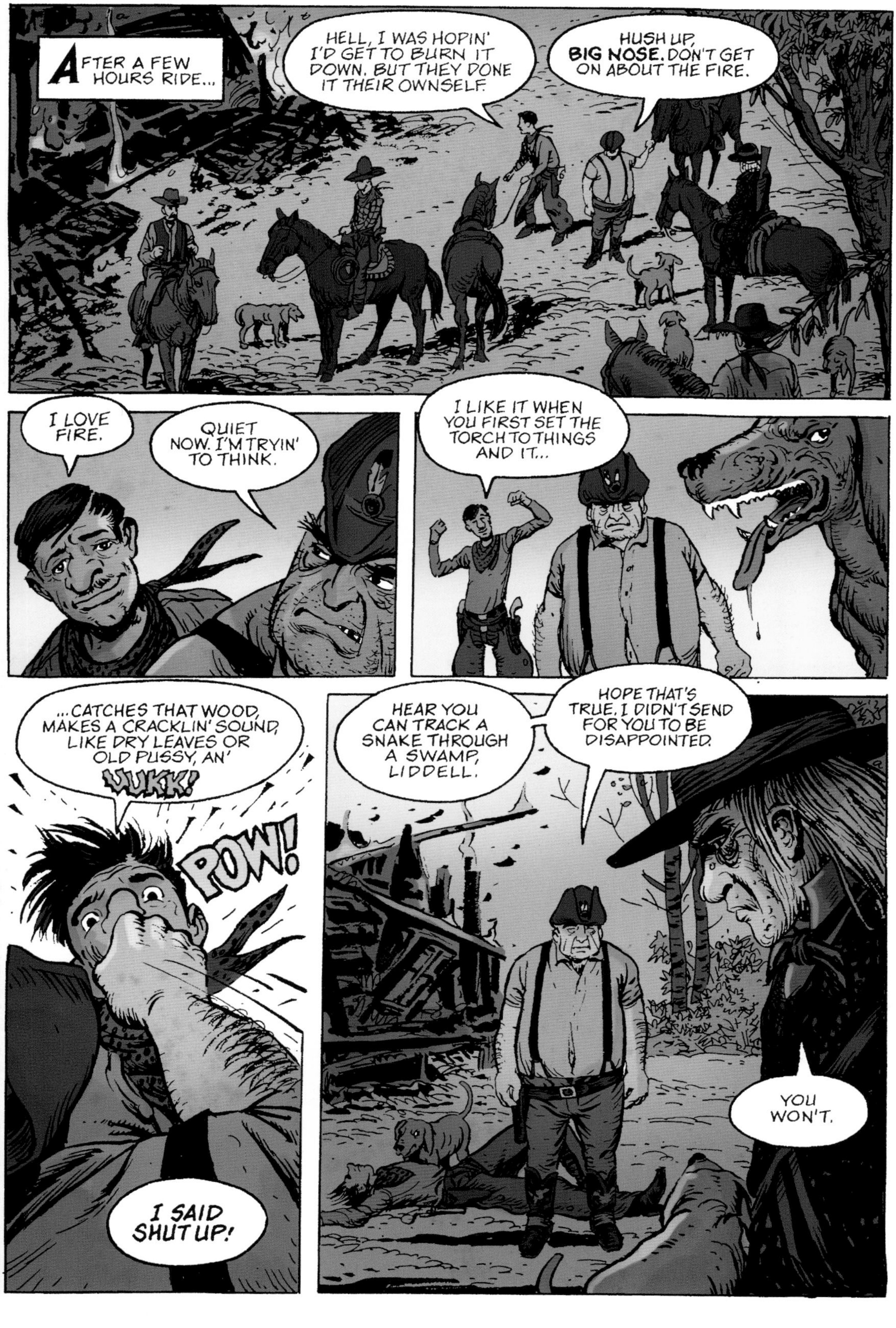
AFTER A FEW HOURS RIDE...
HELL, I WAS HOPIN' I'D GET TO BURN IT DOWN. BUT THEY DONE IT THEIR OWNSELF.
HUSH UP, BIG NOSE. DON'T GET ON ABOUT THE FIRE.
I LOVE FIRE.
QUIET NOW. I'M TRYIN' TO THINK.
I LIKE IT WHEN YOU FIRST SET THE TORCH TO THINGS AND IT...
...CATCHES THAT WOOD, MAKES A CRACKLIN' SOUND, LIKE DRY LEAVES OR OLD PUSSY, AN'
UUKK!
POW!
I SAID SHUT UP!
HEAR YOU CAN TRACK A SNAKE THROUGH A SWAMP, LIDDELL.
HOPE THAT'S TRUE. I DIDN'T SEND FOR YOU TO BE DISAPPOINTED.
YOU WON'T.

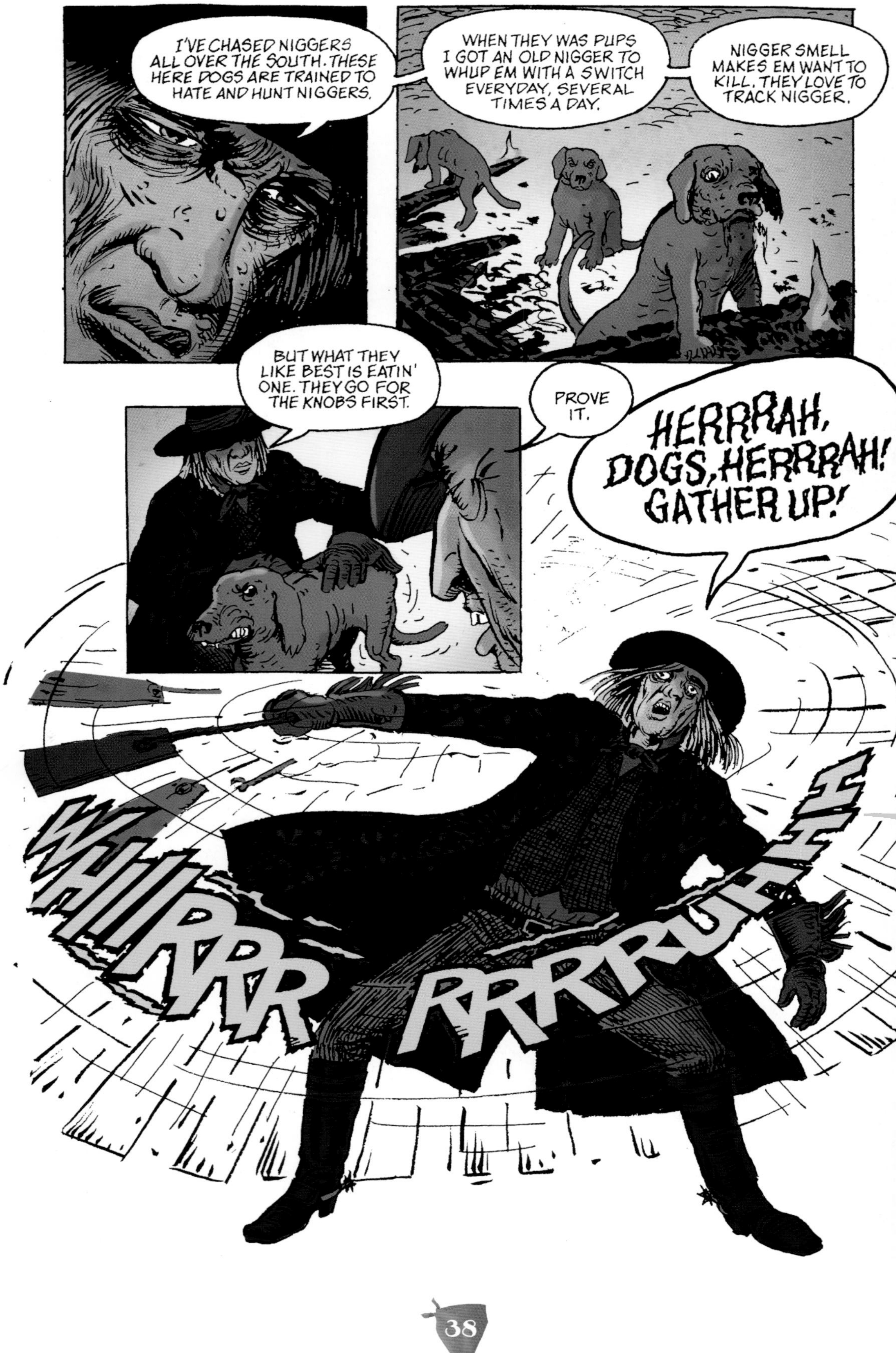
I'VE CHASED NIGGERS ALL OVER THE SOUTH. THESE HERE DOGS ARE TRAINED TO HATE AND HUNT NIGGERS.
WHEN THEY WAS PUPS I GOT AN OLD NIGGER TO WHUP EM WITH A SWITCH EVERYDAY, SEVERAL TIMES A DAY.
NIGGER SMELL MAKES EM WANT TO KILL. THEY LOVE TO TRACK NIGGER.
BUT WHAT THEY LIKE BEST IS EATIN' ONE. THEY GO FOR THE KNOBS FIRST.
PROVE IT.
HERRRAH, DOGS, HERRRAH! GATHER UP!
WHIIRRR RRRRUHII

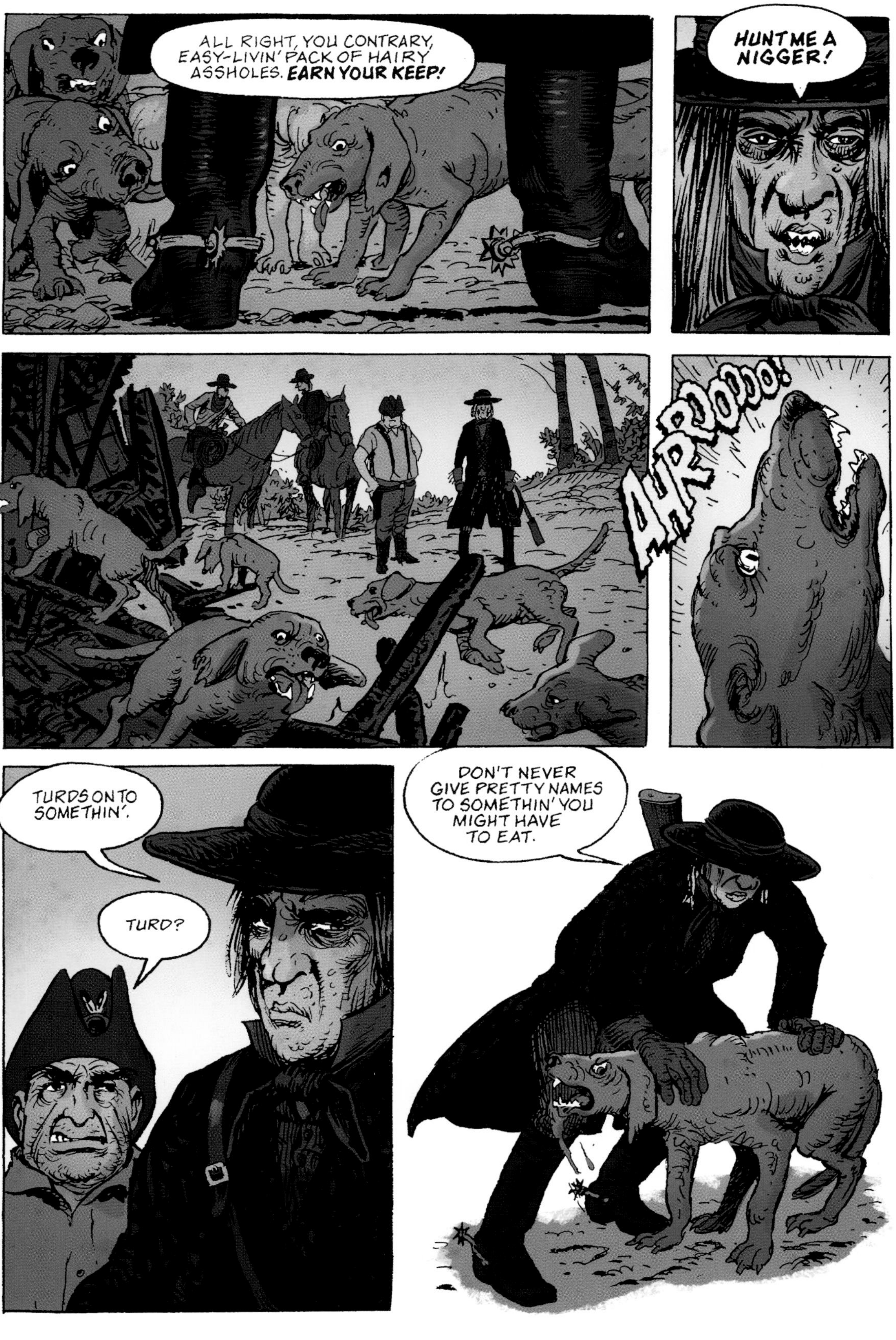
ALL RIGHT, YOU CONTRARY, EASY-LIVIN' PACK OF HAIRY ASSHOLES. **EARN YOUR KEEP!**
HUNT ME A NIGGER!
AURROOOO!
TURDS ON TO SOMETHIN'.
TURD?
DON'T NEVER GIVE PRETTY NAMES TO SOMETHIN' YOU MIGHT HAVE TO EAT.

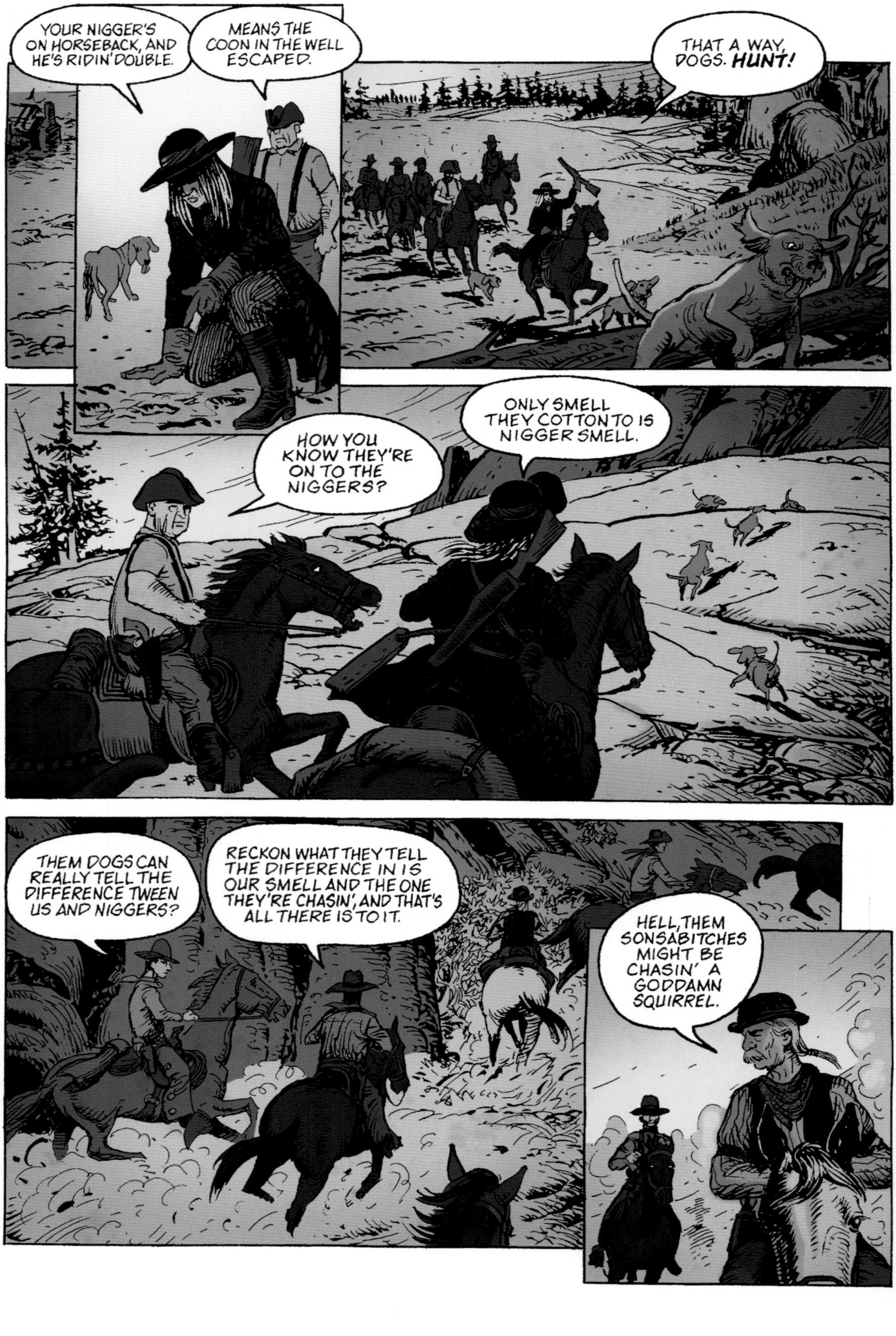
YOUR NIGGER'S ON HORSEBACK, AND HE'S RIDIN' DOUBLE.
MEANS THE COON IN THE WELL ESCAPED.
THAT A WAY, DOGS. HUNT!
HOW YOU KNOW THEY'RE ON TO THE NIGGERS?
ONLY SMELL THEY COTTON TO IS NIGGER SMELL.
THEM DOGS CAN REALLY TELL THE DIFFERENCE 'TWEEN US AND NIGGERS?
RECKON WHAT THEY TELL THE DIFFERENCE IN IS OUR SMELL AND THE ONE THEY'RE CHASIN', AND THAT'S ALL THERE IS TO IT.
HELL, THEM SONSABITCHES MIGHT BE CHASIN' A GODDAMN SQUIRREL.

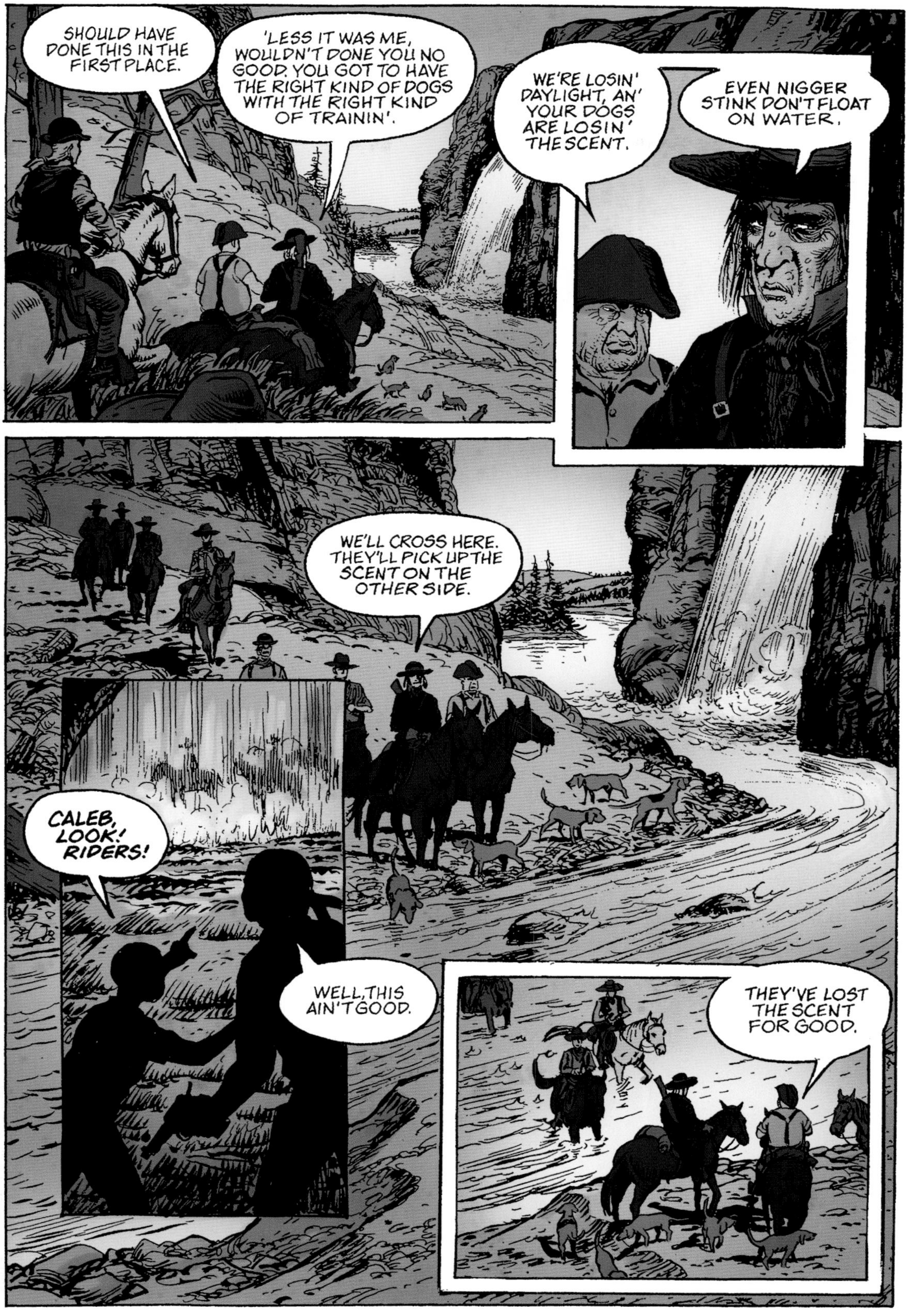
SHOULD HAVE DONE THIS IN THE FIRST PLACE.
'LESS IT WAS ME, WOULDN'T DONE YOU NO GOOD. YOU GOT TO HAVE THE RIGHT KIND OF DOGS WITH THE RIGHT KIND OF TRAININ'.
WE'RE LOSIN' DAYLIGHT, AN' YOUR DOGS ARE LOSIN' THE SCENT.
EVEN NIGGER STINK DON'T FLOAT ON WATER.
WE'LL CROSS HERE. THEY'LL PICK UP THE SCENT ON THE OTHER SIDE.
CALEB, LOOK! RIDERS!
WELL, THIS AIN'T GOOD.
THEY'VE LOST THE SCENT FOR GOOD.

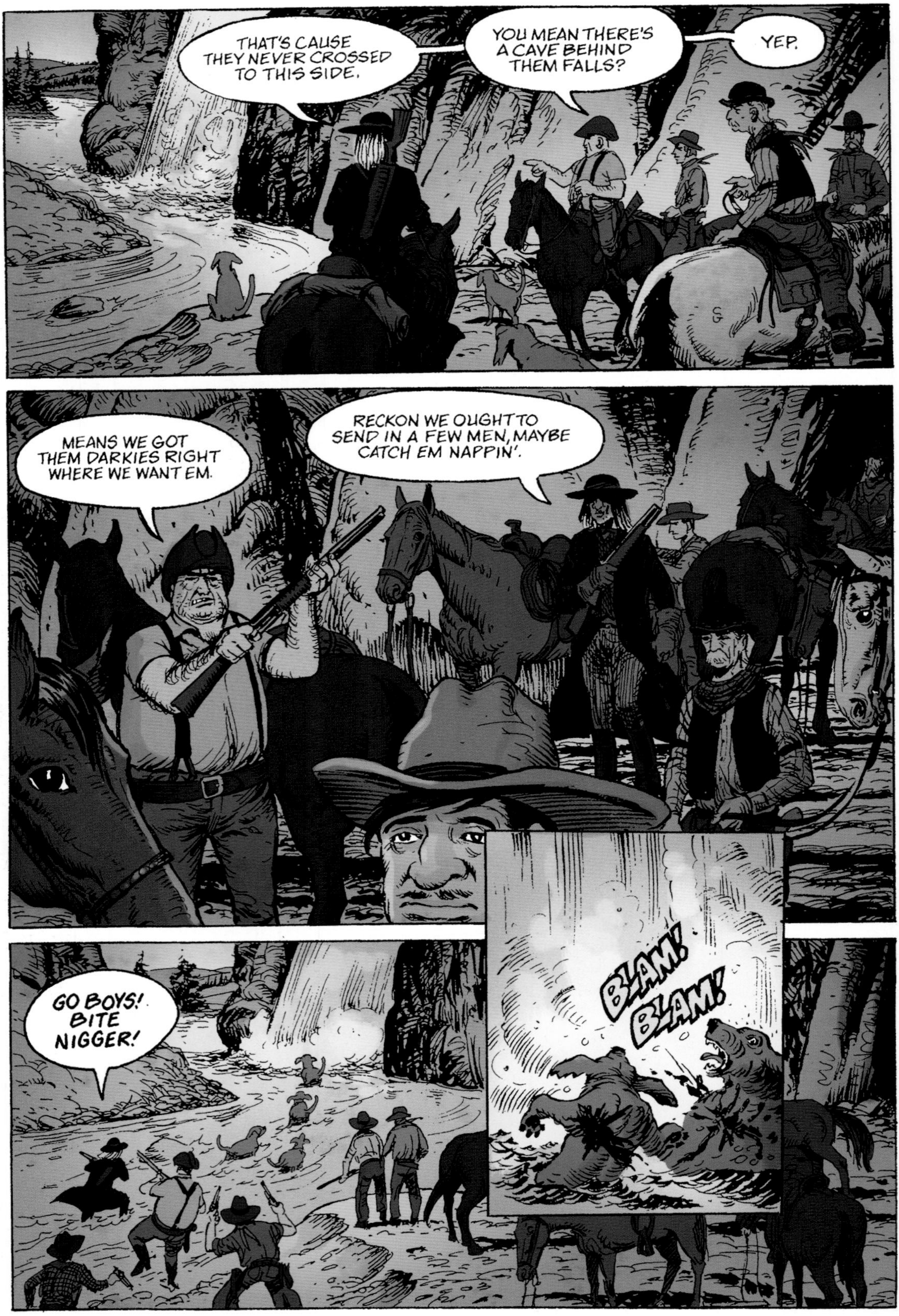
THAT'S CAUSE THEY NEVER CROSSED TO THIS SIDE.
YOU MEAN THERE'S A CAVE BEHIND THEM FALLS?
YEP.
MEANS WE GOT THEM DARKIES RIGHT WHERE WE WANT EM.
RECKON WE OUGHT TO SEND IN A FEW MEN, MAYBE CATCH EM NAPPIN'.
GO BOYS! BITE NIGGER!
BLAM! BLAM!

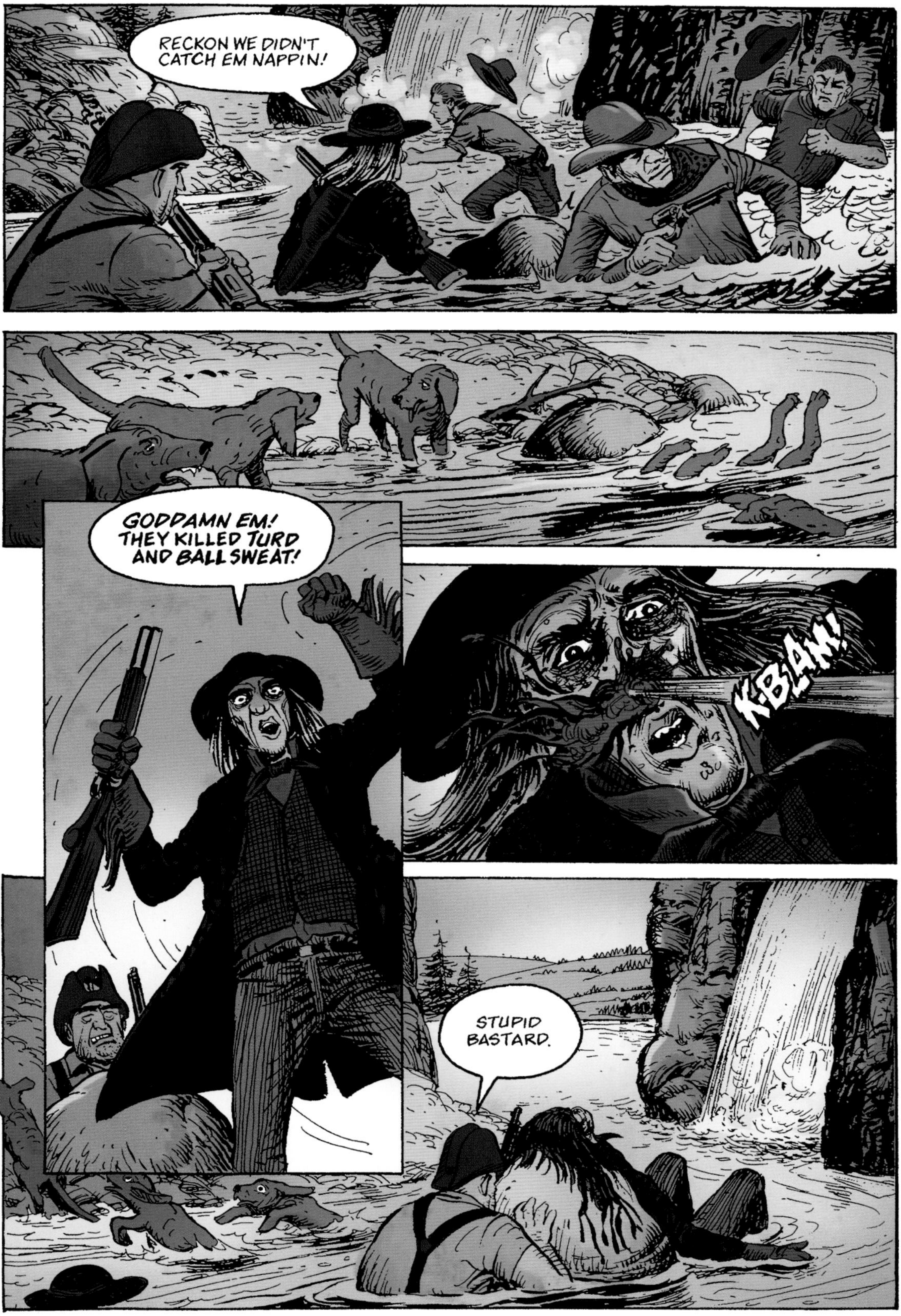
RECKON WE DIDN'T CATCH EM NAPPIN!
GODDAMN EM! THEY KILLED TURD AND BALL SWEAT!
K-BLAM!
STUPID BASTARD.

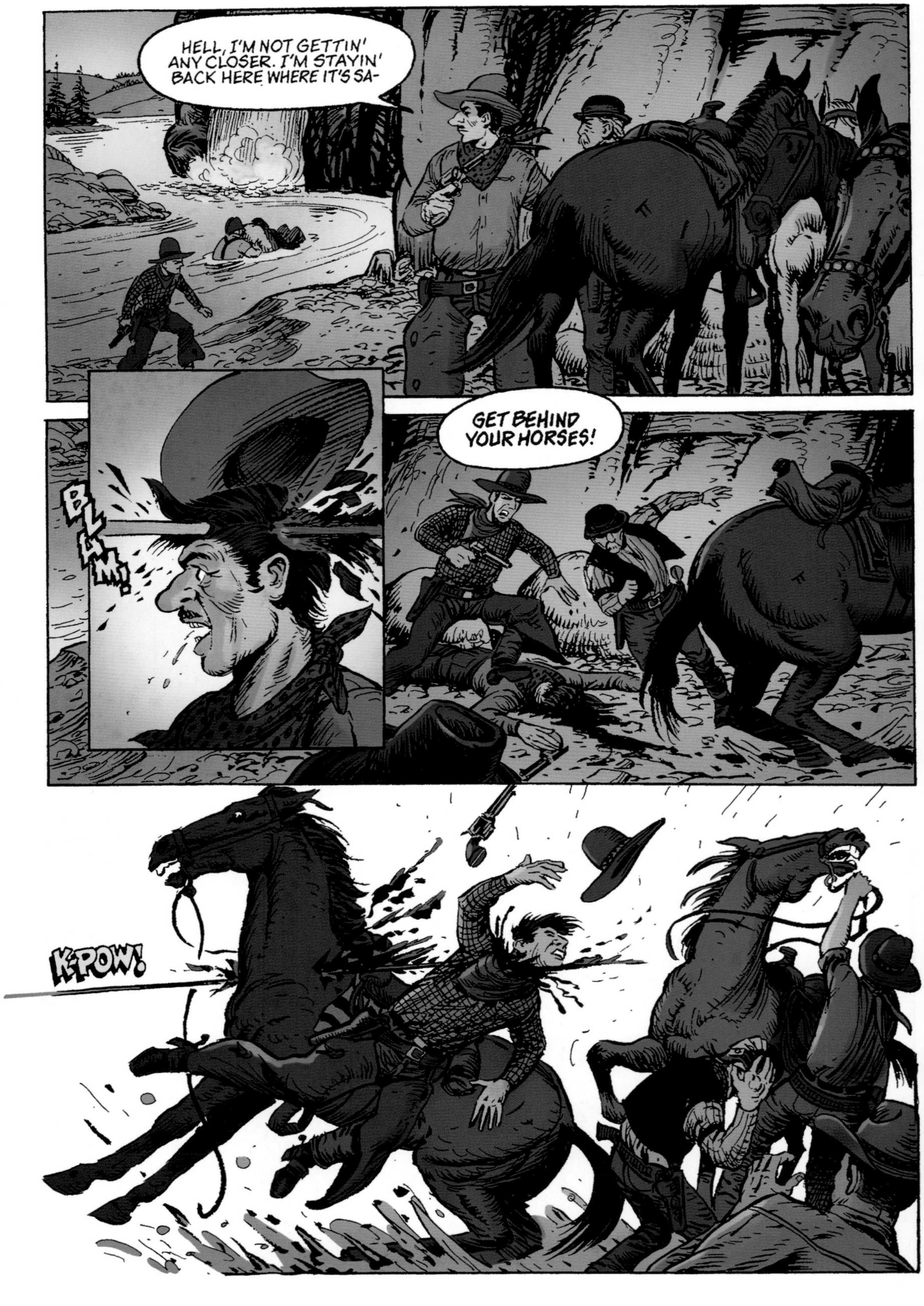
HELL, I'M NOT GETTIN' ANY CLOSER. I'M STAYIN' BACK HERE WHERE IT'S SA-
BLAM!
GET BEHIND YOUR HORSES!
K-POW!

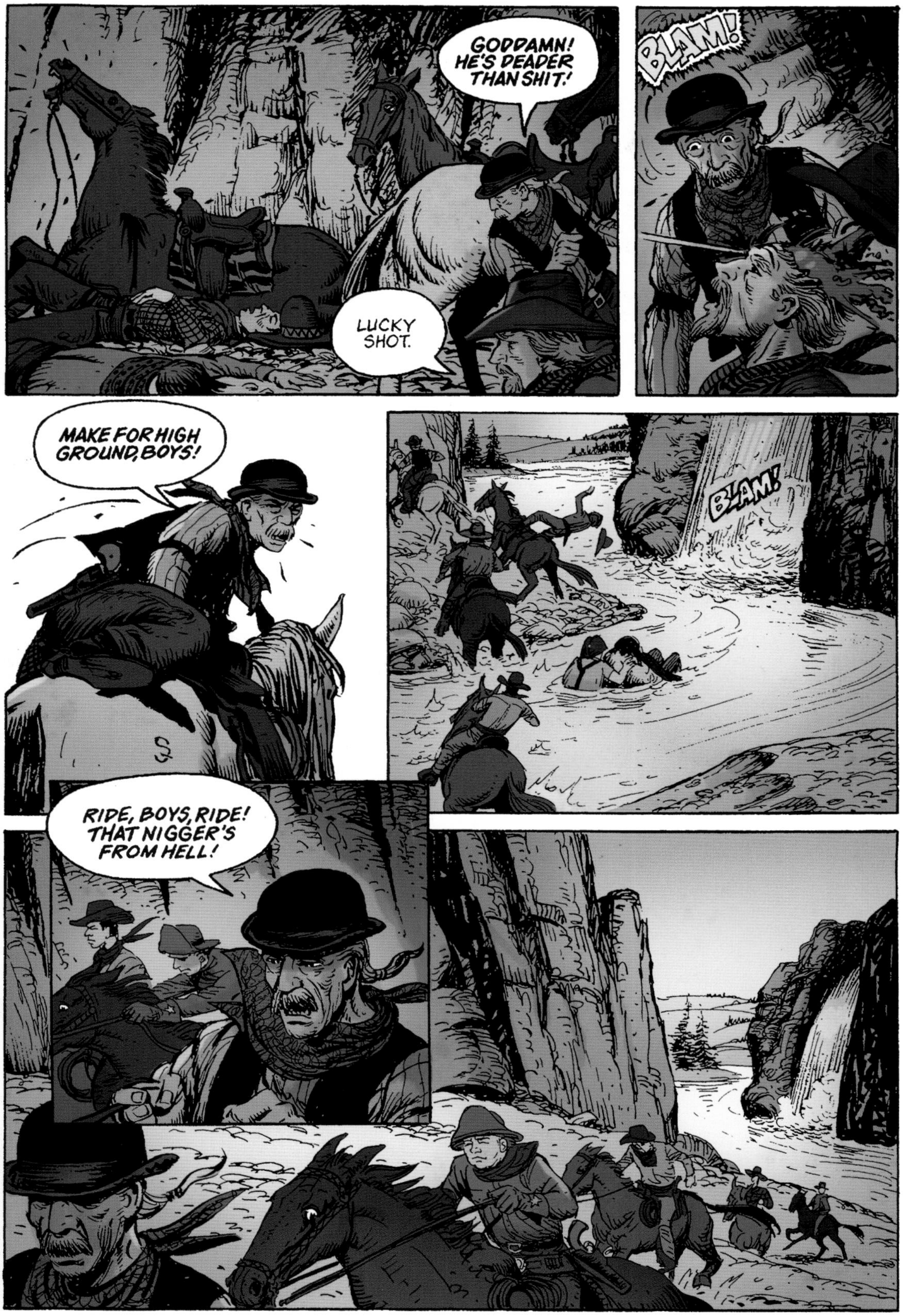
GODDAMN! HE'S DEADER THAN SHIT!
LUCKY SHOT.
BLAM!
MAKE FOR HIGH GROUND, BOYS!
BLAM!
RIDE, BOYS, RIDE! THAT NIGGER'S FROM HELL!

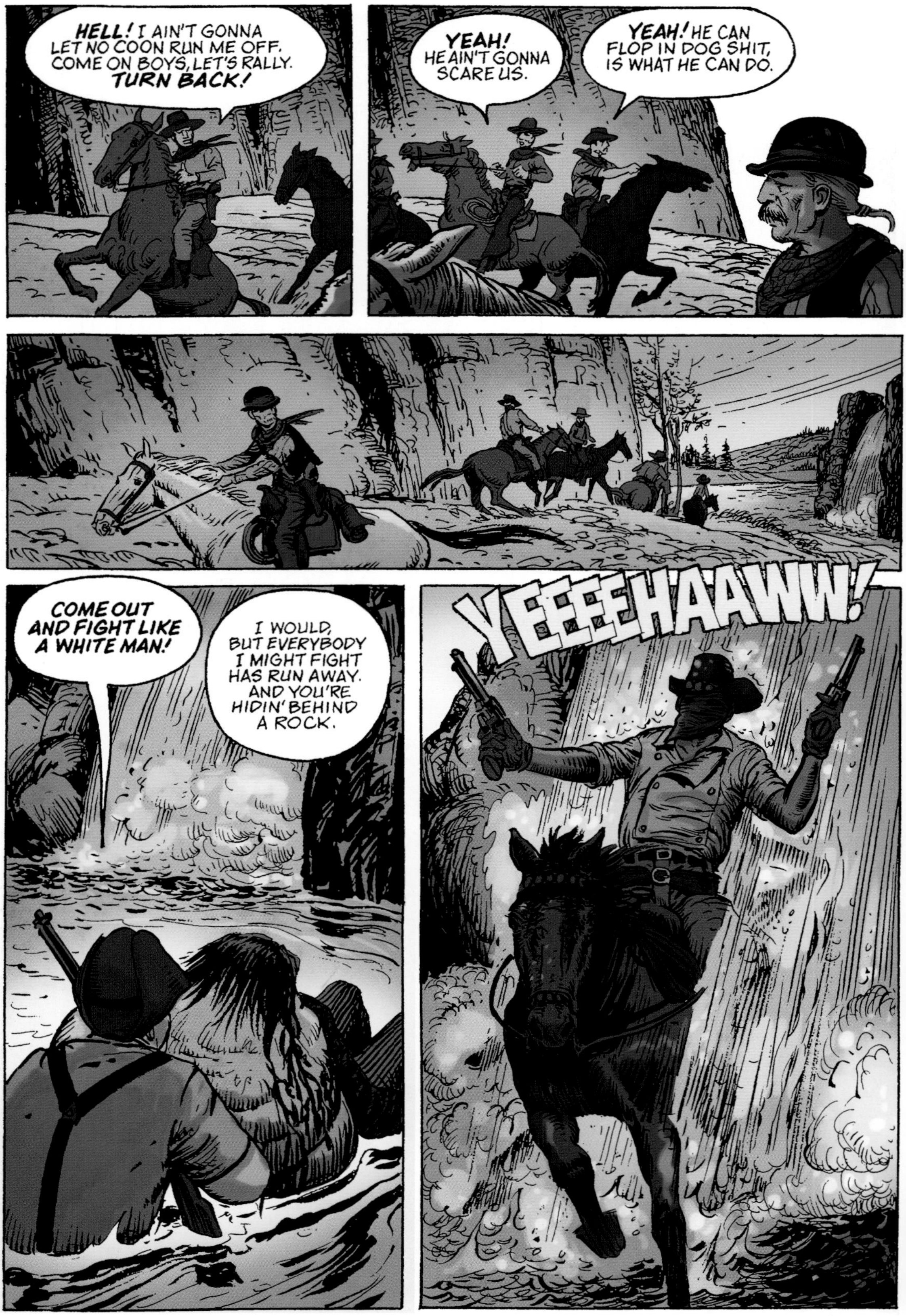
HELL! I AIN'T GONNA LET NO COON RUN ME OFF. COME ON BOYS, LET'S RALLY. TURN BACK!
YEAH! HE AIN'T GONNA SCARE US.
YEAH! HE CAN FLOP IN DOG SHIT, IS WHAT HE CAN DO.
COME OUT AND FIGHT LIKE A WHITE MAN!
I WOULD, BUT EVERYBODY I MIGHT FIGHT HAS RUN AWAY. AND YOU'RE HIDIN' BEHIND A ROCK.
YEEEEHAAWW!

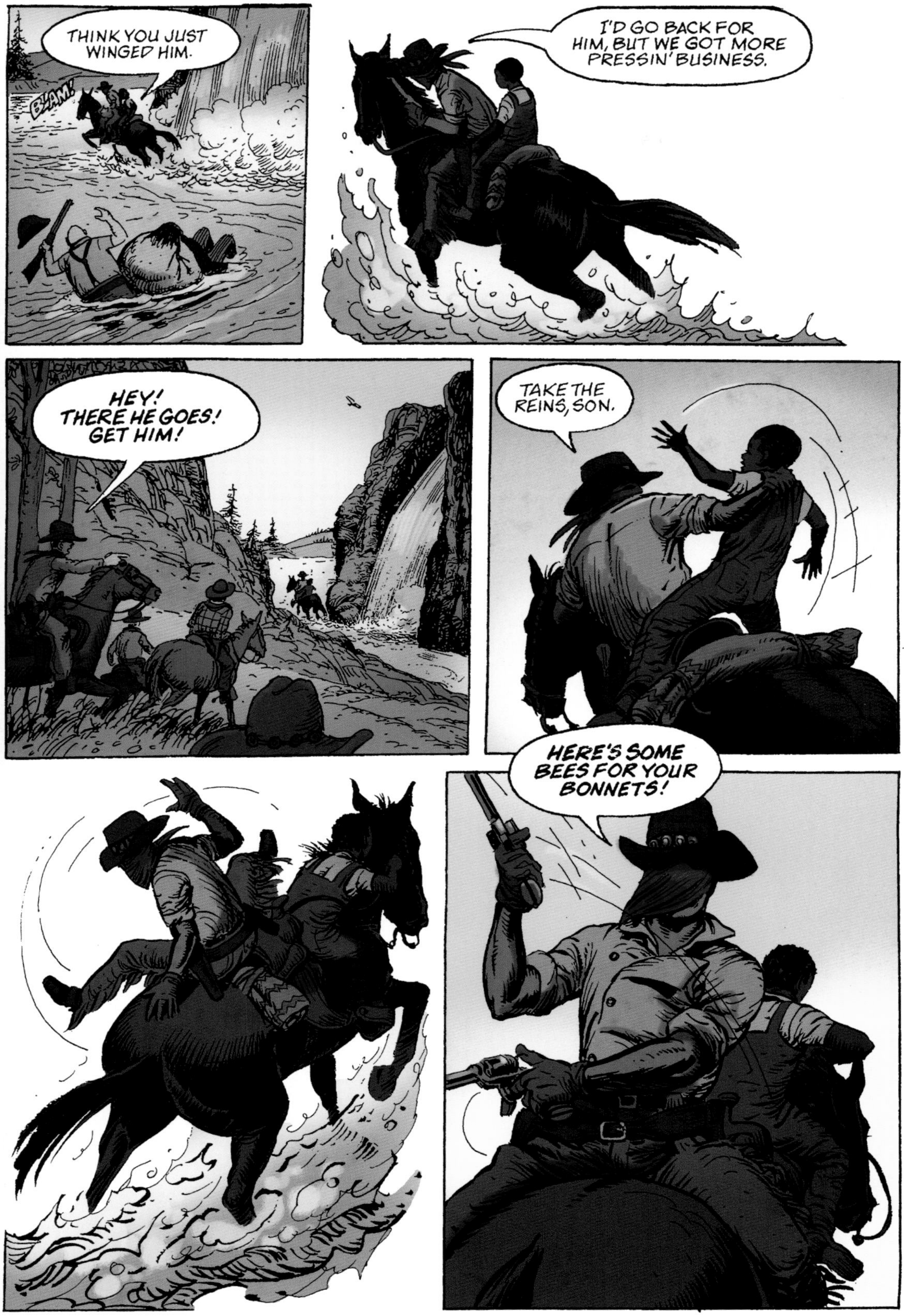
THINK YOU JUST WINGED HIM.
BLAM!
I'D GO BACK FOR HIM, BUT WE GOT MORE PRESSIN' BUSINESS.
HEY! THERE HE GOES! GET HIM!
TAKE THE REINS, SON.
HERE'S SOME BEES FOR YOUR BONNETS!

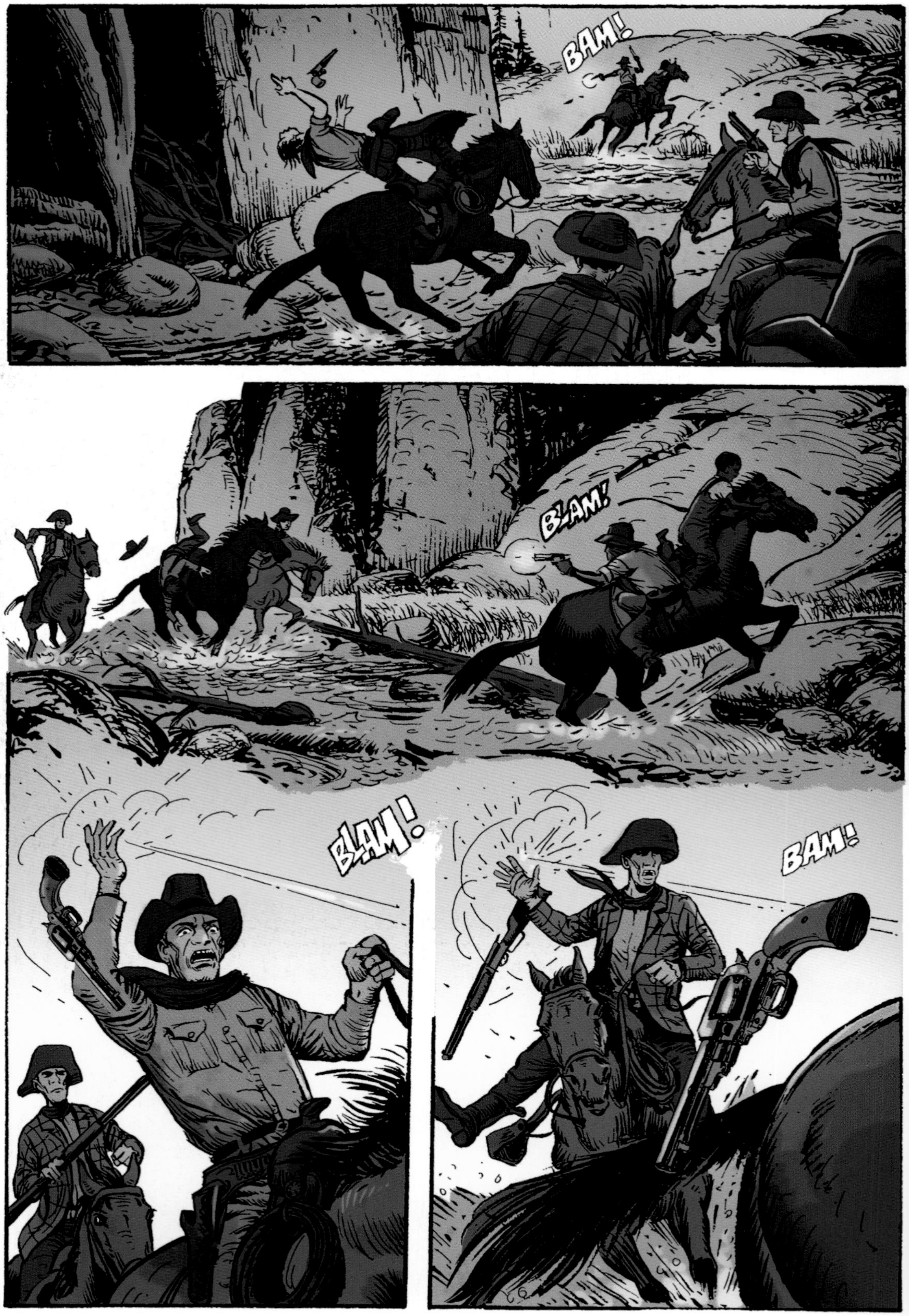
BAM!
BLAM!
BLAM!
BAM!

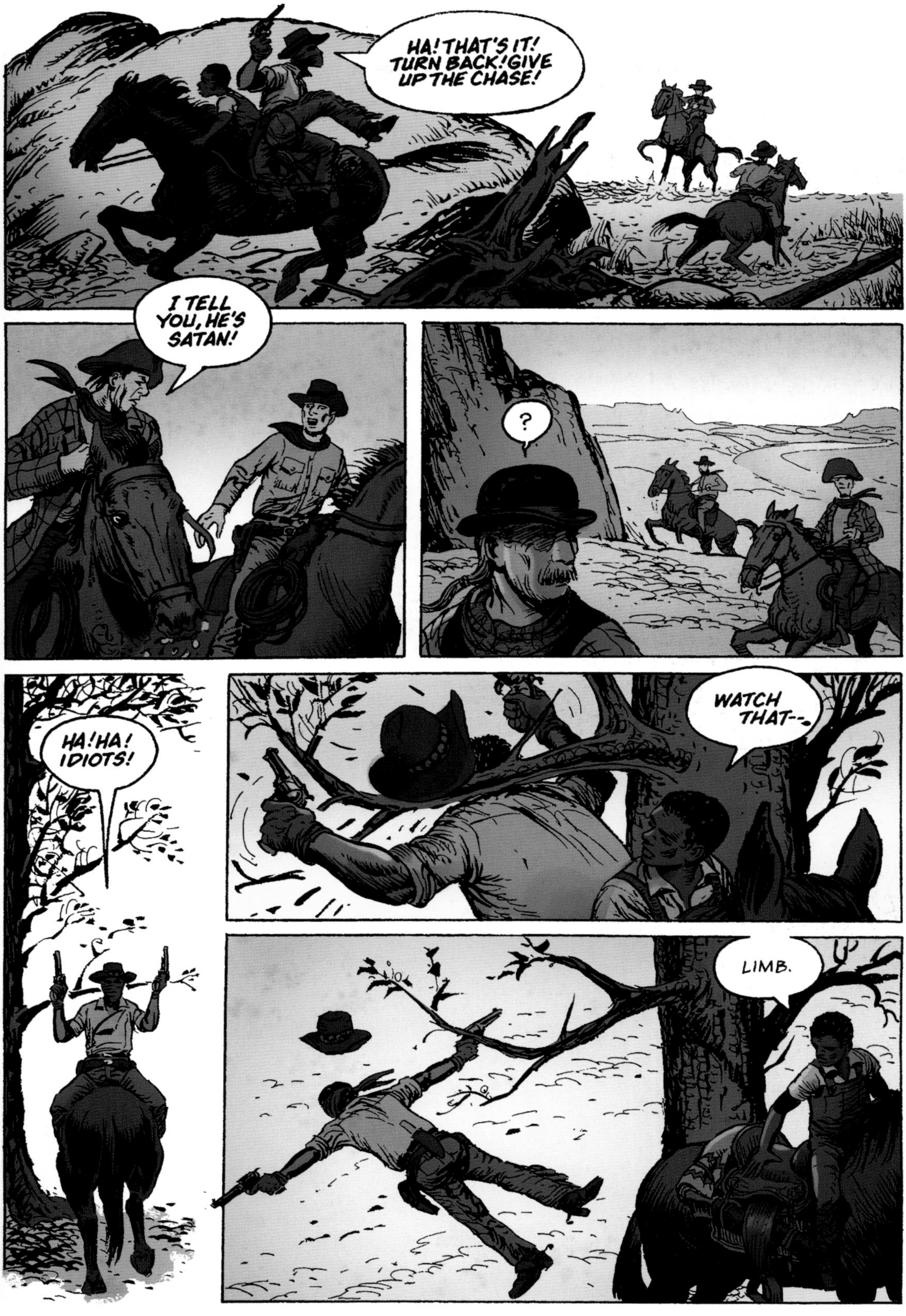
HA! THAT'S IT! TURN BACK! GIVE UP THE CHASE!
I TELL YOU, HE'S SATAN!
?
HA! HA! IDIOTS!
WATCH THAT--
LIMB.

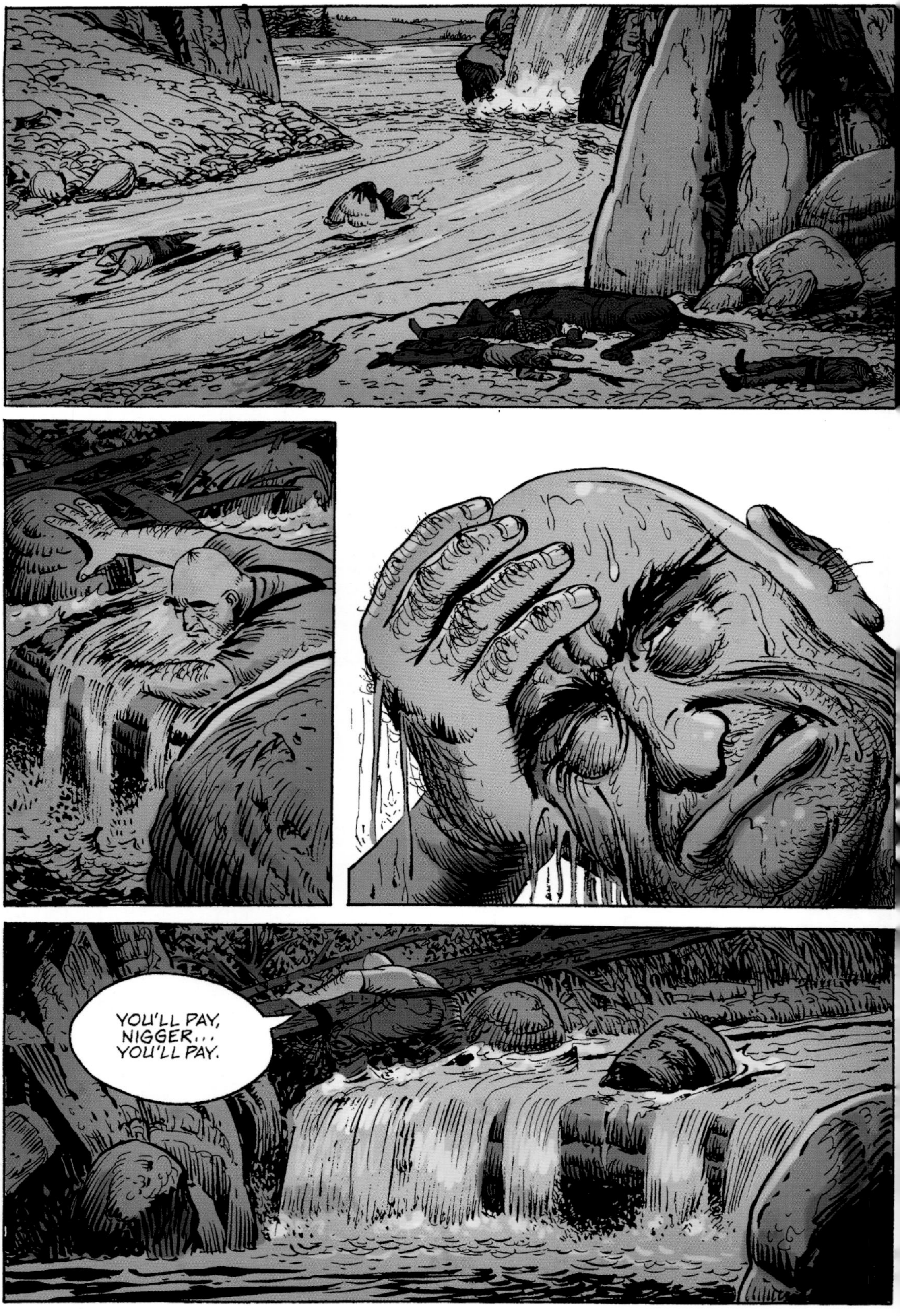
YOU'LL PAY, NIGGER... YOU'LL PAY.

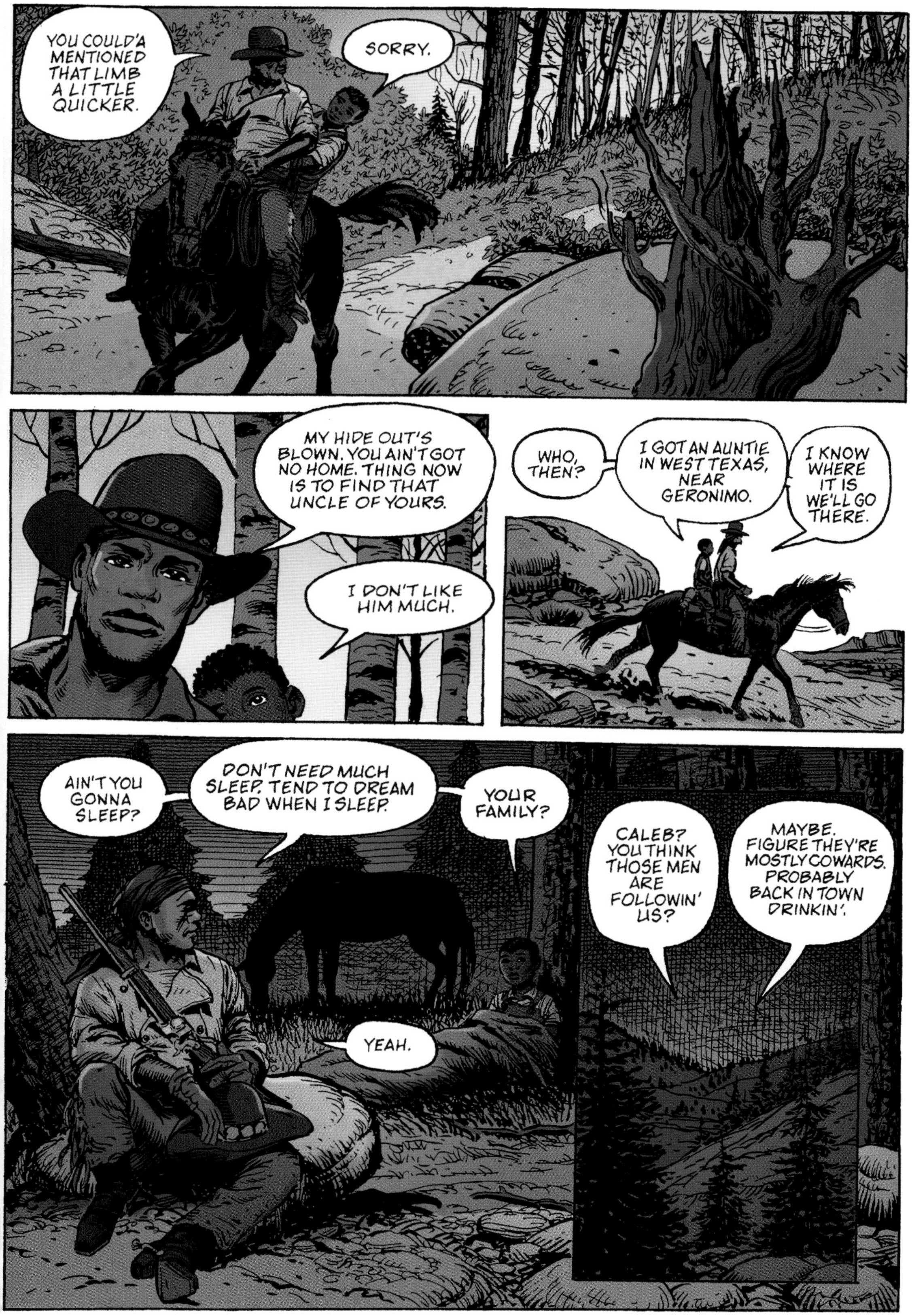
YOU COULD'A MENTIONED THAT LIMB A LITTLE QUICKER.
SORRY.
MY HIDE OUT'S BLOWN. YOU AIN'T GOT NO HOME. THING NOW IS TO FIND THAT UNCLE OF YOURS.
I DON'T LIKE HIM MUCH.
WHO, THEN?
I GOT AN AUNTIE IN WEST TEXAS, NEAR GERONIMO.
I KNOW WHERE IT IS WE'LL GO THERE.
AIN'T YOU GONNA SLEEP?
DON'T NEED MUCH SLEEP. TEND TO DREAM BAD WHEN I SLEEP.
YOUR FAMILY?
YEAH.
CALEB? YOU THINK THOSE MEN ARE FOLLOWIN' US?
MAYBE. FIGURE THEY'RE MOSTLY COWARDS. PROBABLY BACK IN TOWN DRINKIN'.

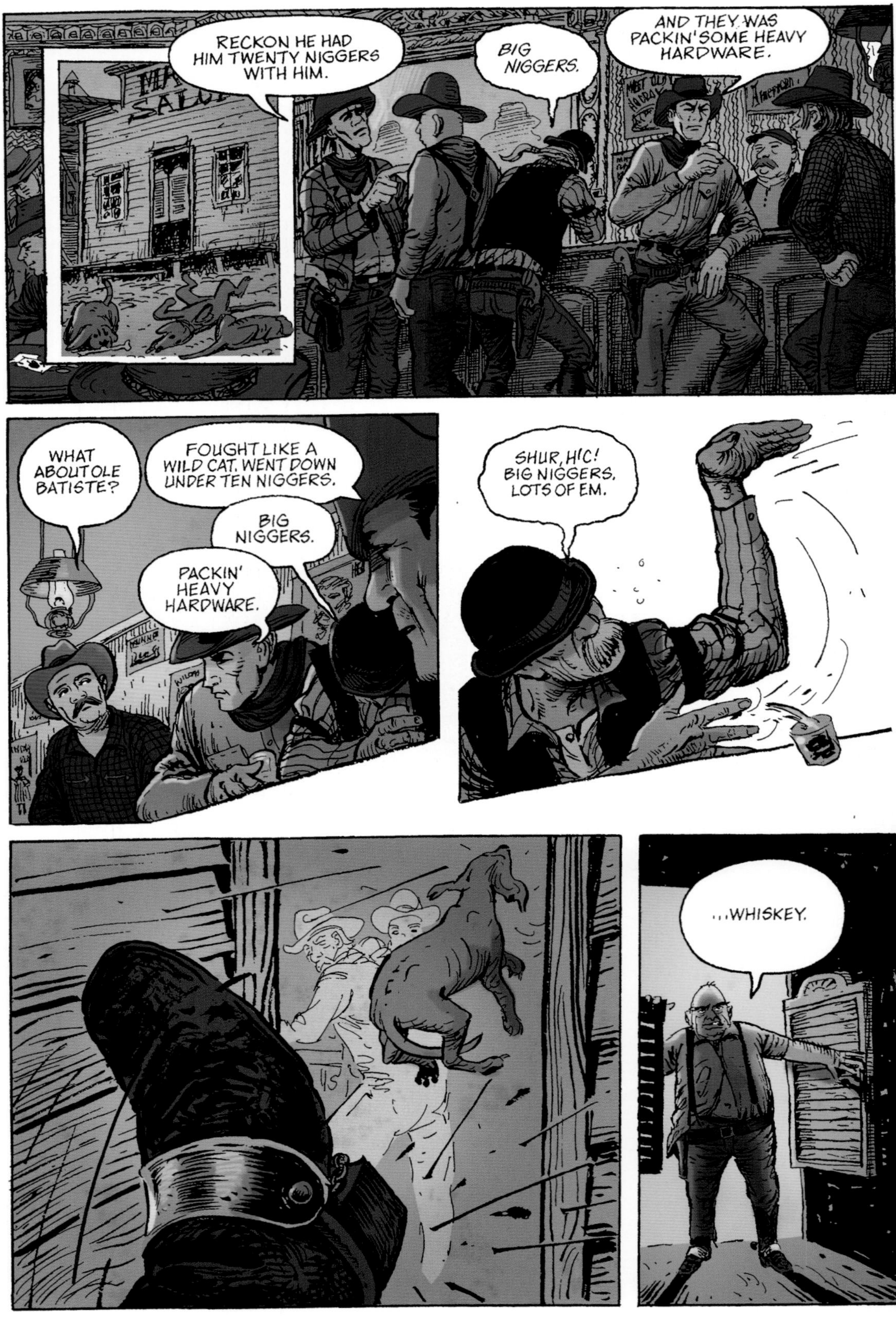
RECKON HE HAD HIM TWENTY NIGGERS WITH HIM.
BIG NIGGERS.
AND THEY WAS PACKIN' SOME HEAVY HARDWARE.
WHAT ABOUT OLE BATISTE?
FOUGHT LIKE A WILD CAT. WENT DOWN UNDER TEN NIGGERS.
BIG NIGGERS.
PACKIN' HEAVY HARDWARE.
SHUR, HIC! BIG NIGGERS, LOTS OF EM.
...WHISKEY.

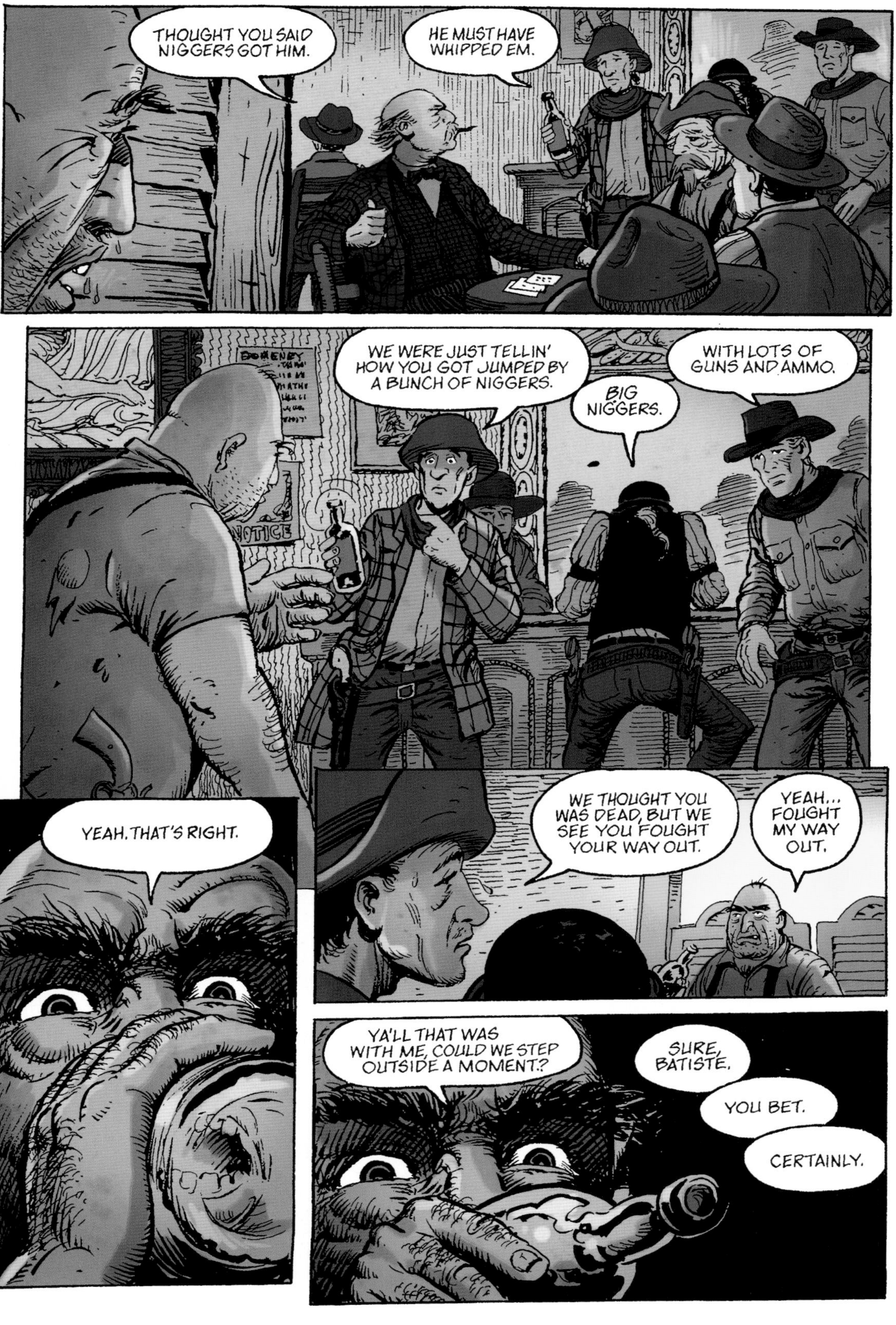
THOUGHT YOU SAID NIGGERS GOT HIM.
HE MUST HAVE WHIPPED EM.
WE WERE JUST TELLIN' HOW YOU GOT JUMPED BY A BUNCH OF NIGGERS.
BIG NIGGERS.
WITH LOTS OF GUNS AND AMMO.
NOTICE
YEAH. THAT'S RIGHT.
WE THOUGHT YOU WAS DEAD, BUT WE SEE YOU FOUGHT YOUR WAY OUT.
YEAH... FOUGHT MY WAY OUT.
YA'LL THAT WAS WITH ME, COULD WE STEP OUTSIDE A MOMENT.?
SURE, BATISTE.
YOU BET.
CERTAINLY.

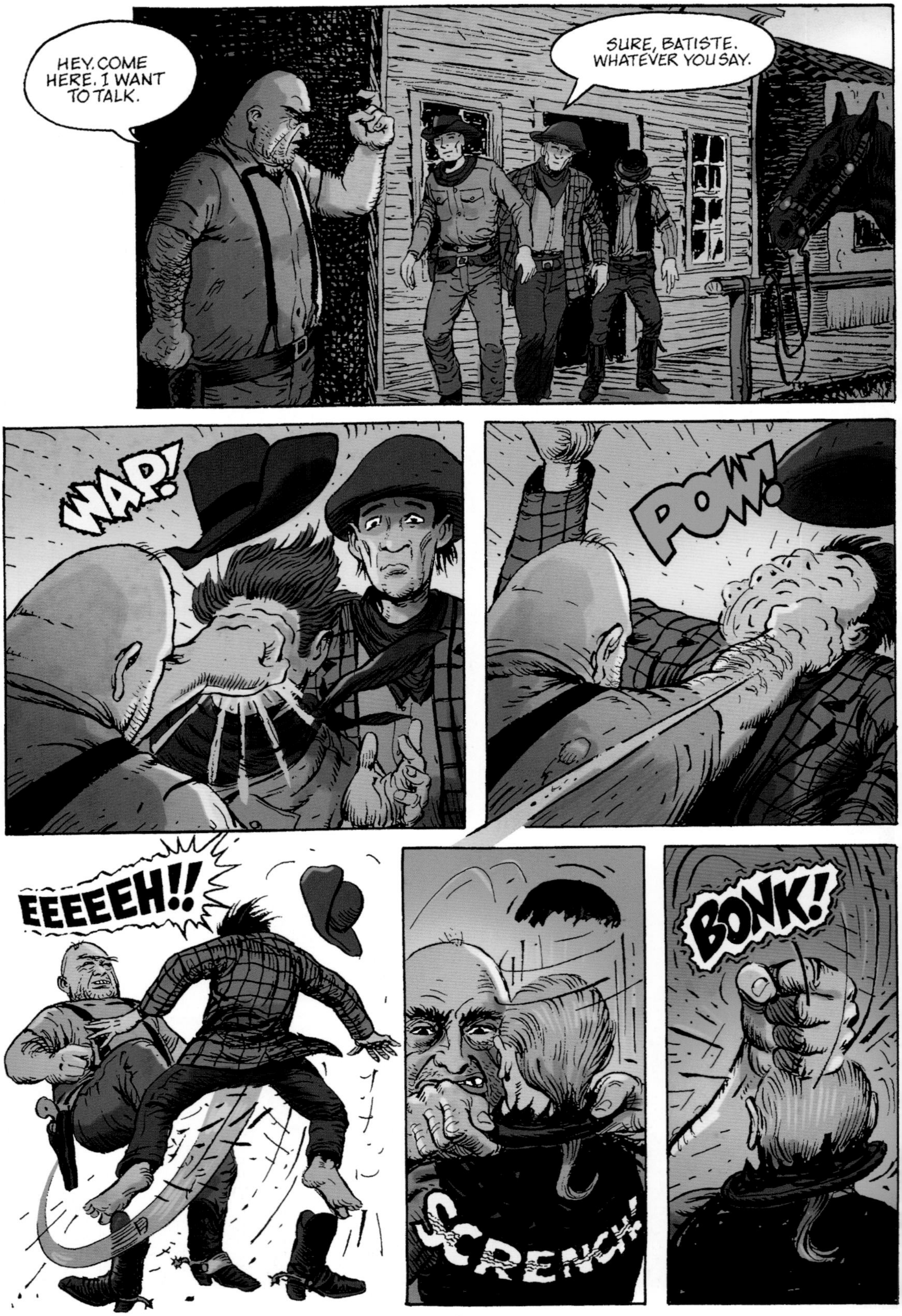
HEY. COME HERE. I WANT TO TALK.
SURE, BATISTE. WHATEVER YOU SAY.
WAP!
POW!
EEEEEH!!
SCRENCH!
BONK!

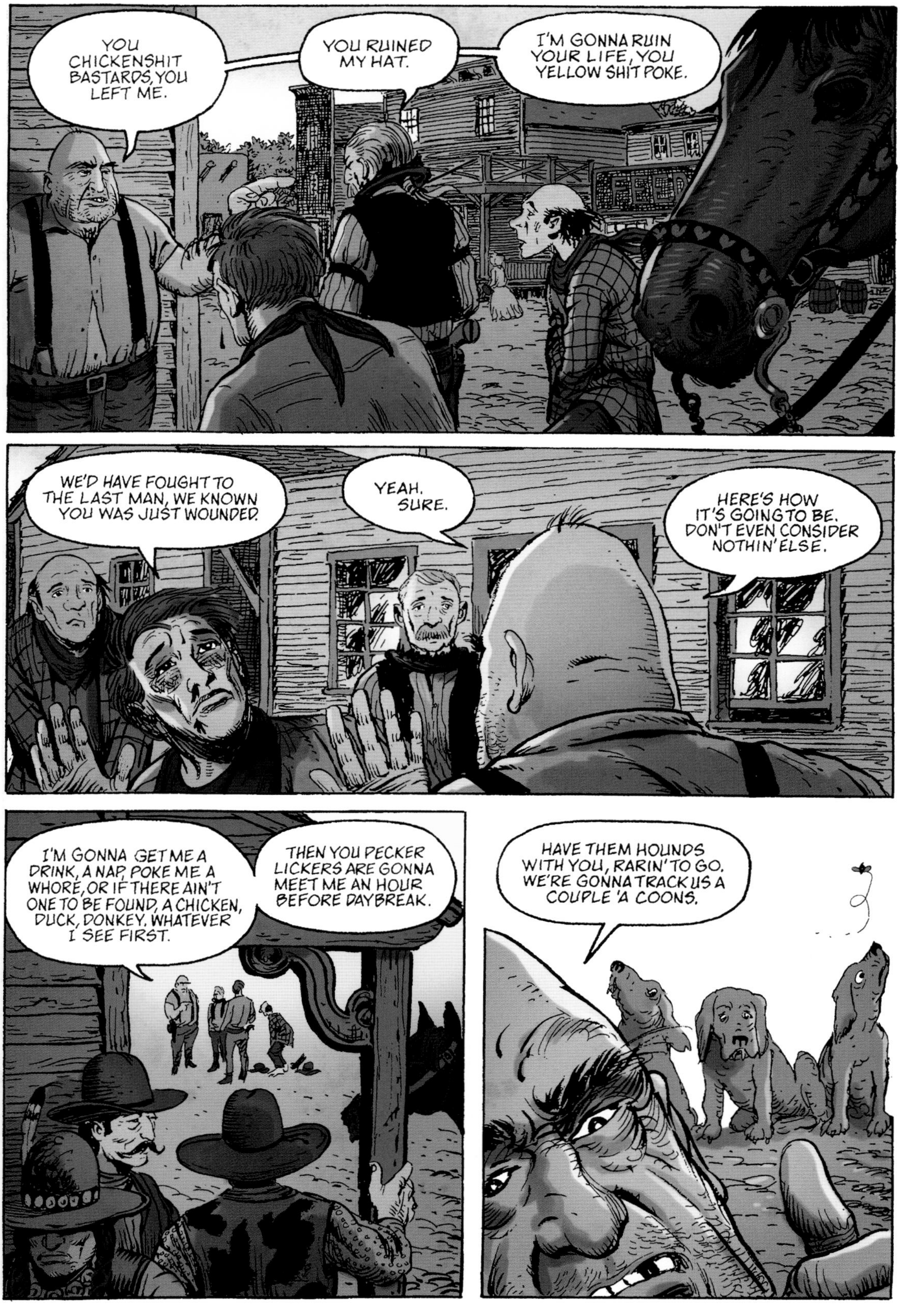
YOU CHICKENSHIT BASTARDS, YOU LEFT ME.
YOU RUINED MY HAT.
I'M GONNA RUIN YOUR LIFE, YOU YELLOW SHIT POKE.
WE'D HAVE FOUGHT TO THE LAST MAN, WE KNOWN YOU WAS JUST WOUNDED.
YEAH. SURE.
HERE'S HOW IT'S GOING TO BE. DON'T EVEN CONSIDER NOTHIN' ELSE.
I'M GONNA GET ME A DRINK, A NAP, POKE ME A WHORE, OR IF THERE AIN'T ONE TO BE FOUND, A CHICKEN, DUCK, DONKEY. WHATEVER I SEE FIRST.
THEN YOU PECKER LICKERS ARE GONNA MEET ME AN HOUR BEFORE DAYBREAK.
HAVE THEM HOUNDS WITH YOU, RARIN' TO GO. WE'RE GONNA TRACK US A COUPLE 'A COONS.

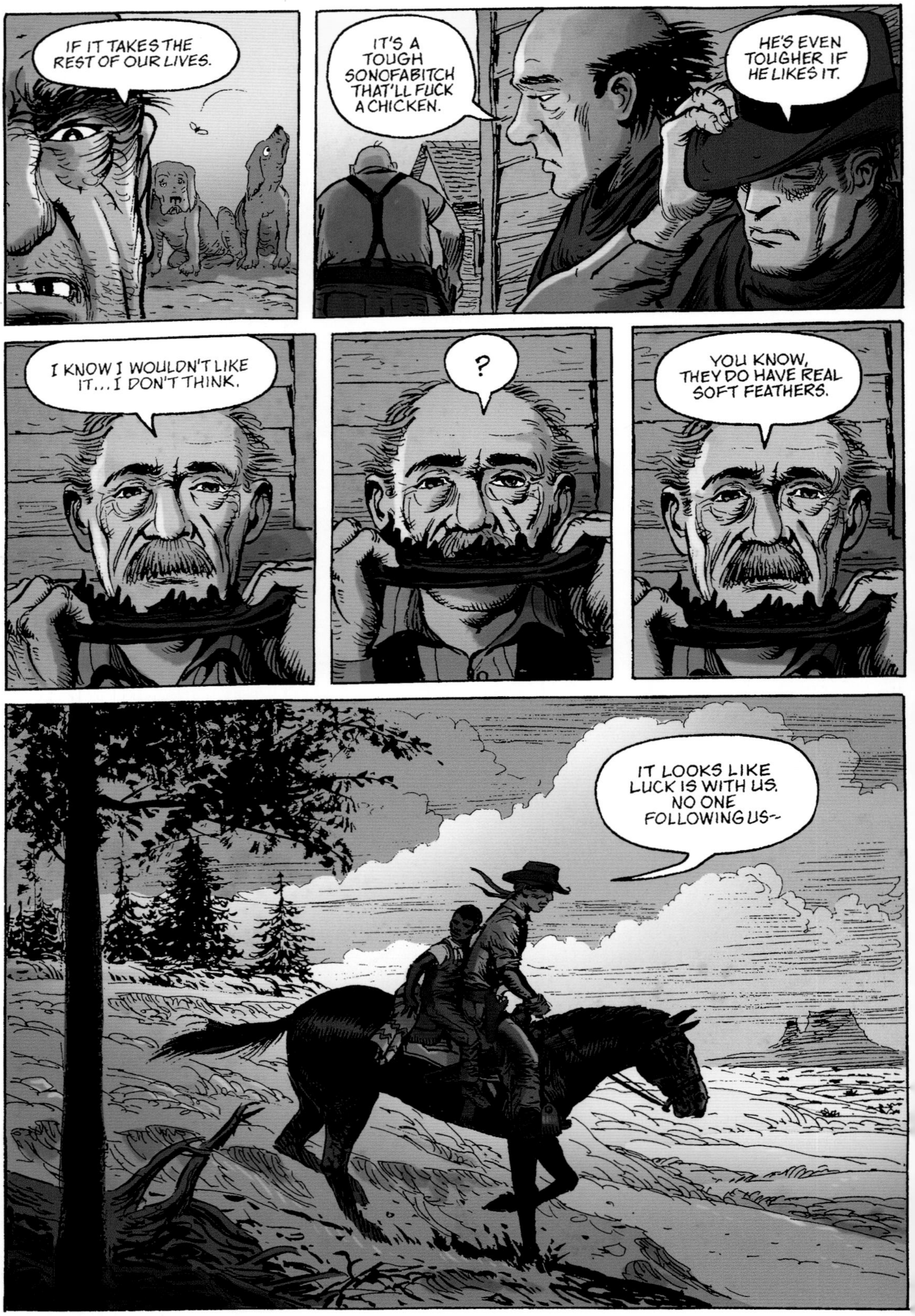

IF IT TAKES THE REST OF OUR LIVES.
IT'S A TOUGH SONOFABITCH THAT'LL FUCK A CHICKEN.
HE'S EVEN TOUGHER IF HE LIKES IT.
I KNOW I WOULDN'T LIKE IT... I DON'T THINK.
?
YOU KNOW, THEY DO HAVE REAL SOFT FEATHERS.
IT LOOKS LIKE LUCK IS WITH US. NO ONE FOLLOWING US-

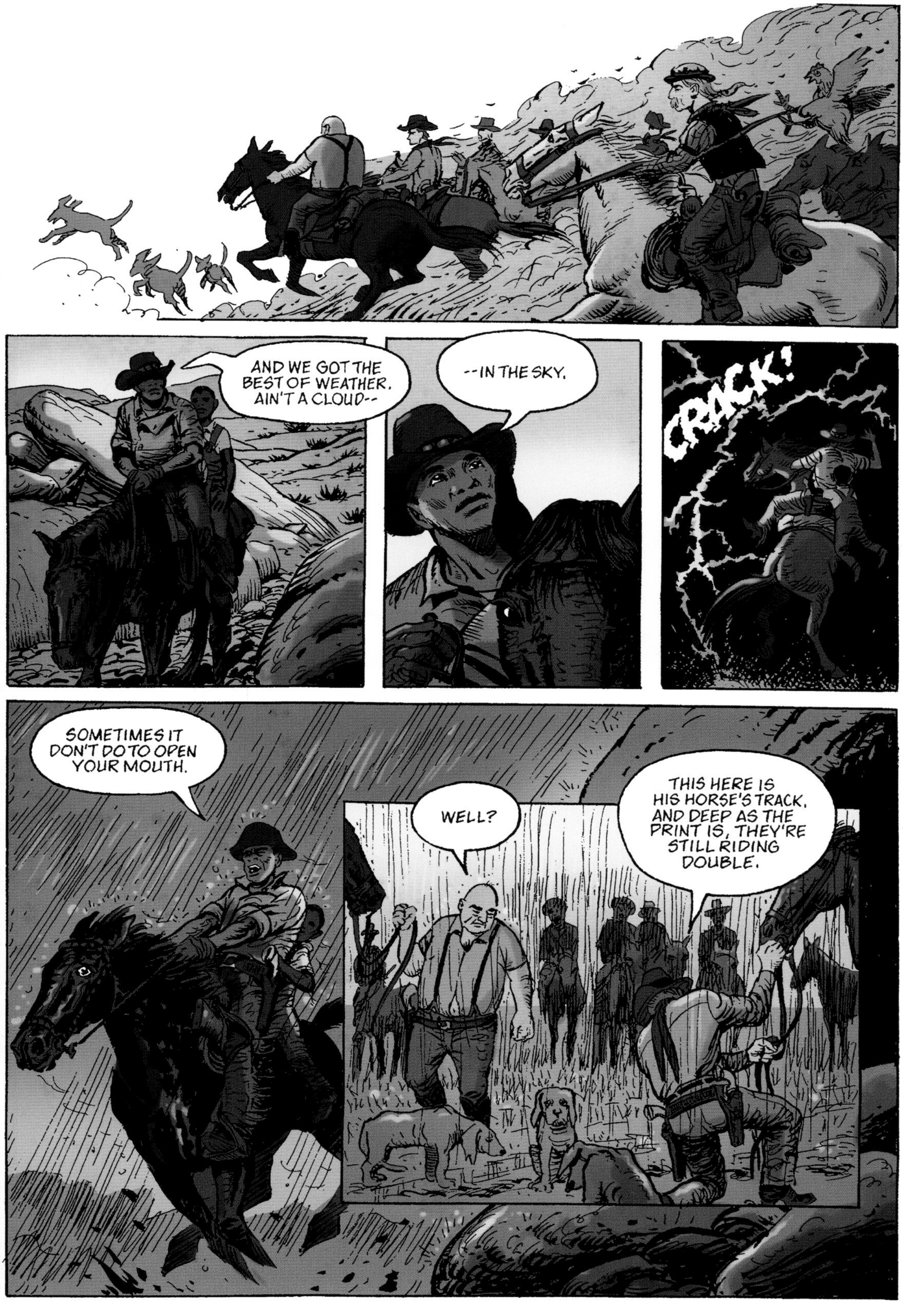
AND WE GOT THE BEST OF WEATHER. AIN'T A CLOUD--
--IN THE SKY.
CRACK!
SOMETIMES IT DON'T DO TO OPEN YOUR MOUTH.
WELL?
THIS HERE IS HIS HORSE'S TRACK, AND DEEP AS THE PRINT IS, THEY'RE STILL RIDING DOUBLE.

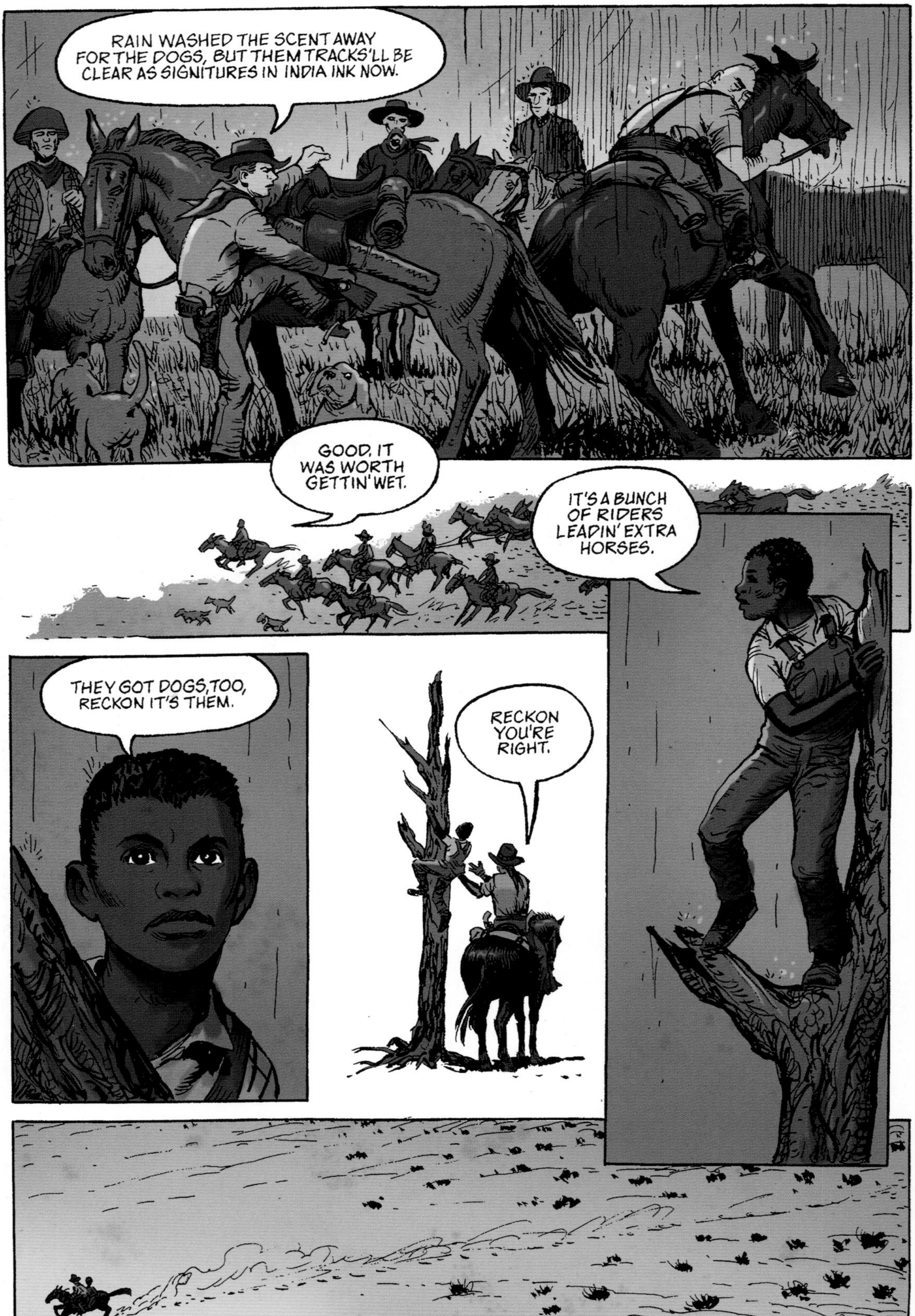
RAIN WASHED THE SCENT AWAY FOR THE DOGS, BUT THEM TRACKS'LL BE CLEAR AS SIGNITURES IN INDIA INK NOW.
GOOD, IT WAS WORTH GETTIN' WET.
IT'S A BUNCH OF RIDERS LEADIN' EXTRA HORSES.
THEY GOT DOGS, TOO, RECKON IT'S THEM.
RECKON YOU'RE RIGHT.

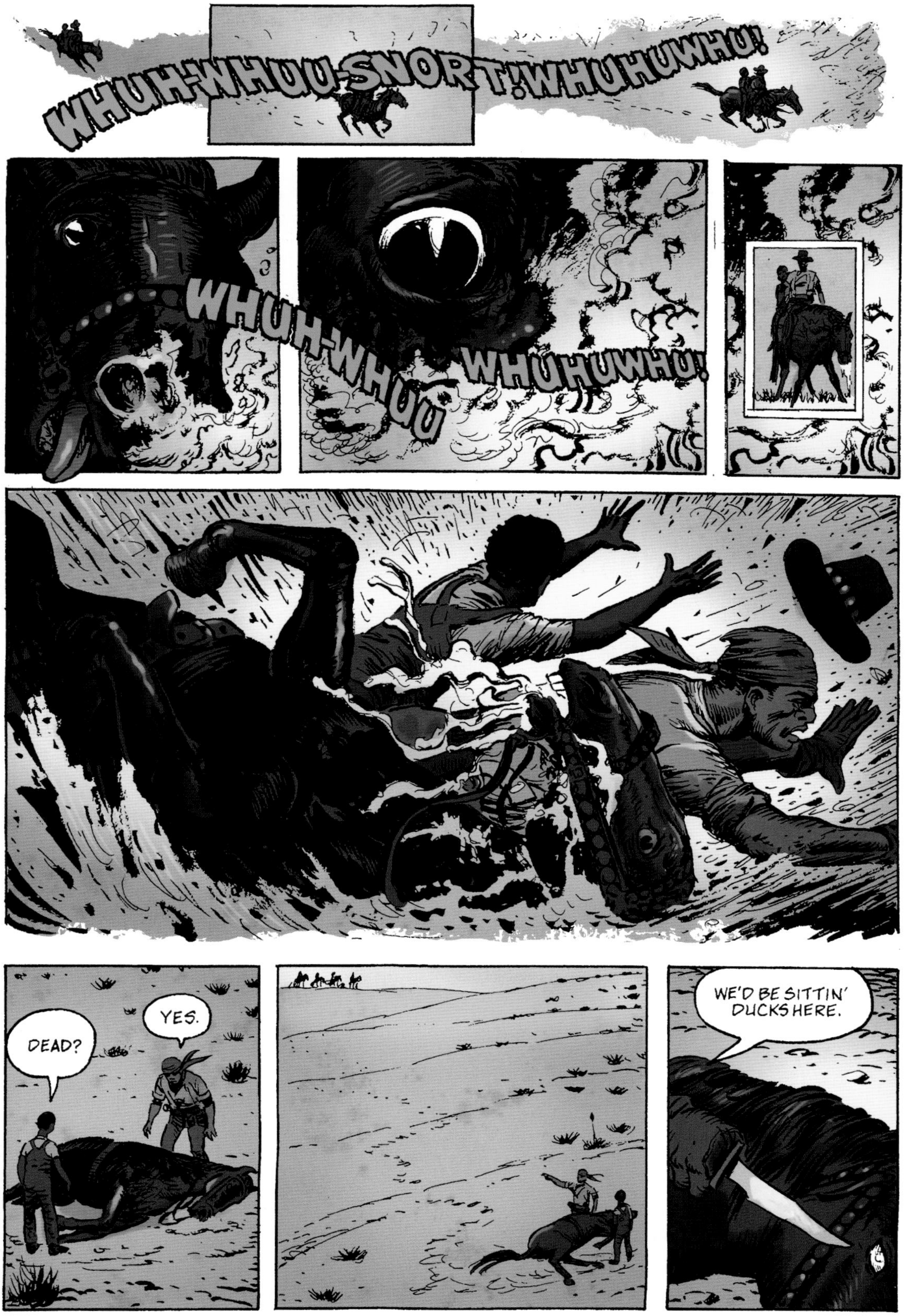
WHUH-WHUU-SNORT! WHUHUWHU!
WHUH-WHUU
WHUHUWHU!
DEAD?
YES.
WE'D BE SITTIN' DUCKS HERE.

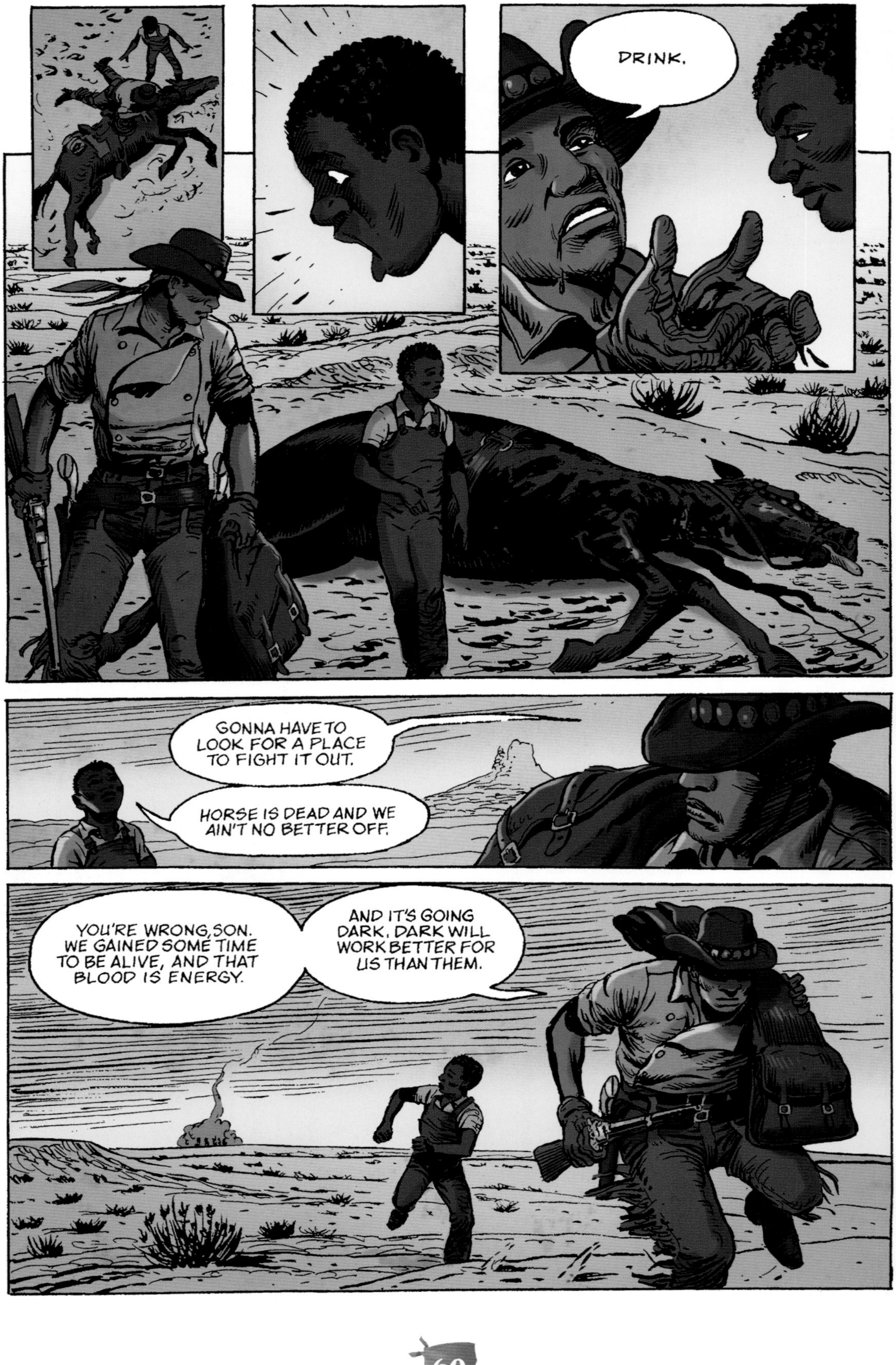
DRINK.
GONNA HAVE TO LOOK FOR A PLACE TO FIGHT IT OUT.
HORSE IS DEAD AND WE AIN'T NO BETTER OFF.
YOU'RE WRONG, SON. WE GAINED SOME TIME TO BE ALIVE, AND THAT BLOOD IS ENERGY.
AND IT'S GOING DARK. DARK WILL WORK BETTER FOR US THAN THEM.

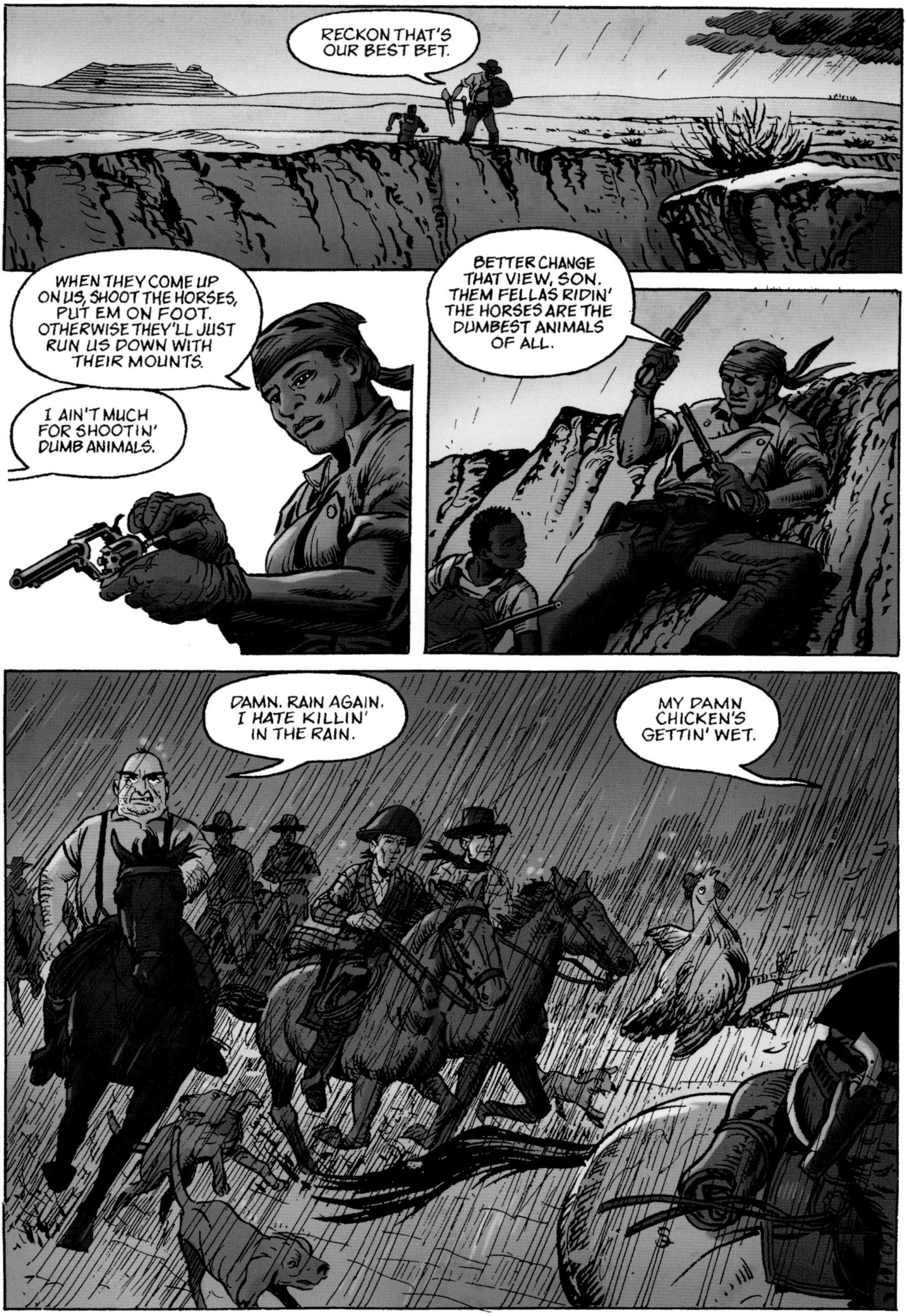
RECKON THAT'S OUR BEST BET.
WHEN THEY COME UP ON US, SHOOT THE HORSES, PUT EM ON FOOT. OTHERWISE THEY'LL JUST RUN US DOWN WITH THEIR MOUNTS.
I AIN'T MUCH FOR SHOOTIN' DUMB ANIMALS.
BETTER CHANGE THAT VIEW, SON. THEM FELLAS RIDIN' THE HORSES ARE THE DUMBEST ANIMALS OF ALL.
DAMN. RAIN AGAIN. I HATE KILLIN' IN THE RAIN.
MY DAMN CHICKEN'S GETTIN' WET.

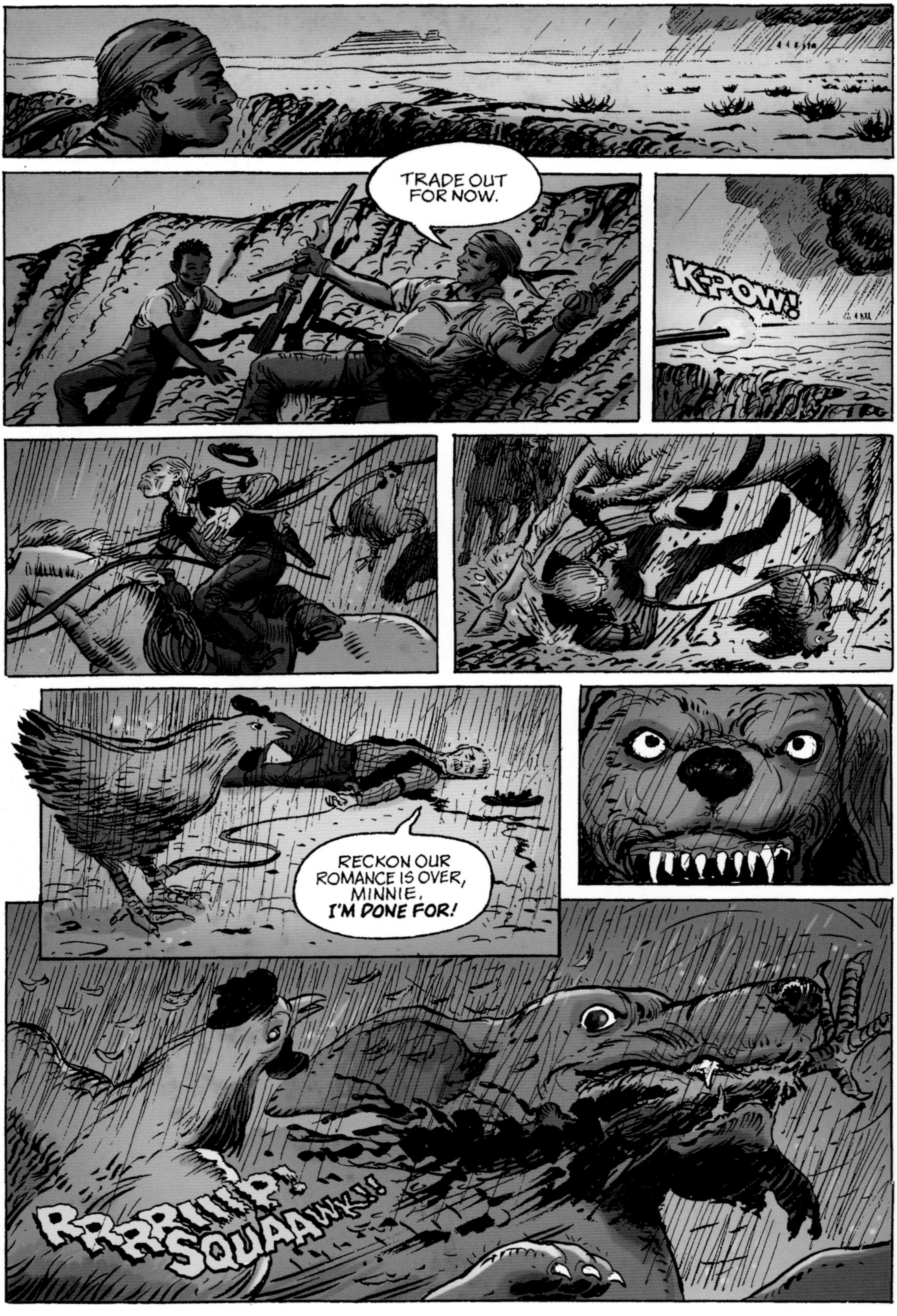
TRADE OUT FOR NOW.
K-POW!
RECKON OUR ROMANCE IS OVER, MINNIE. I'M DONE FOR!
RRRRIIIIP! SQUAAAWK!!

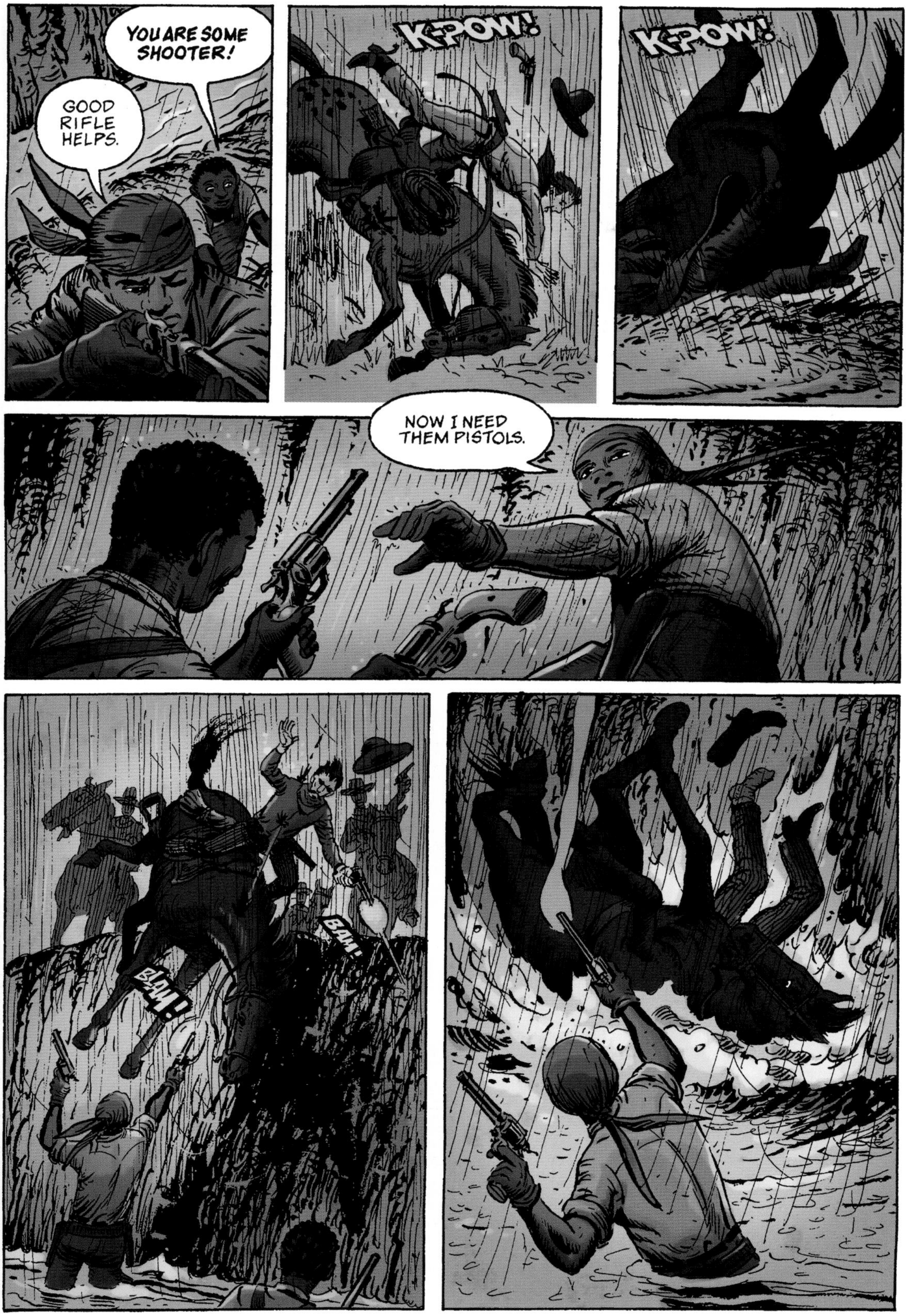
YOU ARE SOME SHOOTER!
GOOD RIFLE HELPS.
K-POW!
K-POW!
NOW I NEED THEM PISTOLS.
BAM!
BLAM!

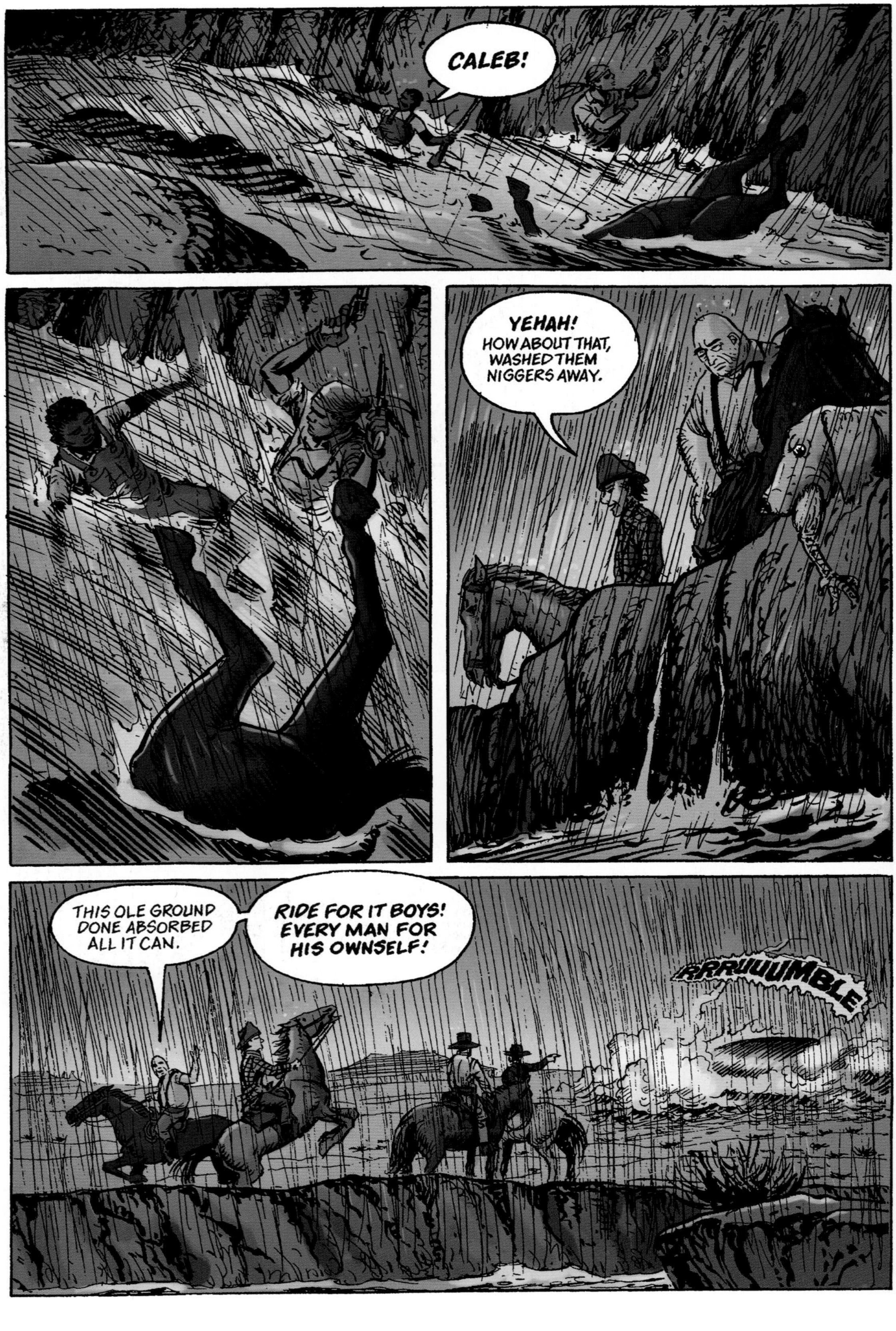
CALEB!
YEHAH! HOW ABOUT THAT, WASHED THEM NIGGERS AWAY.
THIS OLE GROUND DONE ABSORBED ALL IT CAN.
RIDE FOR IT BOYS! EVERY MAN FOR HIS OWNSELF!
RRRUUUUMBLE

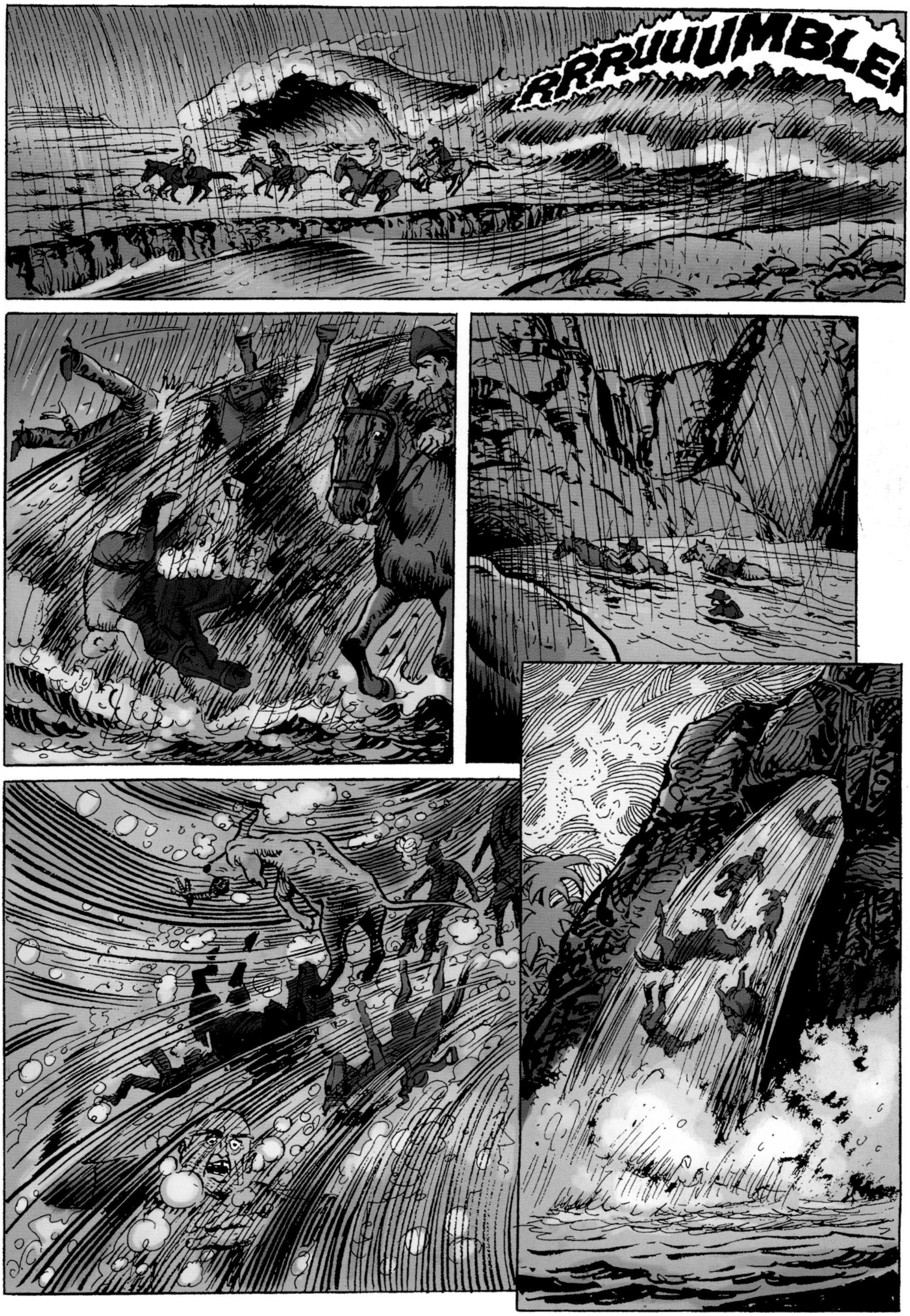
RRRUUUMBLE!

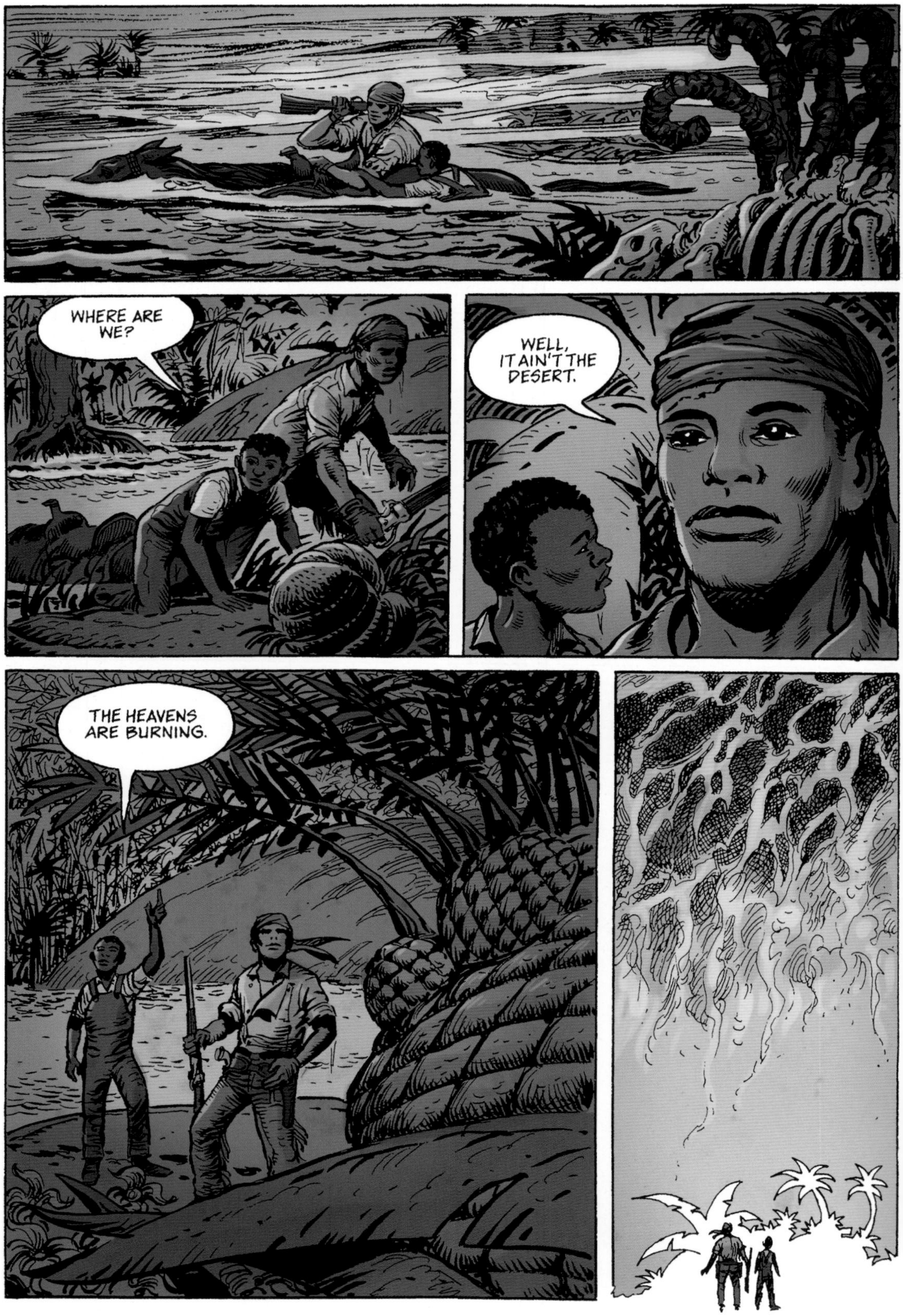
WHERE ARE WE?
WELL, IT AIN'T THE DESERT.
THE HEAVENS ARE BURNING.

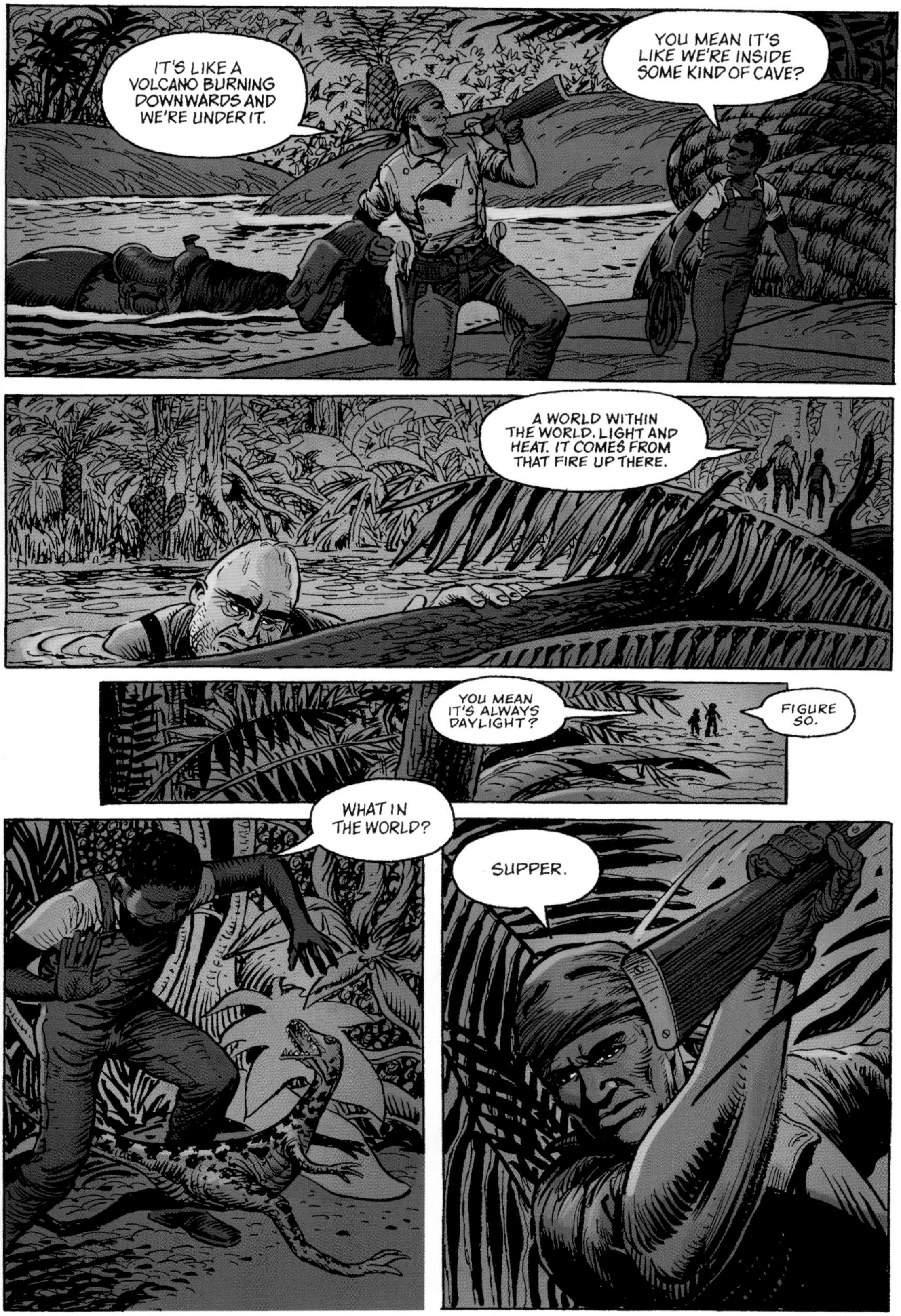
IT'S LIKE A VOLCANO BURNING DOWNWARDS AND WE'RE UNDER IT.
YOU MEAN IT'S LIKE WE'RE INSIDE SOME KIND OF CAVE?
A WORLD WITHIN THE WORLD. LIGHT AND HEAT. IT COMES FROM THAT FIRE UP THERE.
YOU MEAN IT'S ALWAYS DAYLIGHT?
FIGURE SO.
WHAT IN THE WORLD?
SUPPER.

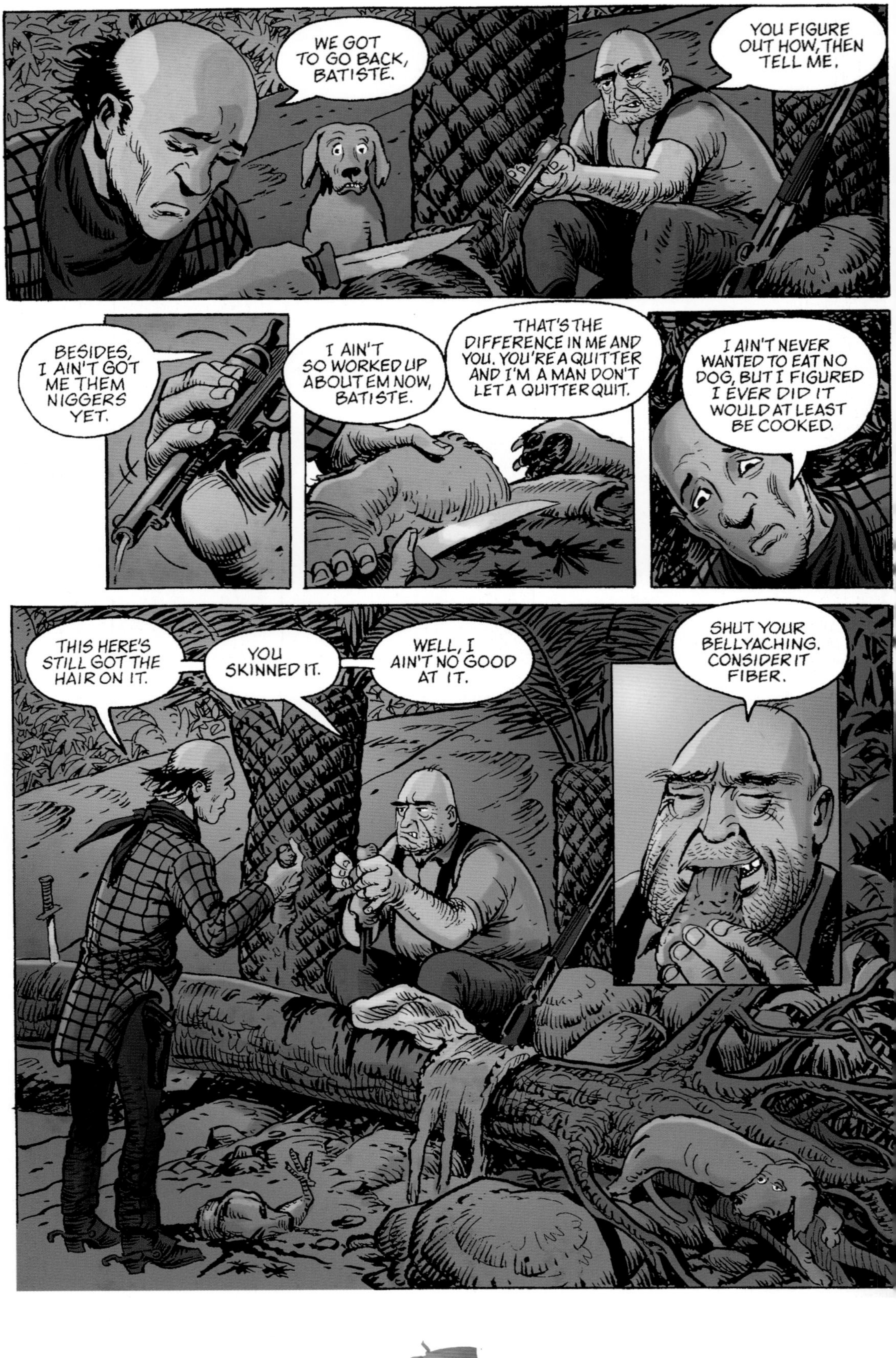
WE GOT TO GO BACK, BATISTE.
YOU FIGURE OUT HOW, THEN TELL ME.
BESIDES, I AIN'T GOT ME THEM NIGGERS YET.
I AIN'T SO WORKED UP ABOUT EM NOW, BATISTE.
THAT'S THE DIFFERENCE IN ME AND YOU. YOU'RE A QUITTER AND I'M A MAN DON'T LET A QUITTER QUIT.
I AIN'T NEVER WANTED TO EAT NO DOG, BUT I FIGURED I EVER DID IT WOULD AT LEAST BE COOKED.
THIS HERE'S STILL GOT THE HAIR ON IT.
YOU SKINNED IT.
WELL, I AIN'T NO GOOD AT IT.
SHUT YOUR BELLYACHING. CONSIDER IT FIBER.

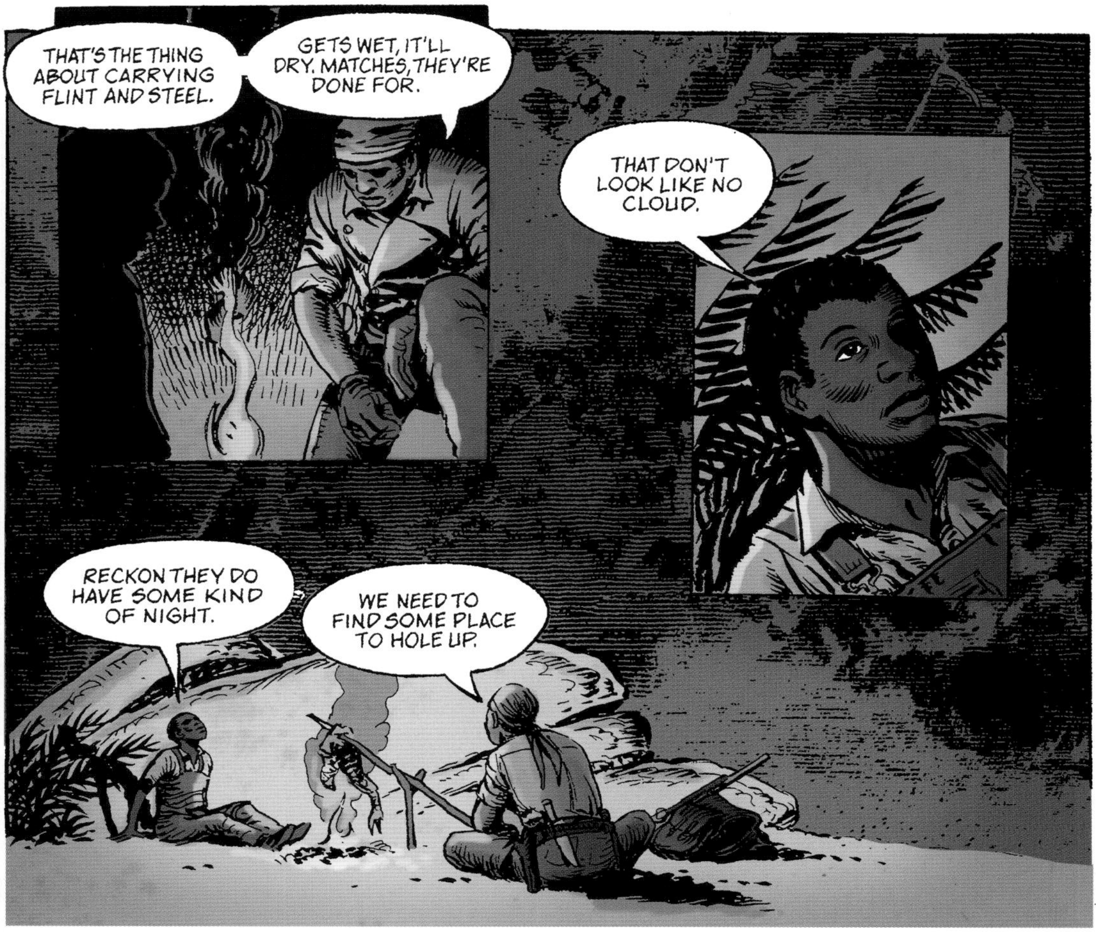
THAT'S THE THING ABOUT CARRYING FLINT AND STEEL.
GETS WET, IT'LL DRY. MATCHES, THEY'RE DONE FOR.
THAT DON'T LOOK LIKE NO CLOUD.
RECKON THEY DO HAVE SOME KIND OF NIGHT.
WE NEED TO FIND SOME PLACE TO HOLE UP.

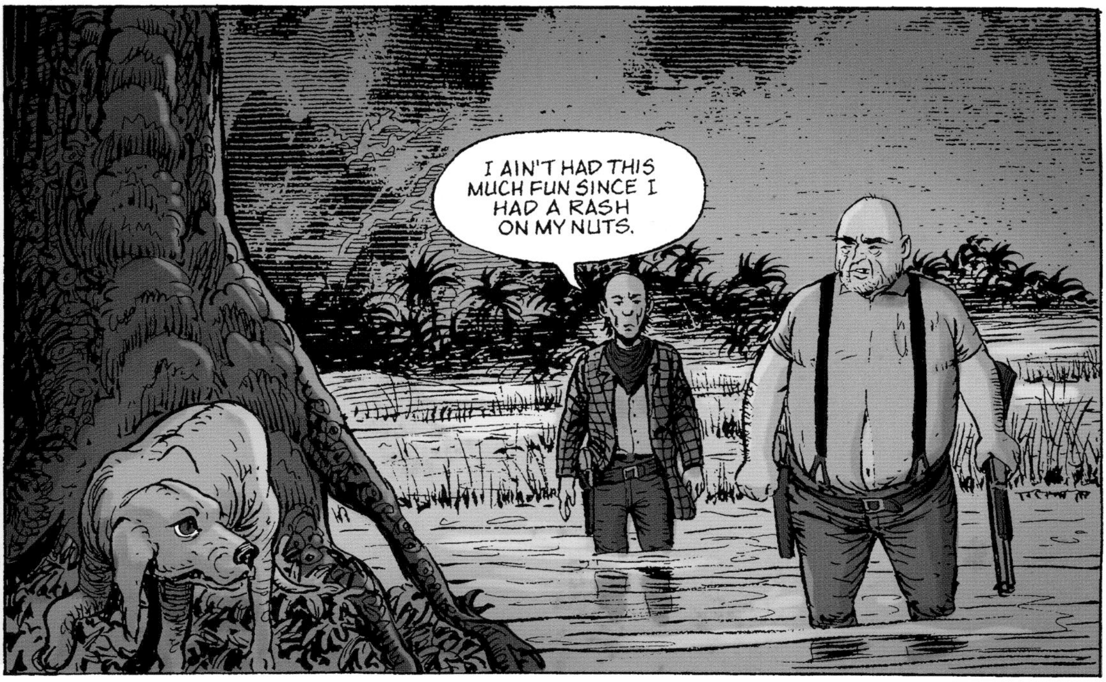
I AIN'T HAD THIS MUCH FUN SINCE I HAD A RASH ON MY NUTS.

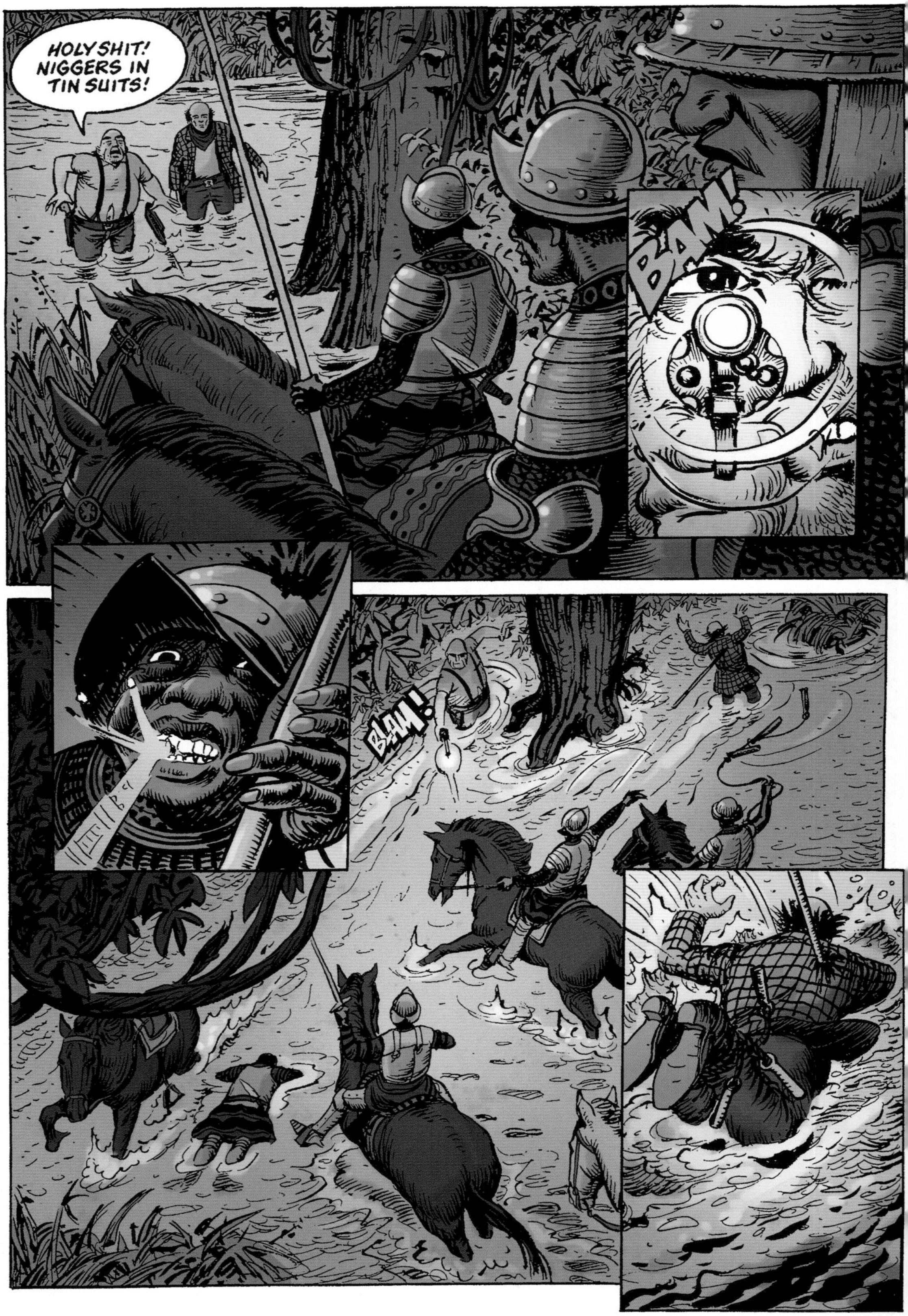
HOLY SHIT! NIGGERS IN TIN SUITS!
BAM!
BLAM!

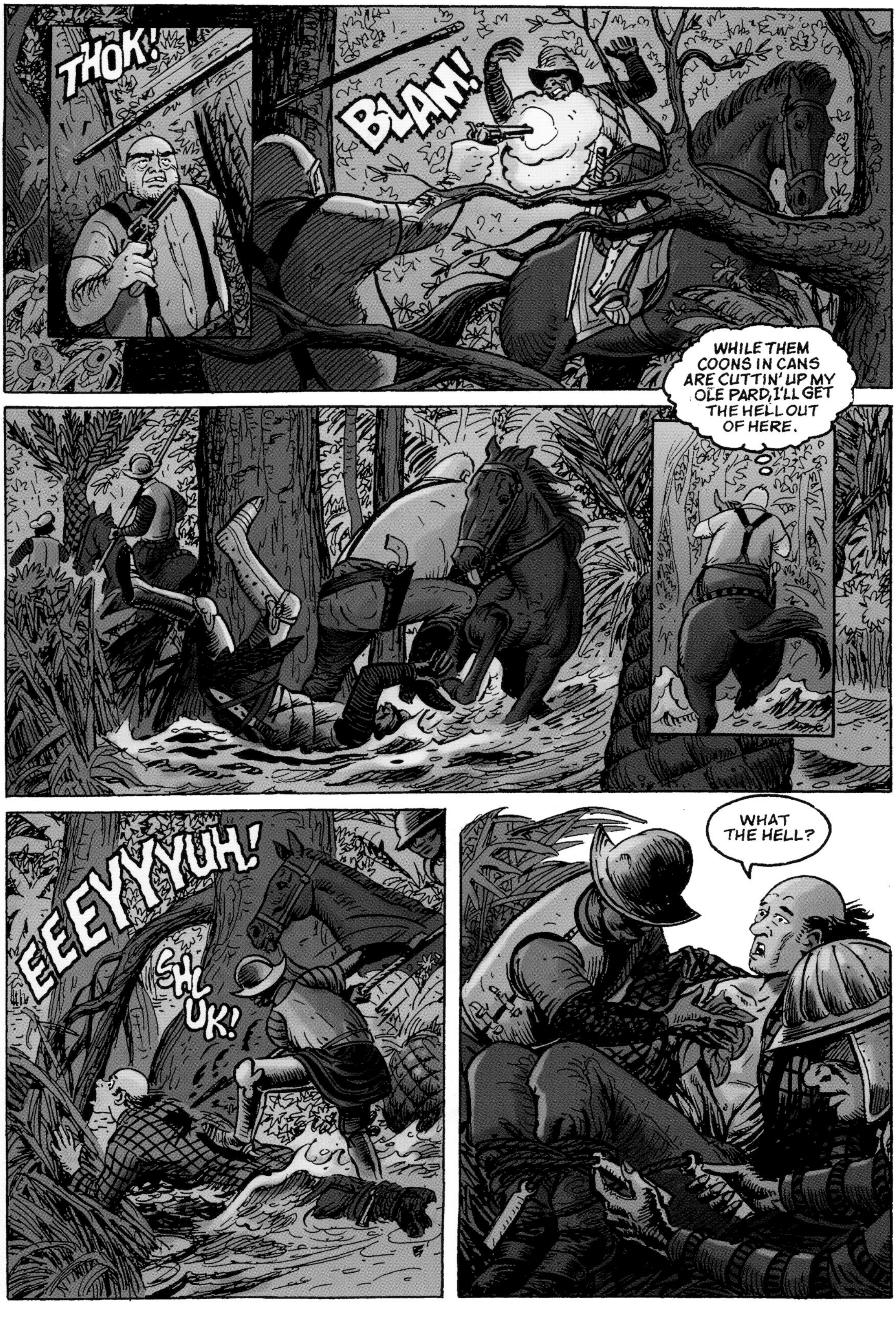
THOK!
BLAM!
WHILE THEM COONS IN CANS ARE CUTTIN' UP MY OLE PARD, I'LL GET THE HELL OUT OF HERE.
EEEYYYUH!
SHLUK!
WHAT THE HELL?

LEAVES STOPPED THE BLEEDING.

YOU BOYS ARE GONNA HELP ME?

THIS IS SOME SHIT, FELLAS. FIRST YOU POKE ME, NOW YOU'RE GONNA TAKE CARE OF ME.

RECKON IN ALL THE CONFUSION, BAD LIGHT AND ALL, THEY JUST NOW REALIZED I'M A WHITE MAN.

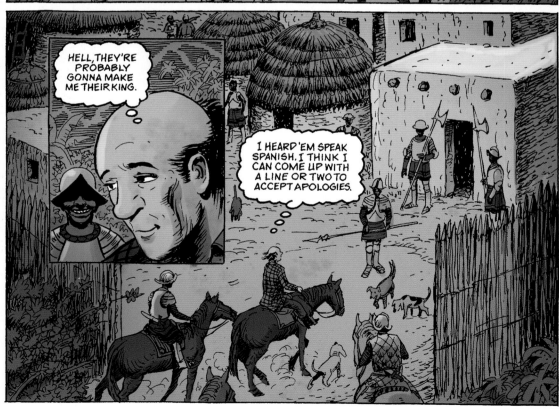

HELL, THEY'RE PROBABLY GONNA MAKE ME THEIR KING.

I HEARD 'EM SPEAK SPANISH. I THINK I CAN COME UP WITH A LINE OR TWO TO ACCEPT APOLOGIES.

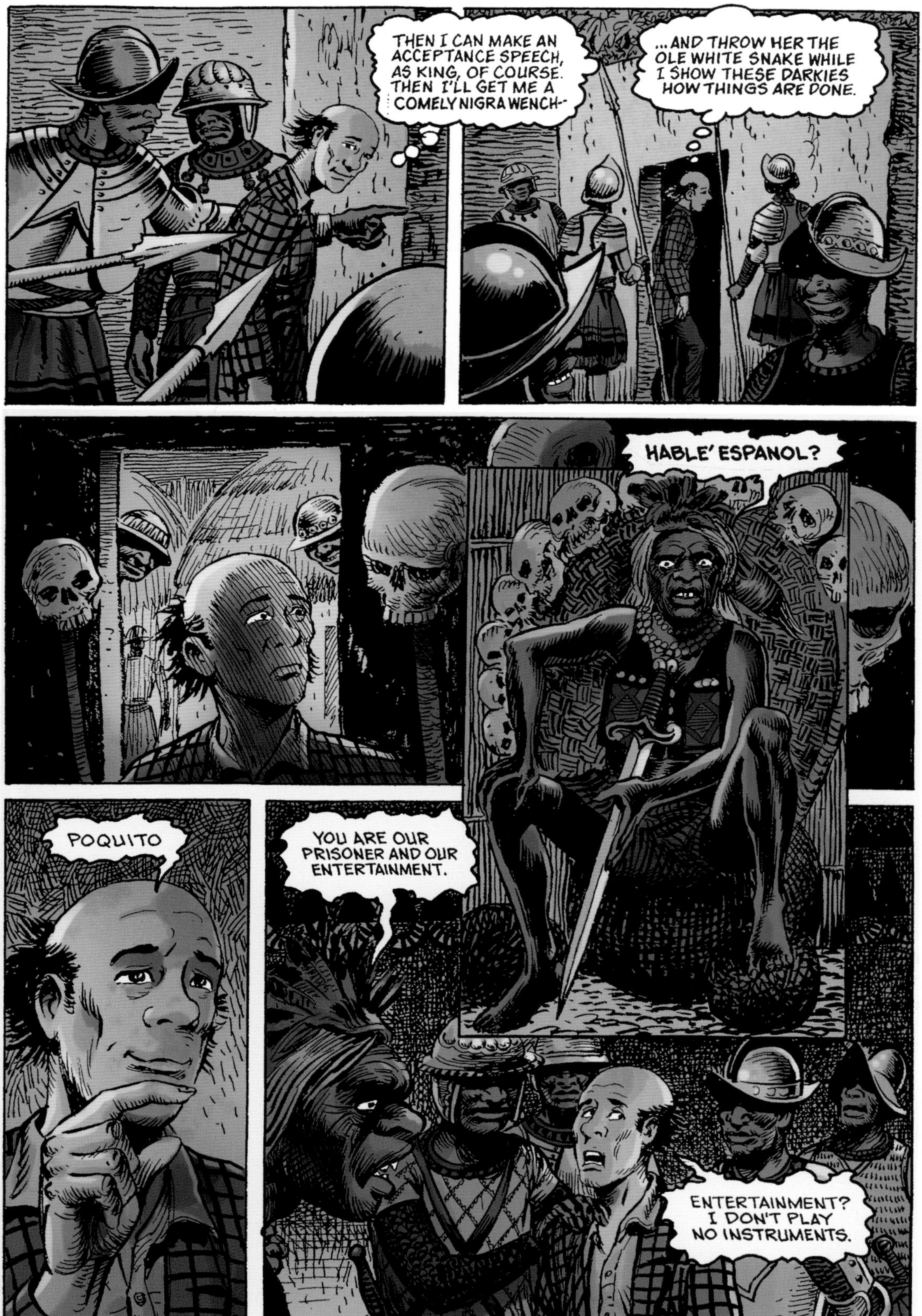
THEN I CAN MAKE AN ACCEPTANCE SPEECH, AS KING, OF COURSE. THEN I'LL GET ME A COMELY NIGRA WENCH-
...AND THROW HER THE OLE WHITE SNAKE WHILE I SHOW THESE DARKIES HOW THINGS ARE DONE.
HABLE' ESPANOL?
POQUITO
YOU ARE OUR PRISONER AND OUR ENTERTAINMENT.
ENTERTAINMENT? I DON'T PLAY NO INSTRUMENTS.

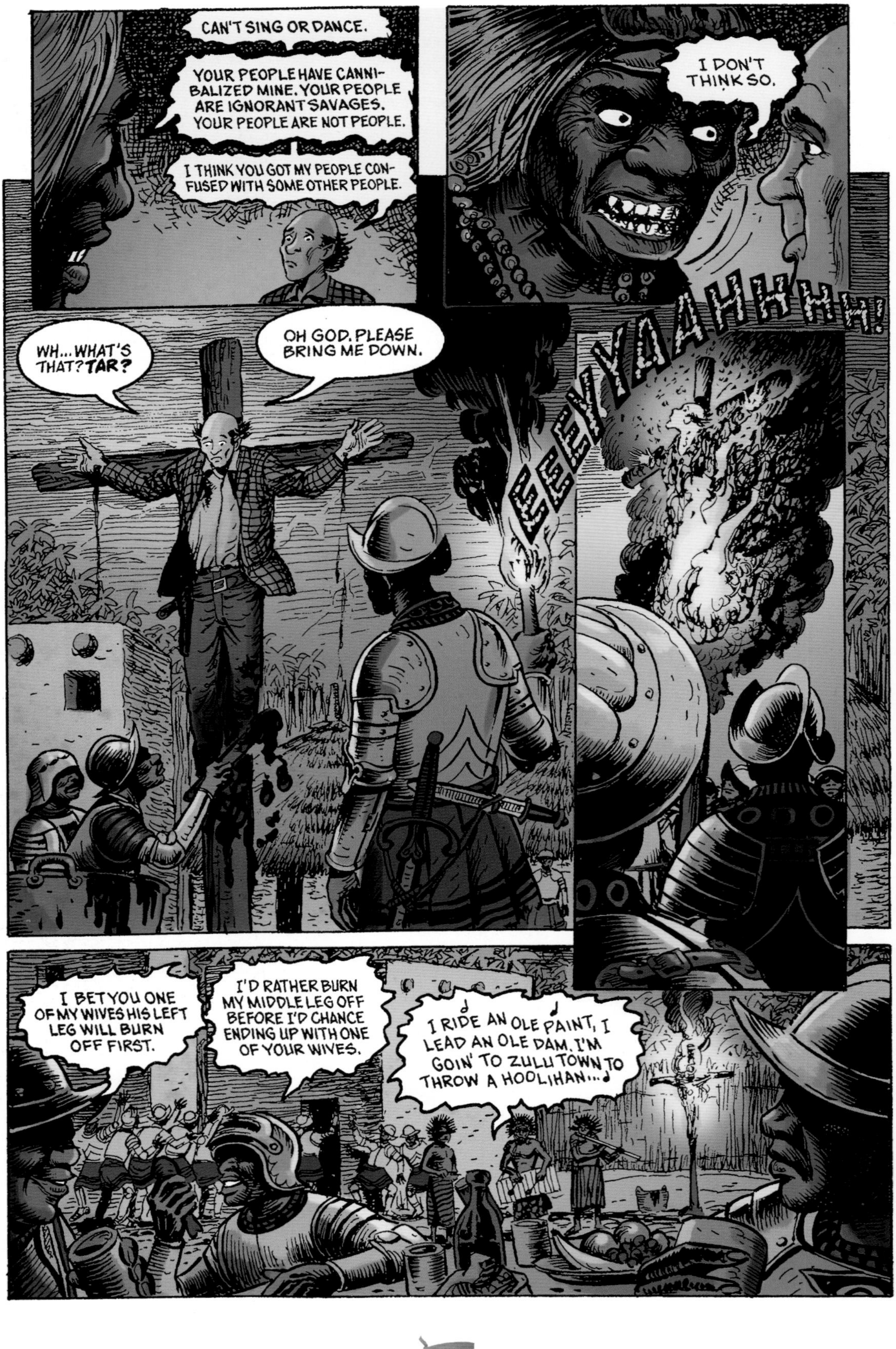
CAN'T SING OR DANCE.
YOUR PEOPLE HAVE CANNIBALIZED MINE. YOUR PEOPLE ARE IGNORANT SAVAGES. YOUR PEOPLE ARE NOT PEOPLE.
I THINK YOU GOT MY PEOPLE CONFUSED WITH SOME OTHER PEOPLE.
I DON'T THINK SO.
WH... WHAT'S THAT? TAR?
OH GOD. PLEASE BRING ME DOWN.
EEEYAAHHHHH!
I BET YOU ONE OF MY WIVES HIS LEFT LEG WILL BURN OFF FIRST.
I'D RATHER BURN MY MIDDLE LEG OFF BEFORE I'D CHANCE ENDING UP WITH ONE OF YOUR WIVES.
I RIDE AN OLE PAINT, I LEAD AN OLE DAM. I'M GOIN' TO ZULU TOWN TO THROW A HOOLIHAN...

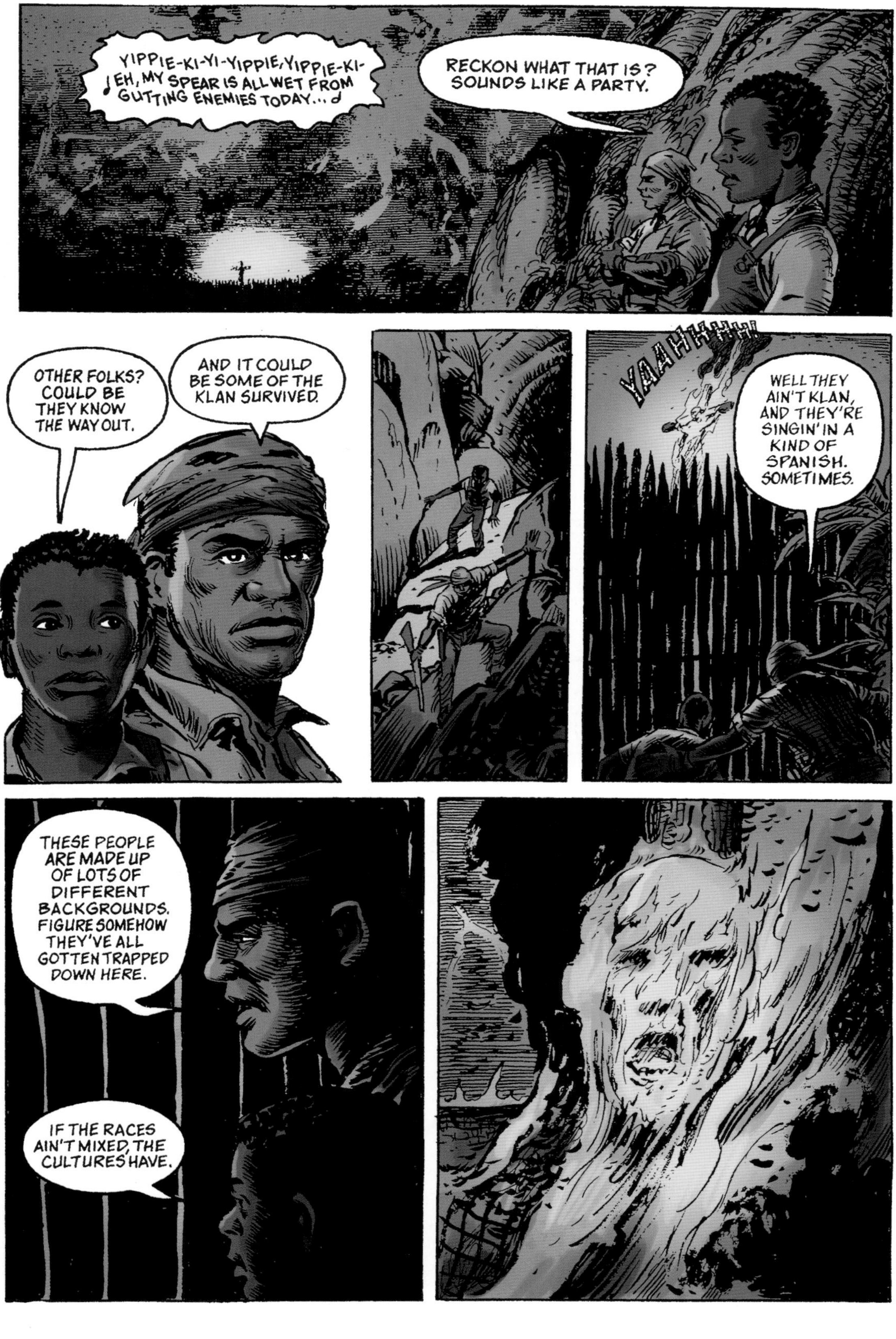
YIPPIE-KI-YI-YIPPIE, YIPPIE-KI-EH, MY SPEAR IS ALL WET FROM GUTTING ENEMIES TODAY...
RECKON WHAT THAT IS? SOUNDS LIKE A PARTY.
OTHER FOLKS? COULD BE THEY KNOW THE WAY OUT.
AND IT COULD BE SOME OF THE KLAN SURVIVED.
YAAHHHHH!
WELL THEY AIN'T KLAN, AND THEY'RE SINGIN' IN A KIND OF SPANISH. SOMETIMES.
THESE PEOPLE ARE MADE UP OF LOTS OF DIFFERENT BACKGROUNDS. FIGURE SOMEHOW THEY'VE ALL GOTTEN TRAPPED DOWN HERE.
IF THE RACES AIN'T MIXED, THE CULTURES HAVE.

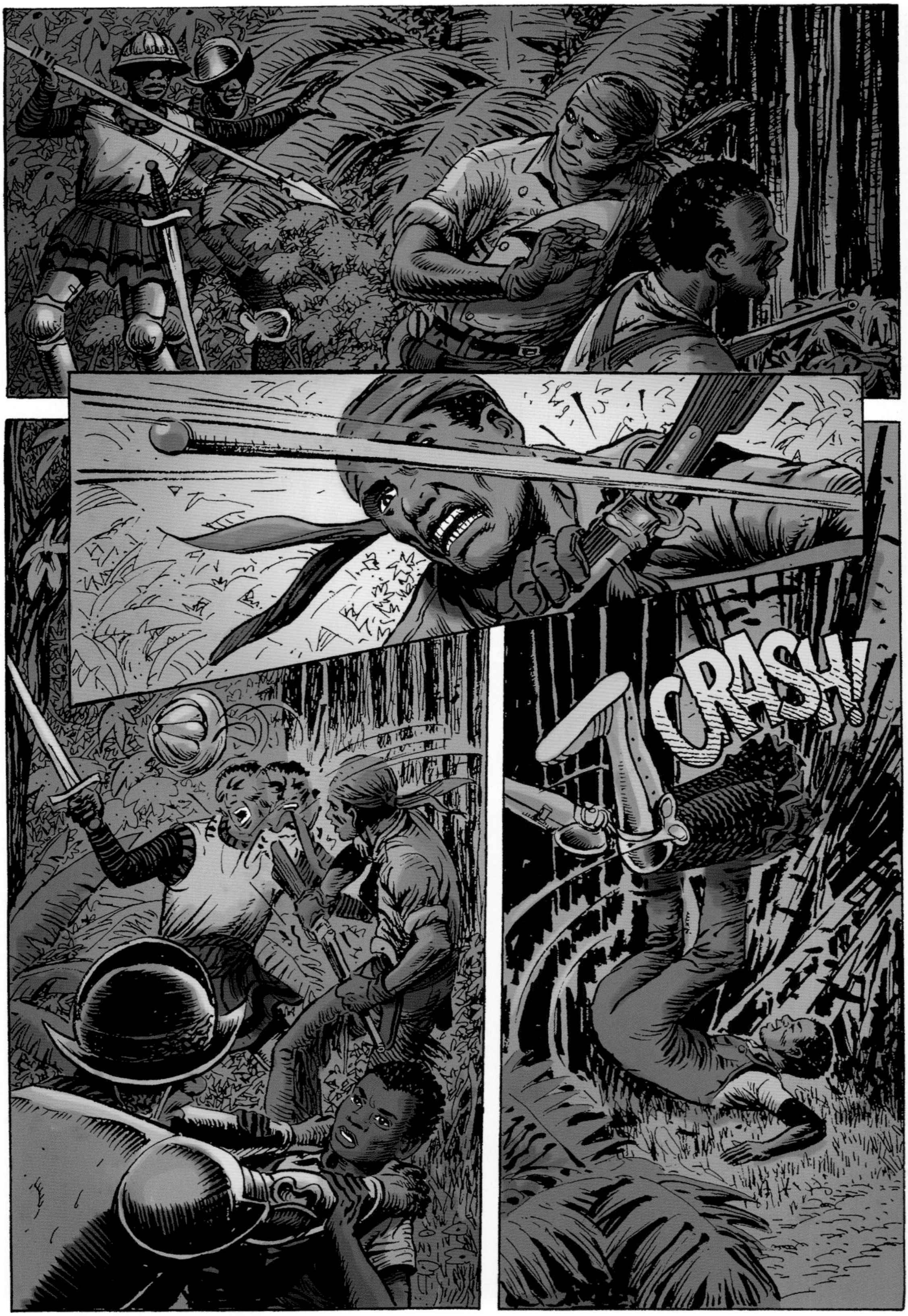
CRASH!

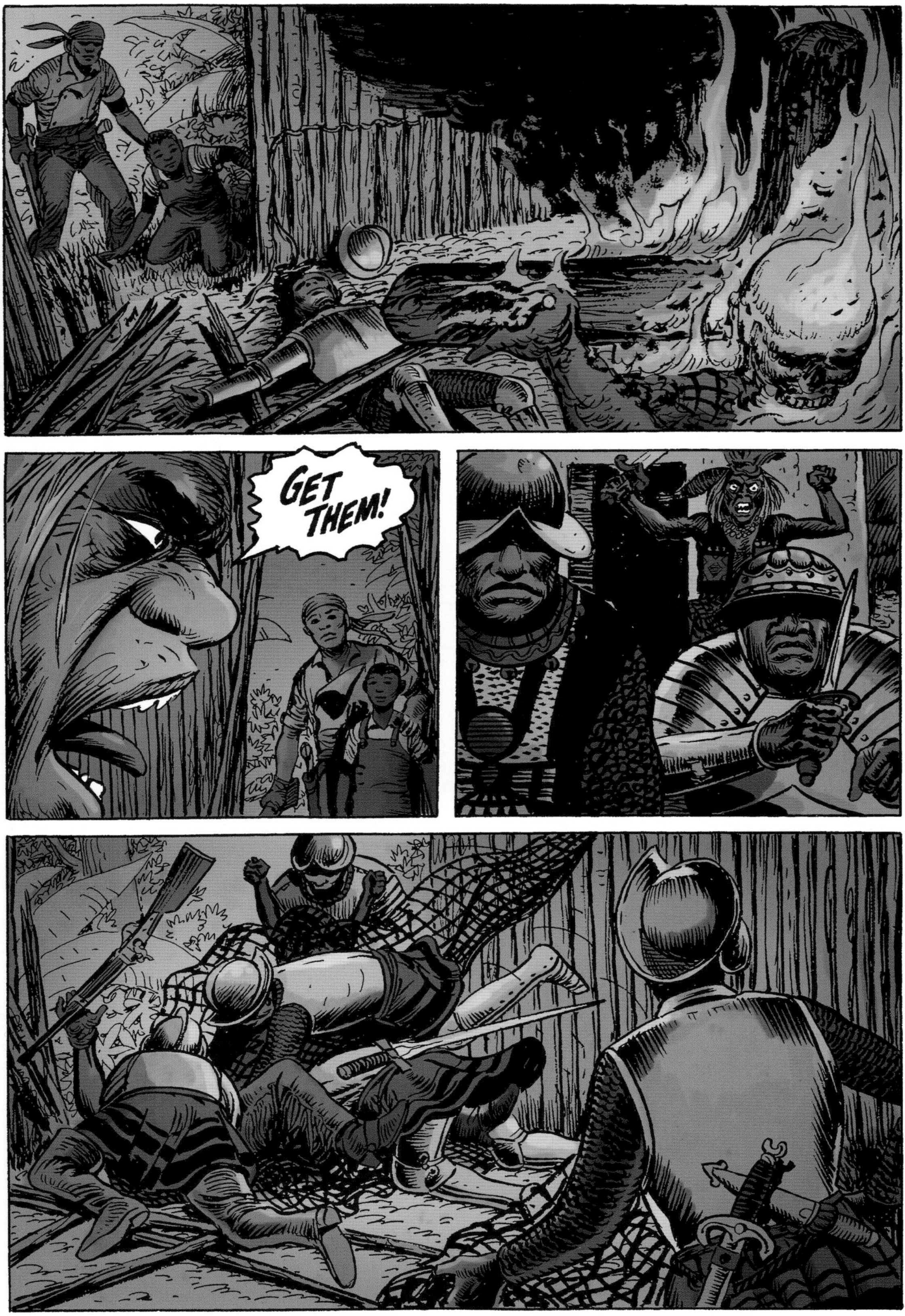
GET THEM!

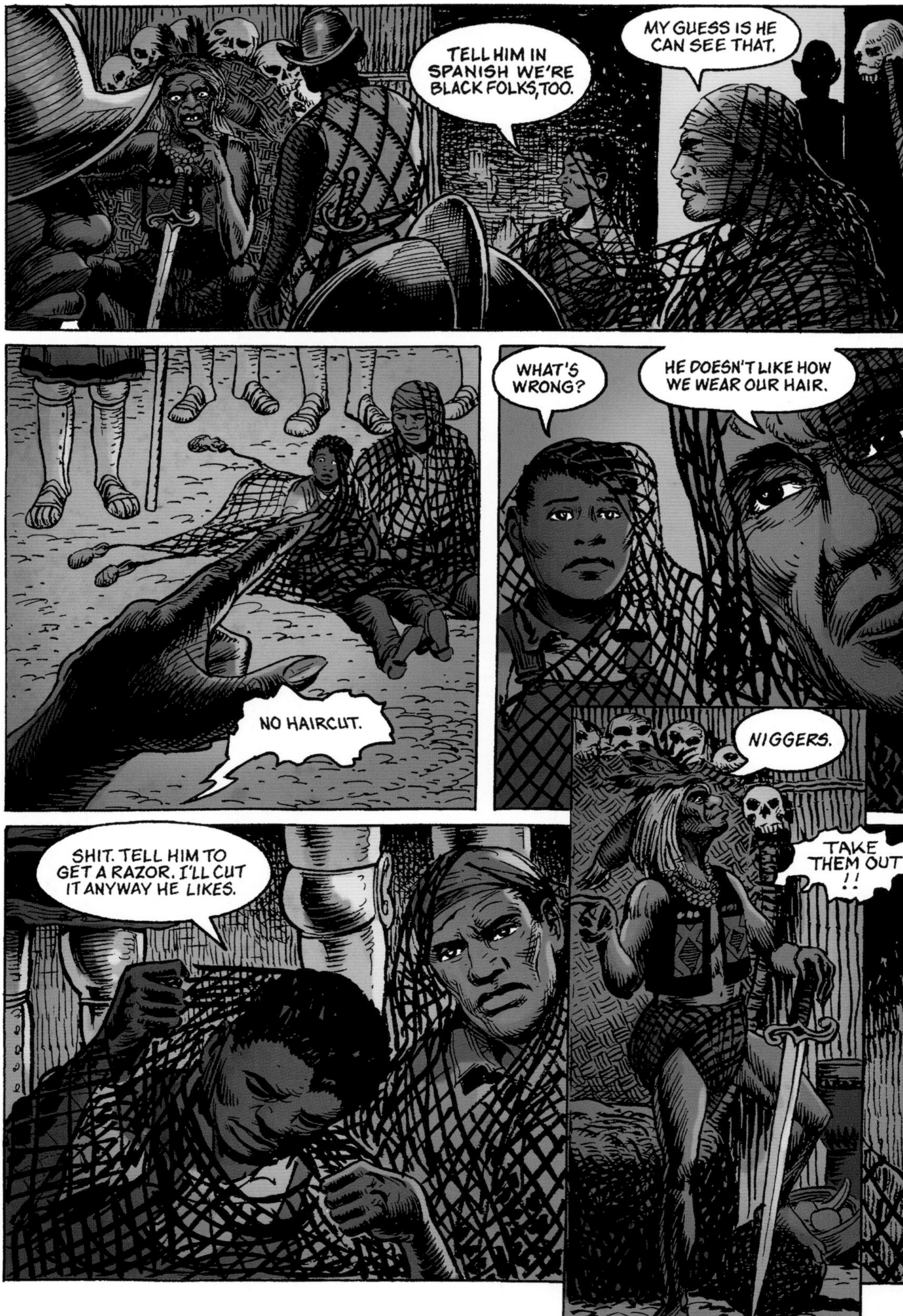
TELL HIM IN SPANISH WE'RE BLACK FOLKS, TOO.
MY GUESS IS HE CAN SEE THAT.
NO HAIRCUT.
WHAT'S WRONG?
HE DOESN'T LIKE HOW WE WEAR OUR HAIR.
NIGGERS.
SHIT. TELL HIM TO GET A RAZOR. I'LL CUT IT ANYWAY HE LIKES.
TAKE THEM OUT !!

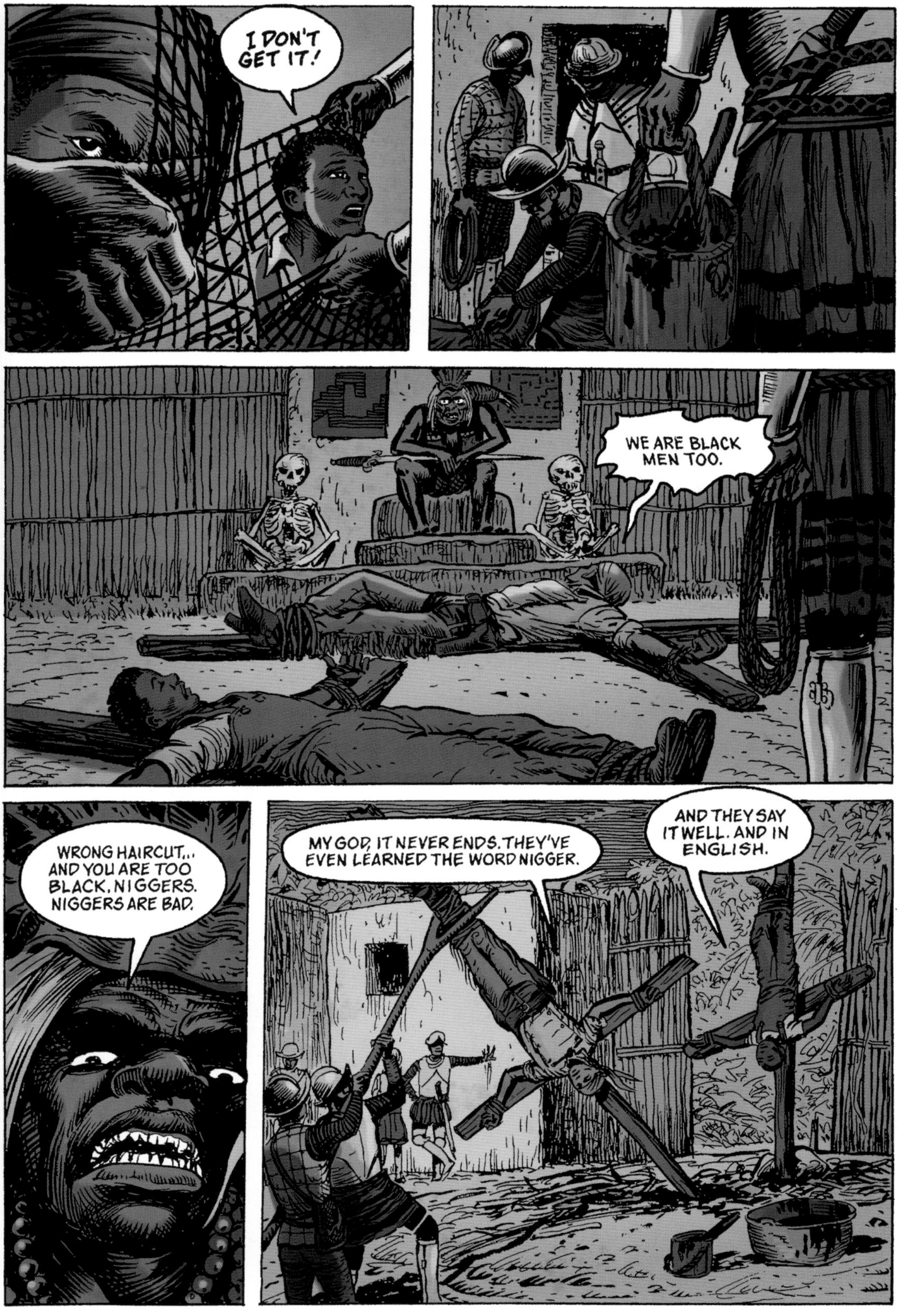
I DON'T GET IT!
WE ARE BLACK MEN TOO.
WRONG HAIRCUT... AND YOU ARE TOO BLACK, NIGGERS. NIGGERS ARE BAD.
MY GOD, IT NEVER ENDS. THEY'VE EVEN LEARNED THE WORD NIGGER.
AND THEY SAY IT WELL. AND IN ENGLISH.

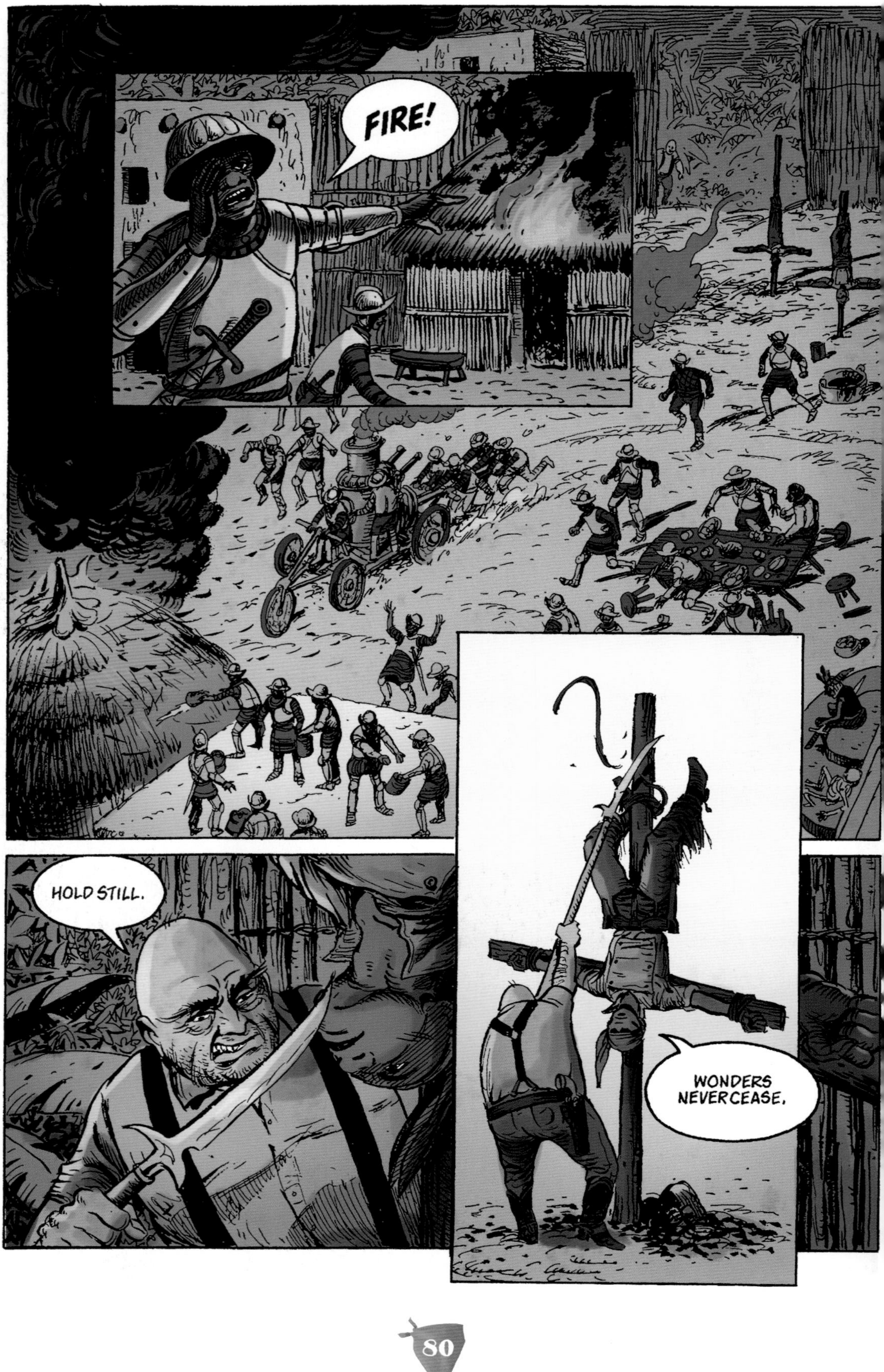
FIRE!
HOLD STILL.
WONDERS NEVER CEASE.

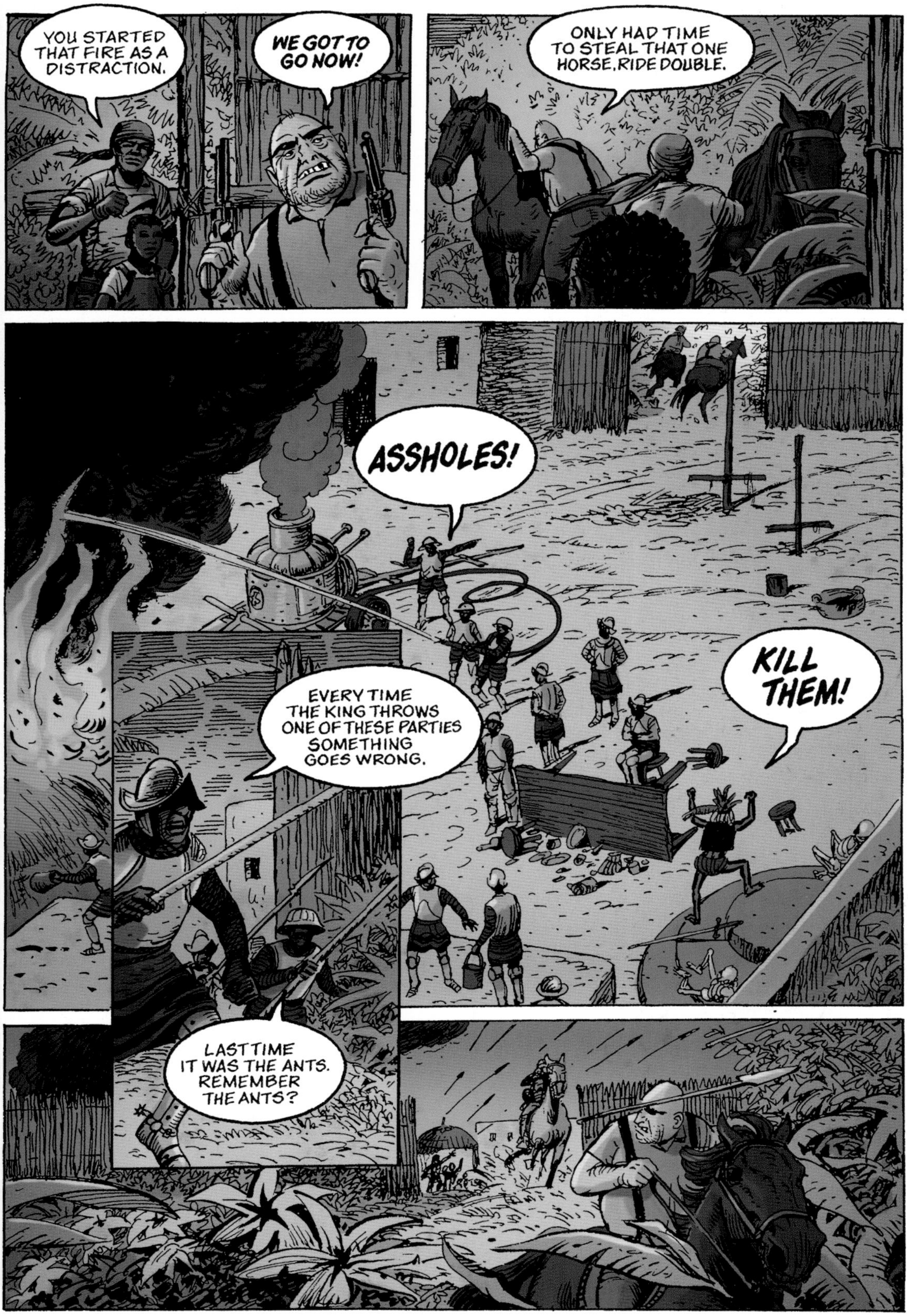
YOU STARTED THAT FIRE AS A DISTRACTION.
WE GOT TO GO NOW!
ONLY HAD TIME TO STEAL THAT ONE HORSE, RIDE DOUBLE.
ASSHOLES!
KILL THEM!
EVERY TIME THE KING THROWS ONE OF THESE PARTIES SOMETHING GOES WRONG.
LAST TIME IT WAS THE ANTS. REMEMBER THE ANTS?

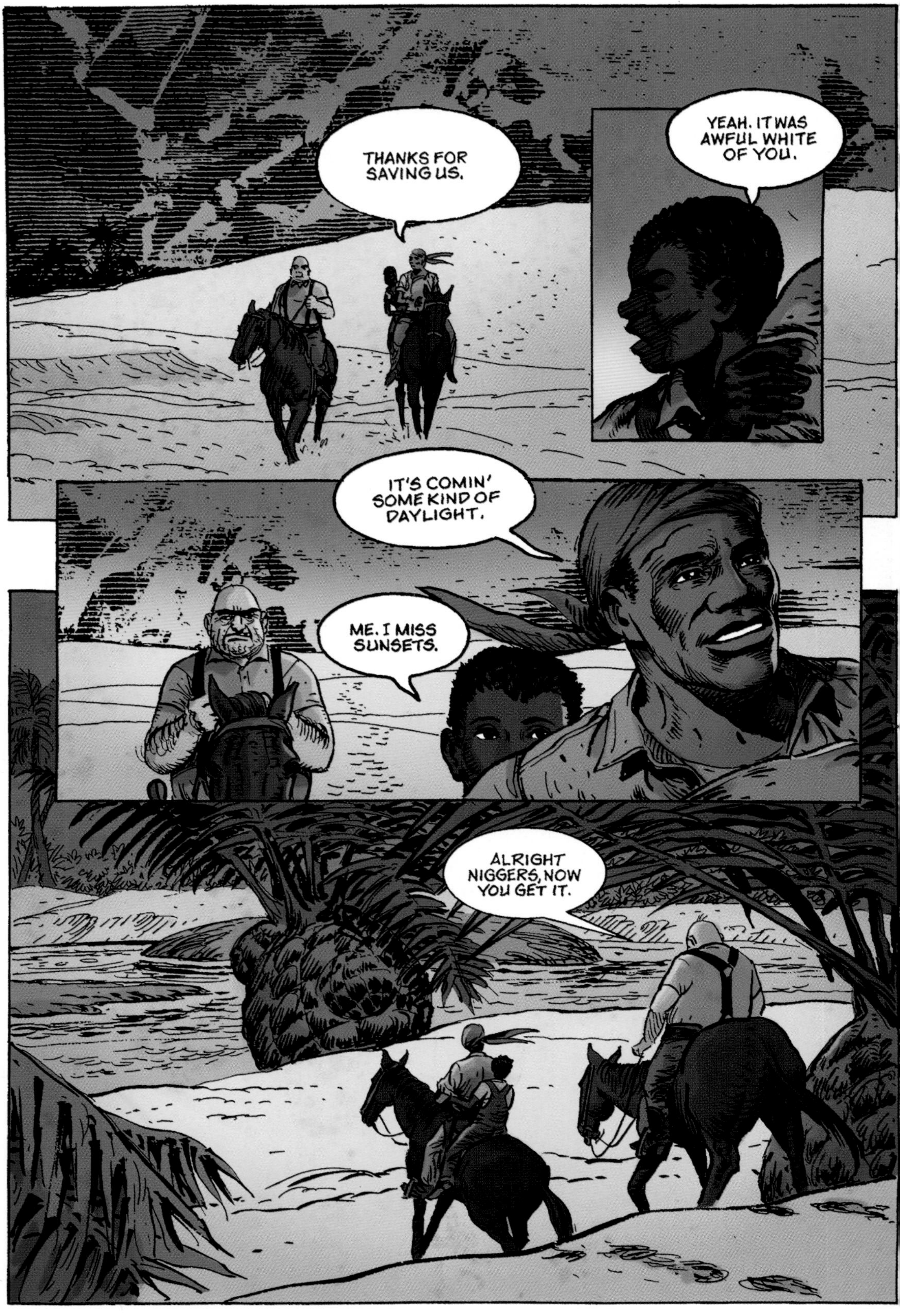
THANKS FOR SAVING US.
YEAH. IT WAS AWFUL WHITE OF YOU.
IT'S COMIN' SOME KIND OF DAYLIGHT.
ME. I MISS SUNSETS.
ALRIGHT NIGGERS, NOW YOU GET IT.

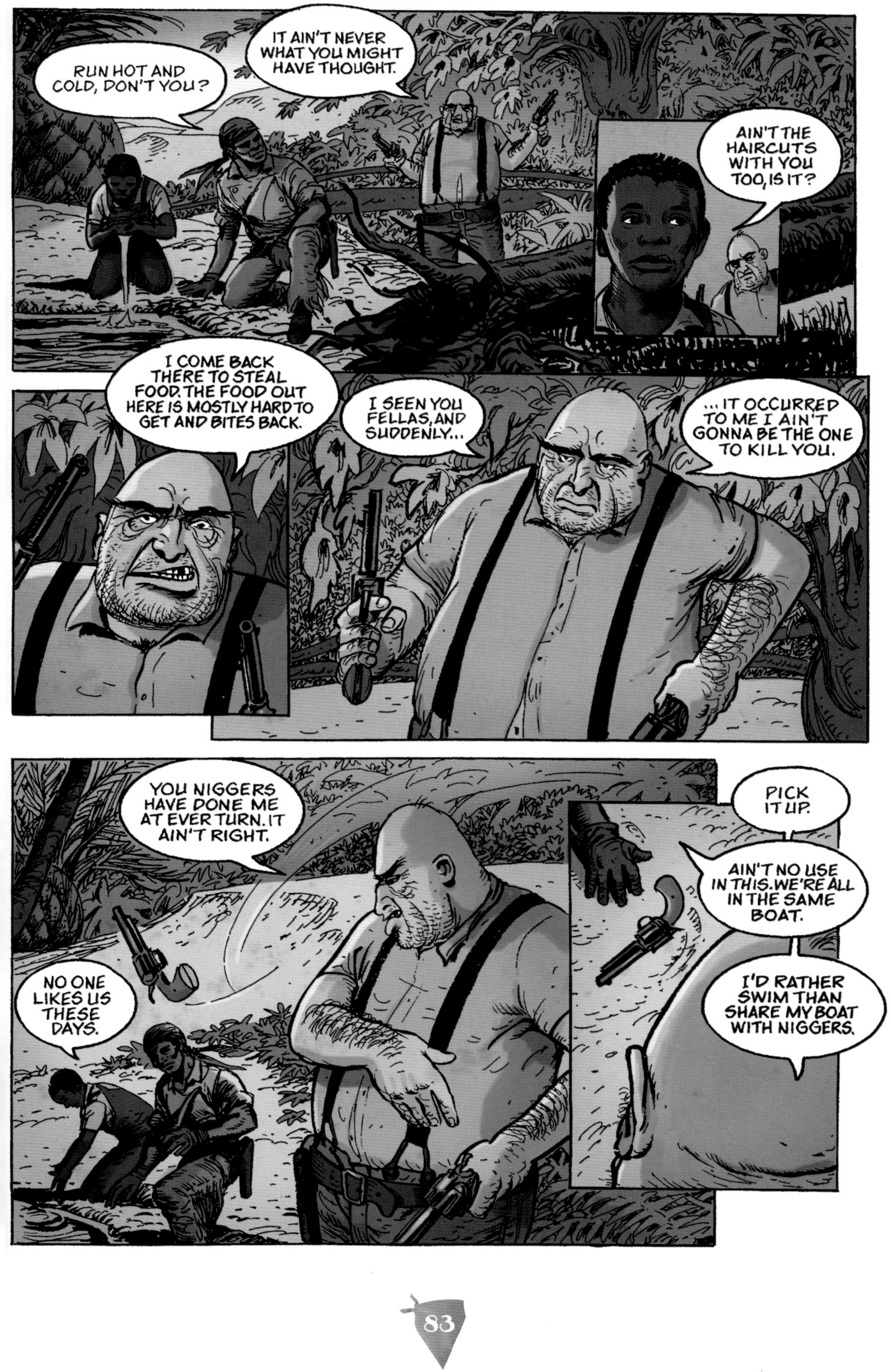

RUN HOT AND COLD, DON'T YOU?
IT AIN'T NEVER WHAT YOU MIGHT HAVE THOUGHT.
AIN'T THE HAIRCUTS WITH YOU TOO, IS IT?
I COME BACK THERE TO STEAL FOOD. THE FOOD OUT HERE IS MOSTLY HARD TO GET AND BITES BACK.
I SEEN YOU FELLAS, AND SUDDENLY...
...IT OCCURRED TO ME I AIN'T GONNA BE THE ONE TO KILL YOU.
YOU NIGGERS HAVE DONE ME AT EVER TURN. IT AIN'T RIGHT.
NO ONE LIKES US THESE DAYS.
PICK IT UP.
AIN'T NO USE IN THIS. WE'RE ALL IN THE SAME BOAT.
I'D RATHER SWIM THAN SHARE MY BOAT WITH NIGGERS.

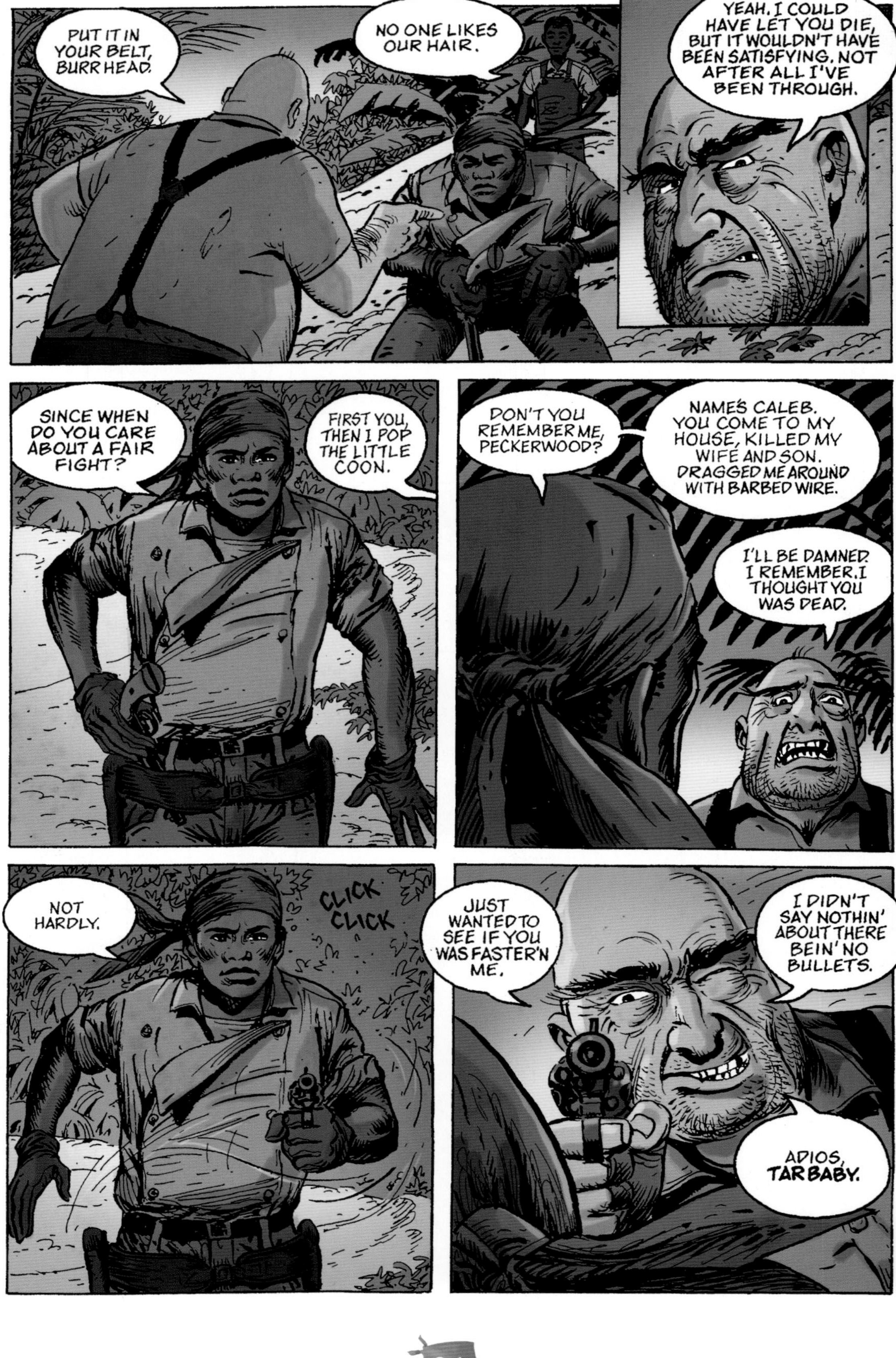
PUT IT IN YOUR BELT, BURR HEAD.
NO ONE LIKES OUR HAIR.
YEAH, I COULD HAVE LET YOU DIE, BUT IT WOULDN'T HAVE BEEN SATISFYING, NOT AFTER ALL I'VE BEEN THROUGH.
SINCE WHEN DO YOU CARE ABOUT A FAIR FIGHT?
FIRST YOU, THEN I POP THE LITTLE COON.
DON'T YOU REMEMBER ME, PECKERWOOD?
NAME'S CALEB. YOU COME TO MY HOUSE, KILLED MY WIFE AND SON. DRAGGED ME AROUND WITH BARBED WIRE.
I'LL BE DAMNED. I REMEMBER. I THOUGHT YOU WAS DEAD.
NOT HARDLY.
CLICK CLICK
JUST WANTED TO SEE IF YOU WAS FASTER'N ME.
I DIDN'T SAY NOTHIN' ABOUT THERE BEIN' NO BULLETS.
ADIOS, **TAR BABY.**

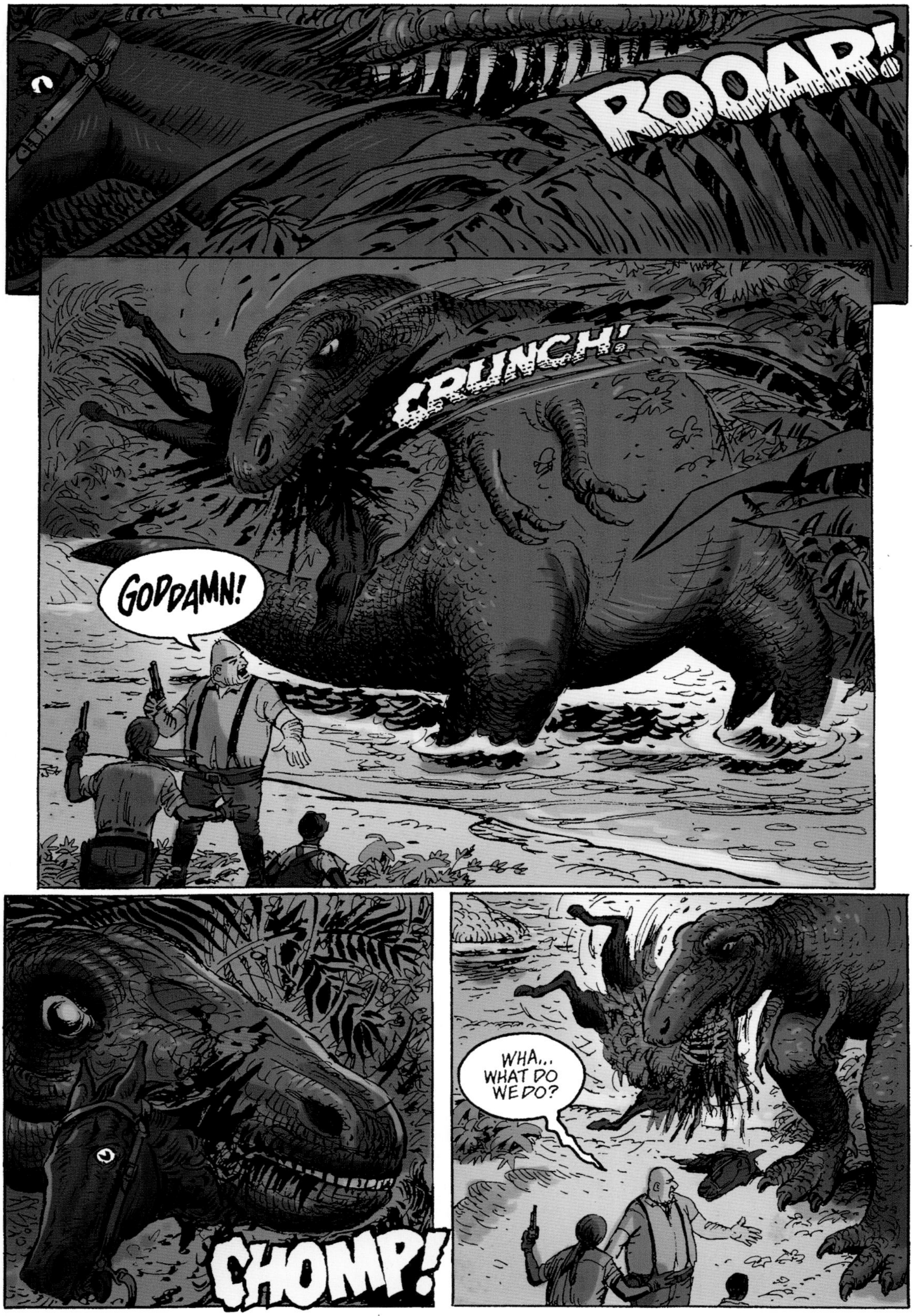
ROOAR!
CRUNCH!
GODDAMN!
CHOMP!
WHA... WHAT DO WE DO?

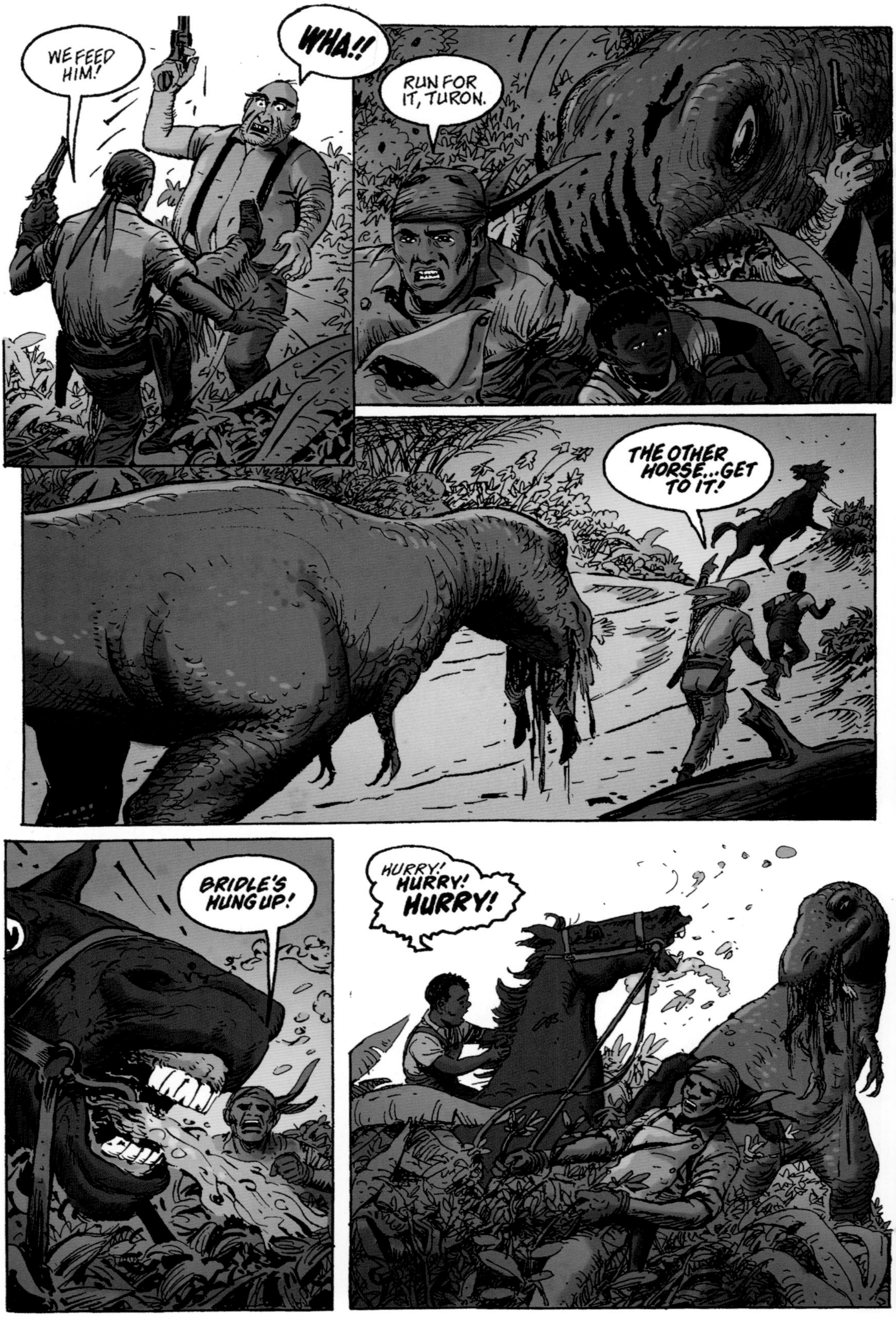
WE FEED HIM!
WHA!!
RUN FOR IT, TURON.
THE OTHER HORSE...GET TO IT!
BRIDLE'S HUNG UP!
HURRY! HURRY! HURRY!

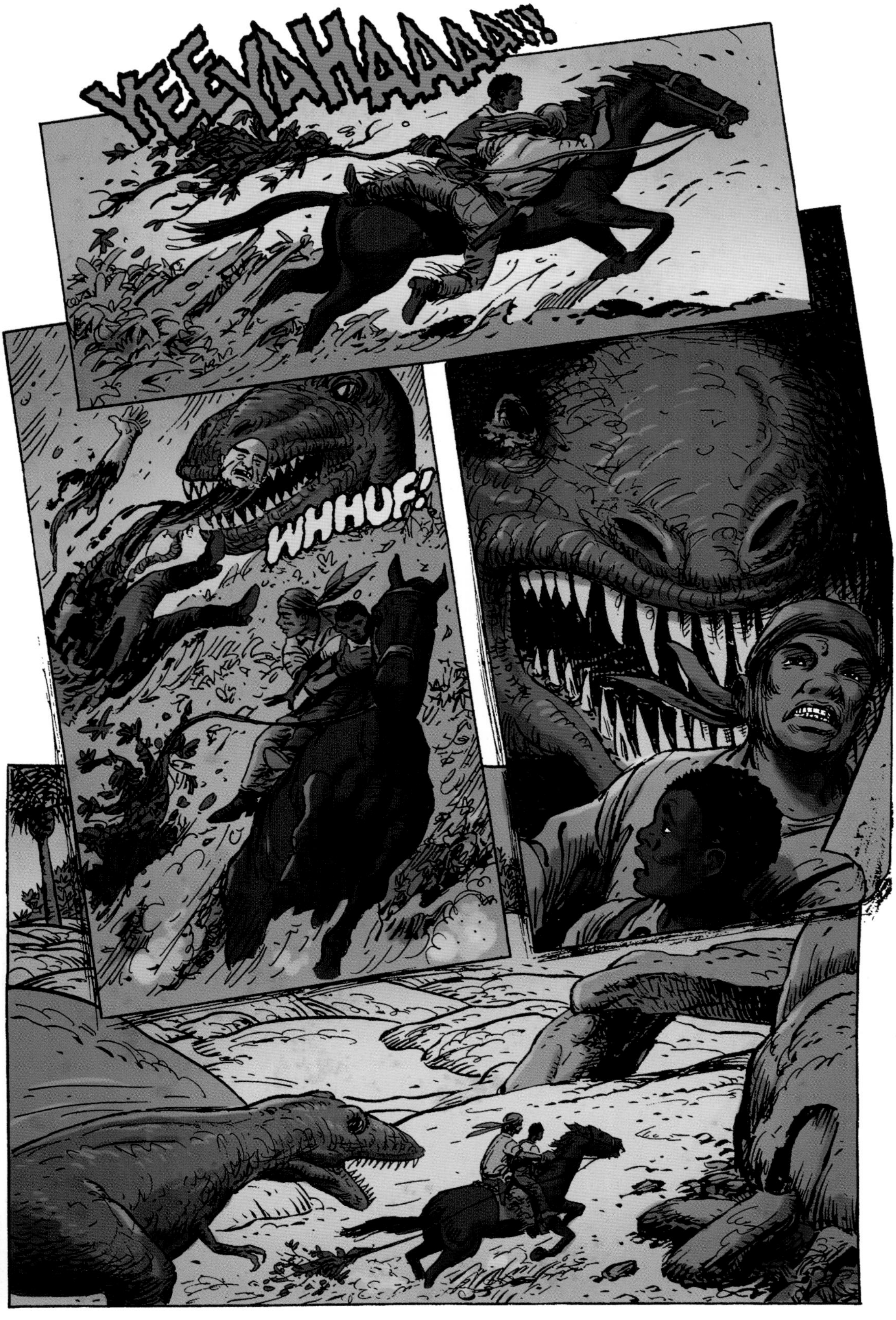
YEEYAHAAAA!!
WHHUF!

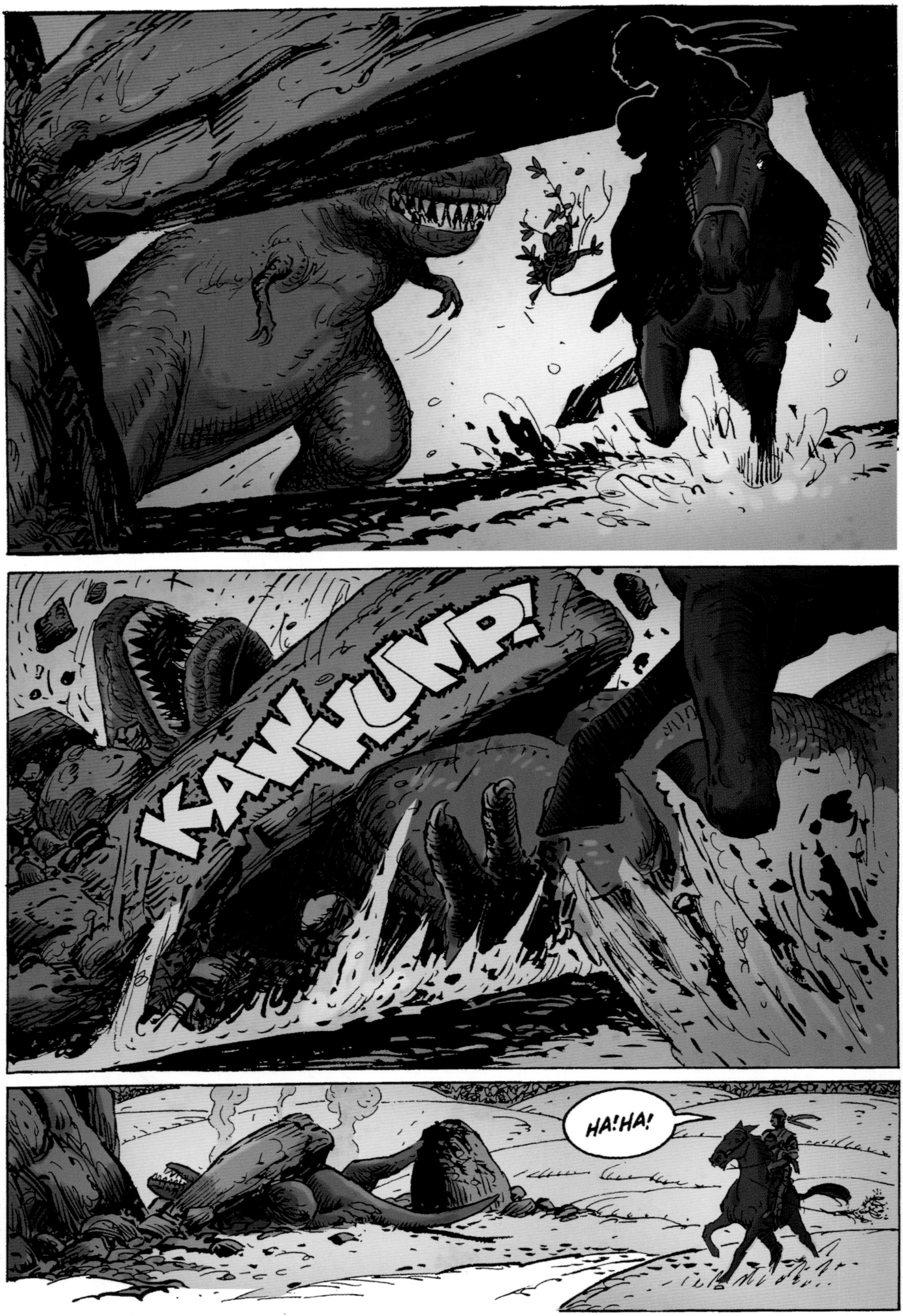
KAWHUMP!
HA!HA!

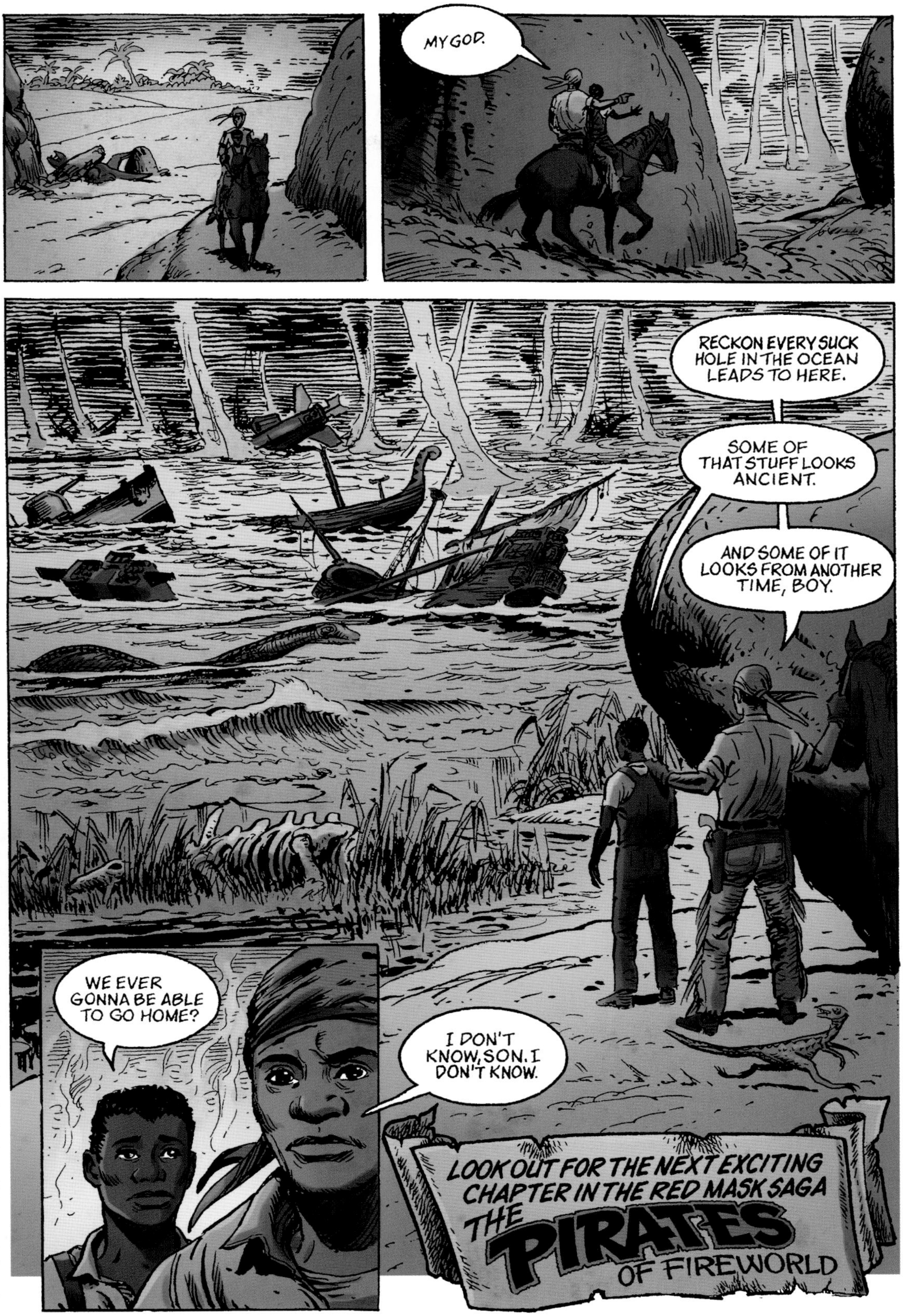
MY GOD.
RECKON EVERY SUCK HOLE IN THE OCEAN LEADS TO HERE.
SOME OF THAT STUFF LOOKS ANCIENT.
AND SOME OF IT LOOKS FROM ANOTHER TIME, BOY.
WE EVER GONNA BE ABLE TO GO HOME?
I DON'T KNOW, SON. I DON'T KNOW.
LOOK OUT FOR THE NEXT EXCITING CHAPTER IN THE RED MASK SAGA
THE PIRATES OF FIREWORLD

BENEATH THE VALLEY OF THE KLAN BUSTERS

(A Sort of) Afterword by Stephen R. Bissette

It's been almost two full decades since Joe R. Lansdale and Sam Glanzman's *Red Range* first saw print (from Mojo Press, in 1999), and damned if Joe and Sam's in-your-face opening pages aren't more timely than ever. As anyone with one unblinkered orb left in their pair of eyes, at least one good tin ear, and half-a-brain left in their skull undoubtedly knows, White Supremacy (never gone, only simmering on some back-burner) reared its ugly head and placed its sorry ass in the White House even as the Black Lives Matter movement arose.

Red Range seemed like an aberration in 1999—an ultraviolent tall tale grounded in America's foulest racist excesses, from Klan purging of innocent families to "you are too black" shades of prejudice within Black circles— but now, it reads like a sequel to Quentin Tarantino's perfectly mainstream, big-budget, 2012 box-office hit, *Django Unchained*, if Jamie Foxx's title character had accidentally stumbled into that lost valley where Turok and Ander were still stuck.

What seemed too over-the-top and unnecessarily mean-spirited to some in 1999, now reads like a somber meditation on Our Nation Way Under God, circa 2017, and if anyone out there is still left wondering "How did we get here?" or (richer yet) "How did this happen?," Joe and Sam's wild and woolly tall tale tells ya, "Pardner, we never left here, it's always been jus' like this."

That's the big picture.

The small picture—that's another story.

What I can report from having been at ground-level is another tale altogether. It's not a tall tale, it's a small tale, but it's mine to tell.

I was a devotee of both Sam Glanzman's and Joe Lansdale's respective

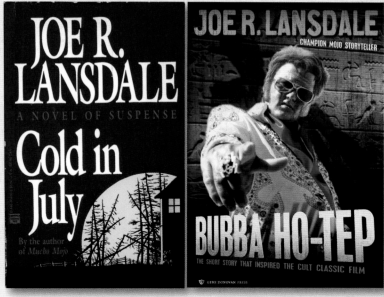

JOE R. LANSDALE
A NOVEL OF SUSPENSE
Cold in July
By the author of *Mucho Mojo*
JOE R. LANSDALE
CHAMPION MOJO STORYTELLER
BUBBA HO-TEP
THE SHORT STORY THAT INSPIRED THE CULT CLASSIC FILM

bodies of work at a time when loving Sam's work was still considered an acquired and rather peculiar taste, if folks rendering such an opinion even knew who Sam was, but loving Joe's work was considered a rarefied pedigree. Lansdale was still an ascending star, especially in genre circles, and the sprawl Joe easily made across blurring genre borders—specifically, horror into noir into Western into mystery into what was being celebrated as Joe's wild-ass breed of all-cylinders-firing fantasy—had only fueled that fiery rise. It could be persuasively argued that the writer and reader's communities Joe's work was being fêted within were, by their very nature, more adventurous than comics fandom circa 1999; but it could be even more convincingly argued that Sam's body of work was far, far harder to access and absorb than Joe's work at that time.

The only work of Sam's most late 1990s comics readers could lay hands on easily were his 1993–99 collaborations with Joe Lansdale and Tim Truman on *Jonah Hex: Two-Gun Mojo* (originally published as a five-issue miniseries, in 1993), *Riders of the Worm and Such* (five issues, 1995), and the then just-completed *Shadows West* (three issues, 1999), all of which Sam inked over Tim's pencils. In the 1990s, Sam had also inked issues of *Zorro* (Topps) and *Turok: Dinosaur Hunter* (Acclaim), meaning that most fans thought of Sam (when they thought of him at all) as an inker, without a clue about the

SO WHO WAS I TO SPOIL ANOTHER FELLA'S FUN?

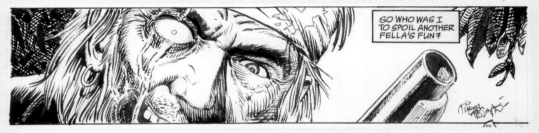

Top: Two of writer Joe R. Lansdale's better known works, *Cold in July,* recently made into a feature film, and *Bubba Ho-Tep*, also adapted for the screen. **Above:** Panel from penciler Tim Truman and inker Sam Glanzman's *Jonah Hex.*

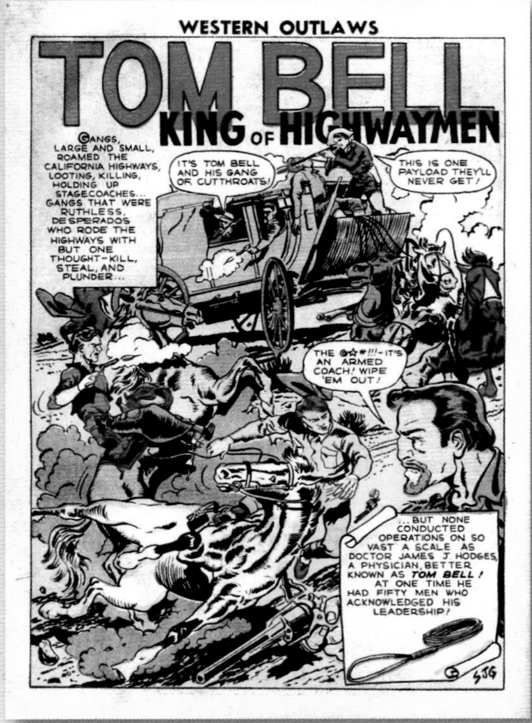
WESTERN OUTLAWS
TOM BELL
KING OF HIGHWAYMEN
GANGS, LARGE AND SMALL, ROAMED THE CALIFORNIA HIGHWAYS, LOOTING, KILLING, HOLDING UP STAGECOACHES... GANGS THAT WERE RUTHLESS, DESPERADOS WHO RODE THE HIGHWAYS WITH BUT ONE THOUGHT–KILL, STEAL, AND PLUNDER...
IT'S TOM BELL AND HIS GANG OF CUTTHROATS!
THIS IS ONE PAYLOAD THEY'LL NEVER GET!
IT'S AN ARMED COACH! WIPE 'EM OUT!
...BUT NONE CONDUCTED OPERATIONS ON SO VAST A SCALE AS DOCTOR JAMES J. HODGES, A PHYSICIAN, BETTER KNOWN AS TOM BELL! AT ONE TIME HE HAD FIFTY MEN WHO ACKNOWLEDGED HIS LEADERSHIP!
SJG

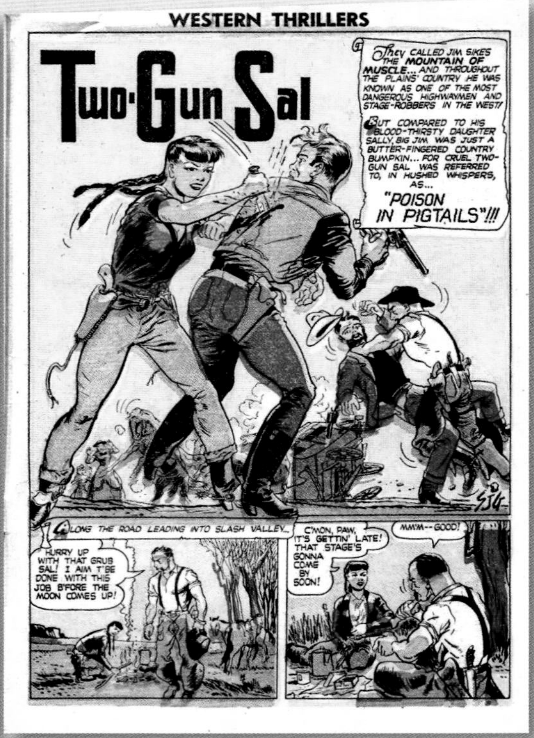
WESTERN THRILLERS
Two-Gun Sal
THEY CALLED JIM SIKES THE MOUNTAIN OF MUSCLE... AND THROUGHOUT THE PLAINS' COUNTRY HE WAS KNOWN AS ONE OF THE MOST DANGEROUS HIGHWAYMEN AND STAGE-ROBBERS IN THE WEST!
BUT COMPARED TO HIS BLOOD-THIRSTY DAUGHTER SALLY, BIG JIM WAS JUST A BUTTER-FINGERED COUNTRY BUMPKIN... FOR CRUEL TWO-GUN SAL WAS REFERRED TO, IN HUSHED WHISPERS, AS... "POISON IN PIGTAILS"!!!
SJG
ALONG THE ROAD LEADING INTO SLASH VALLEY...
HURRY UP WITH THAT GRUB SAL! I AIM T'BE DONE WITH THIS JOB B'FORE THE MOON COMES UP!
C'MON, PAW, IT'S GETTIN' LATE! THAT STAGE'S GONNA COME BY SOON!
MMM--GOOD!

Above: A pair of splash pages of Sam J. Glanzman's late '40s comics work in the Western genre. At left is *Western Outlaws* #18 [Nov. '48, Fox] and, at right, *Western Thrillers* #1 [Aug. '48, Fox]. Note Sam's ubiquitous "S.J.G." signature.

vast body of work Sam had done over the decades. Black-&-white comics publisher Avalon Communications, under its America's Comic Group imprint, was busily reprinting pages upon pages of Sam's Charlton Comics work from the 1960s, sans payment or fanfare, but those, too, fell beneath the notice of the mainstream comics readers and fans of the 1990s. All—and I do mean *all*—of Sam's primo earlier work was still relegated to those long white back-issue boxes in the imploding direct sales comic-book marketplace and private comic-book collections, where sorry saps like Scott Shaw!, Tim Truman, and yours truly were singing the praises of Sam's runs on *Kona: Monarch of Monster Isle, Combat,* and the historic *U.S.S. Stevens* back-up stories in DC's war comics. Only the first couple *Jonah Hex* Vertigo/DC miniseries were available in trade paperback format, and nothing else. Sam's excellent Marvel graphic novels, *A Sailor's Story* (1987) and *A Sailor's Story: Winds, Dreams, and Dragons,* were long out-of-print. Sam's brave experiments with working outside of mainstream comics publishing, specifically *Attu* (via Four Winds, an independent publishing house co-founded by Tim Truman) and his brand-new solo art collaboration with Lansdale on *Red Range* with Dripping Springs, Texas publisher, Mojo Press, were barely bubbles in the *X-Men, Batman*, and Image Comics dominated ocean of monthly comic books.

Who among those who ignored *Red Range* (or, if they cast it a sideways glance, disparaged) knew that Sam had in fact drawn Westerns way back in the early 1950s—and for *John Wayne Adventure Comics* (Toby Press, 1951), for God's sake? You can't get anymore hardcore American red-white-&-blue Western cartoonist pedigree than that, drawing for *John Wayne* and *Jonah Hex* in one lifetime!

Still, Sam wasn't box-office, baby.

Joe, on the other hand, had ten novels (plus the first half-dozen of his Hap and Leonard tomes), nine anthologies, and three novellas out there in the world, as well as his comics work with a variety of artists. Go ahead, look 'im up. Google "Joe R. Lansdale." Check the dates.

Who in hell do you think was the most popular kid on the block?

Be that as it may, Lansdale's rising star didn't propel hot sales for *Red Range*, either.

I was also in the rather unique position at the time of being both a cartoonist and a horror writer (fiction and non-fiction)—until the end of the 1990s, an active member of the Horror Writers of America, a.k.a. the Horror Writers Association—and I was the bozo who convinced the HWA (against stern opposition, initially) that the writer's organization should be recognizing graphic novels in their annual Bram Stoker Awards (and that didn't last long: "Illustrated Narrative" was a Stoker Award category from 1998 to 2004). Furthermore, I was in the even more singular position of being the upstart writer who shared a Stoker with Joe Lansdale—in the "Long Fiction" category for 1992, the official roster reads: "*Aliens: Tribes* by Stephen Bissette, Winner (Tie); *The Events Concerning a Nude Fold-Out Found*

Right: Pin-up of the star of Sam Glanzman's legendary '60s Dell comic book, *Kona, Monarch of Monster Isle*.

Kona TM & © the respective copyright holder.

DC
VERTIGO
JONAH HEX
RIDERS OF THE WORM AND SUCH
JOE R. LANSDALE
TIMOTHY TRUMAN
SAM GLANZMAN
DIRECT SALES

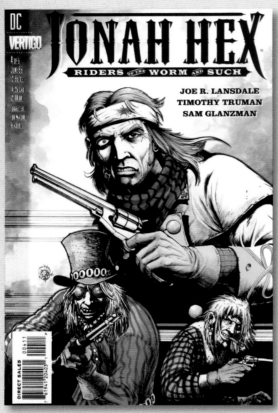

Above: Famed musician siblings Johnny and Edgar Winter took such offense to the "Autumn brothers" characters in the mini-series *Jonah Hex: Riders of the Worm and Such* [1995] that they sued DC Comics and the storytellers, Joe R. Lansdale, Tim Truman, and Sam Glanzman. The California Supreme Court finally ruled in favor of the writer and artists.

in a Harlequin Romance by Joe R. Lansdale, Winner (Tie)."

So there I was in 1999, buying up all the Mojo Press graphic novels I could find available (space doesn't permit me a proper overview of the imprint's fleeting but sterling publishing history here), stunned by how potent, punchy, and entertaining *Red Range* was, and dang it, I couldn't find a single friend who shared my enthusiasm for it.

"Ah, you're crazy, Bissette," one fellow comics creator pal told me, "Sam should retire if this is what he's sunk to," after only looking at the first three pages of *Red Range* and kicking it across the floor.

"Why is Joe wasting his talents on this shit?" one of my HWA buddies scowled, tossing my copy of *Red Range* across the room after glancing at the first five pages of the book, then flipping ahead and dead-stopping on the page with a dinosaur bloodily tearing into a horse. "You only like this 'cuz there's a dinosaur in it, Bissette!"

Not only couldn't I turn anyone onto the book, these fuckers were knockin' the shit out of my copy. It didn't take long for me to just shut the hell up and keep to myself about it.

Lotsa love for Joe, Tim, and Sam's *Jonah Hex* tall tales; not a salt-lick's worth of flavor for *Red Range.* It was tough times, pardners.

And not only was *Jonah Hex* getting the love, it was an honest-to-Christ cause célèbre, something to rally for and around. Speaking of the Strokers—uh, Stokers, Joe, Tim Truman, and Sam Glanzman's *Jonah Hex: Two-Gun Mojo,* by Joe R. Lansdale, was the award-winner in 1993's "Other Media" category, for what that's worth.

Of course, the other "award" Joe, Tim, and Sam shared with DC/Vertigo at the time was landing their asses in court when the rock-star Winter brothers, Johnny and Edgar, took offense at the cannibalistic albino "Autumn brothers" characters in *Jonah Hex: Riders of the Worm and Such*. The sibling musicians filed their suit in Los Angeles County Superior Court, on March 6, 1996, alleging "defamation, invasion of privacy and related claims on two characters, the Autumn brothers, created for the comic book series by Lansdale and Truman." Joe and Tim and Sam's asses were hangin' in the wind for a stretch—brother Tim even had to sell off some of his beloved guitars to cover legal costs at one point—until the Comic Book Legal Defense Fund joined their side in May 1996. According to the CBLDF's website:

I REALLY DON'T WANT TO SEE BIG WORM.
WE GOTTA.
EDGAR, PETE NOT SUPPOSED TO SHIT IN YOU POT, BUT COULD I ASK A FAVOR?
SURE.
YOU GOT TO STOP SHOOTIN' COUSINS, 'CAUSE WE RUN OUT OF 'EM YOU DON'T.
CAN'T WORMS MAKE MORE COUSINS?
DEY OR US GOT TO HAVE WOMEN. WE AIN'T GOT SOME, SO CAN'T MAKE COUSINS.
WE HAVE TO GET SOME WOMEN.
YEAH.
12

Above: The offending caricatures, Johnny and Edgar Autumn, as rendered by artists Tim Truman (pencils) and Sam Glanzman (inks), in *Jonah Hex: Riders of the Worm and Such.*

> Attorneys Gail Migdal Title and Jeffrey Abrams of the Los Angeles office of Katten Muchin Zavis & Weitzman took on the defense of Lansdale, Truman and Glanzman. Title said, "This suit seeks to invade the right of artists and writers to free creative expression, a right that is protected by the First Amendment, parody and other laws. I am happy to assist the CBLDF in its fine work in the support of comic book professionals throughout the country… According to artist and former defendant Tim Truman, "From the creative standpoint, *Jonah Hex: Riders of the Worm and Such* was intended from the beginning as a work of fiction and parody."

Joe Lansdale proclaimed, "It was our intent to use the *Jonah Hex* comic book series as a vehicle for satire and parody of musical genres, Texas music in particular, as well as old radio shows, movie serials, and the like. We feel within our rights to parody music, stage personas, album personas, lyrics, and public figures."

Only after the CBLDF's involvement did DC Comics rise to the occasion, mounting a winning defense "through its insurance company," until in 1998:

> ...[A]ll nine points of the case were thrown out of court in Los Angeles. Truman, in an e-mail to the CBLDF, called it "a victory not only for us, but for any cartoonist who comments upon, or pays tribute to, the legacy of any public figure."

No wonder that only one year later, Joe and Sam opened their next collaborative work, *Red Range,* with as graphic a lynching as any ever to see print in a comic book page.

That, like I said, was the small picture.

But where were all the readers? How could folks "get" that *Jonah Hex* was (ahem) "a work of fiction and parody," (thank ye, Brother Tim!), and that it was Joe's and Tim's and Sam's "intent to use the *Jonah Hex* comic

ACTION-PACKED PRAIRIE ADVENTURE!
MEN OF ACTION BLAZE A TRAIL OF LOVE AND LEAD AS LAW AND ORDER COMES TO THE OLD WEST!
HOLLYWOOD PRODUCTIONS PRESENTS
Herbert JEFFREY AND HIS HORSE "STARDUSK"
in
"Harlem rides the Range"
with SPENCER WILLIAMS - CLARENCE BROOKS
F. E. Miller - Artie Young - Lucius Brooks - Tom Southern - John Thomas
Wade Dumas - Leonard Christmas
THE FOUR TONES and an ALL-COLORED CAST
Story by SPENCER WILLIAMS and F. E. MILLER
A RICHARD C. KAHN PRODUCTION
Distributed by SACK AMUSEMENT ENTERPRISES

Above: A herald (brochure advertisement) spread promoting the 1939 "all-colored" movie Western, *Harlem Rides the Range*, starring Herb Jeffries as "The Happy Cowboy," and featuring an entirely African-American cast.

book series as a vehicle for satire and parody" (thank ye, Brother Joe!), and not "get" *Red Range* was cast and cut in the same savage mold?

It didn't take a long memory to recognize where *Red Range* was coming from. Black Westerns had blazed across movie screens since the 1920s—African-American cowboy Bill Pickett had starred in early "all-colored" Westerns like *The Crimson Skull* (1922) and *The Bull-Dogger* (1923), and those "musical genres, Texas music in particular, as well as old radio shows, movie serials and the like," Lansdale cited had their "all-colored" all-talkie singing-and-shooting incarnations in *Harlem on the Prairie* (1937), *Two-Gun Man from Harlem* (1938), *The Bronze Buckaroo* and *Harlem Rides the Range* (both 1939). Sassy

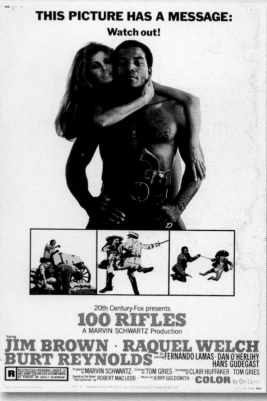

THIS PICTURE HAS A MESSAGE:
Watch out!

20th Century-Fox presents
100 RIFLES
A MARVIN SCHWARTZ Production
Starring
JIM BROWN · RAQUEL WELCH
BURT REYNOLDS also starring FERNANDO LAMAS · DAN O'HERLIHY
HANS GUDEGAST
Produced by MARVIN SCHWARTZ · Directed by TOM GRIES · Screenplay by CLAIR HUFFAKER · TOM GRIES
Based on the Novel "The Californio" by ROBERT MacLEOD · Music by JERRY GOLDSMITH · **COLOR** by De Luxe

Above: Provocative poster for the 1979 Western, *100 Rifles*, starring famed football star Jim Brown and sex symbol Raquel Welch. **Below inset:** Actor/athlete Woody Strode.

saxophonist and singer Louis Jordan (and the Tympany Five) saddled up for *Look-Out Sister* (1947) and *Come on, Cowboy* (1948) and starred comics Mantan Moreland and Johnny Lee (later best known to a generation as "Algonquin J. Calhoun" on the *Amos 'n Andy* TV series). Rarefied history, to be sure, except to fellow Texans like George Turner and Michael H. Price (co-founders and co-authors of the venerable *Forgotten Horrors* book series; Price also authored the only biography of Mantan Moreland, currently in print), but *Red Range* also echoed movies Sam had seen and Joe and I grew up seeing on TV, in nabes, and at drive-ins. John Ford had cast stoic Woody Strode as *Sergeant Rutledge* (1960), and you can't get any more "classical American Western" than John Ford, bunky, or for that matter than Woody Strode, who also rode tall in *The Professionals* (1966), Sergio Leone's *Once Upon A Time In The West* (1968), *Boot Hill* (1969), and joined Muhammad Ali in the documentary *Black Rodeo*

100 Rifles TM & © 20th Century Fox

Django Unchained © The Weinstein Company.

Above: Jamie Foxx plays the titular character, a freed slave turned bounty hunter, in Quentin Tarantino's 2012 hit Western, the outrageously violent — and viscerally entertaining — *Django Unchained*.

(1972). Former football star Jim Brown rode tall and busted cultural taboos via his love scene with Raquel Welch in *100 Rifles* (1969), even as spaghetti Westerns like *Lola Colt* (1967) fed a new breed of Black American Westerns by the 1970s: Bill Cosby's *Man and Boy* (1971), Sydney Poitier's *Buck and the Preacher* (1972, with a scene-stealing performance by Harry Belafonte as the titular "preacher"), and the like.

For those taking instant offense to the "N-word" on page one of *Red Range*, remember that there was a time not so long ago when that loaded word burned on movie theater marquees in two violent, angry Fred Williamson box office hit Black Westerns, *The Legend of Nigger Charley* (1972) and *The Soul of Nigger Charley* (1973), from none other than Paramount Pictures (Gulf+Western, folks). That opened up red ranges a-plenty: *Soul Soldier* (1970), *Thomasine & Bushrod* (1974), *Take a Hard Ride* (1975), *Boss Nigger* (Fred Williamson again, 1975), *Joshua* (ditto, 1976), and so on. It was such a popular explosion that people forget the top box office Western of all time, Mel Brooks' *Blazing Saddles* (1974), was both a goof on and vital entry in the cycle with Cleavon Little's Black Bart making a mockery of die-hard American racism—and the brothers Fred Williamson and Richard Pryor (who Brooks had wanted to cast as Bart) responded with their own spin, *Adiós Amigo* (1976). Tarantino's *Django Unchained*

and Denzel Washington's star turn in the 2016 remake of *The Magnificent Seven* are just the latest permutations of what is now an obvious tradition, punctuated with Mario Van Peeble's *Posse* (1993) and *Los Locos* (1997) twixt then and now.

So, what's the problem with *Red Range*? I reckon back in '99, most folks who even bothered to take a peek were all down but nine. Look, just watch *Blazing Saddles* one more time; if you're made of stronger stuff, read a parcel of Joe's Westerns. Then dive into *Red Range*.

Take it as you will—a commentary on 2017 Amerika, or just Joe and Sam's eccentric tall tale, or a vicious but loving satire of *Harlem Rides the Range* adventures, or an extension of the 1970s Black Western explosion, whatever—*Red Range* is an Arkansas Toothpick of a read. These two will take you on one hell of a ride, and Joe and Sam are just the two saddle tramps for the job.

And if you're going to kick anyone's copy across the room in spite, kick your own Goddamned copy. Me, I stand with Joe and Sam; vindicated, at long last!

> —*Stephen R. Bissette*
> Mountains of Madness, Vermont
> The tail-end of winter 2017

Stephen R. Bissette, a pioneer graduate of the Joe Kubert School, teaches at the Center for Cartoon Studies. Renowned for Swamp Thing, Taboo *(launching* From Hell *and* Lost Girls*), 1963, S.R. Bissette's* Tyrant®*, co-creating John Constantine, and creating the world's second '24-Hour Comic' (invented by Scott McCloud for Bissette), he writes, illustrates, and co-authors many books, include illustrating* The Vermont Monster Guide *(2009), writing* Teen Angels & New Mutants *(2011, '16) and fiction for* The New Dead *(2010),* Mister October *(2013), etc. Bissette regularly writes for* Monster! *and* Weng's Chop*, and is currently completing a Midnight Movies Monograph on David Cronenberg's* The Brood*, and the first volume of S.R. Bissette's* How to Make a Monster.

The following story, "I Could Eat a Horse," was written and drawn by Sam J. Glanzman for editor Richard Klaw, and it originally appeared in the Mojo Press trade paperback collection, *Wild West Show* (1996).

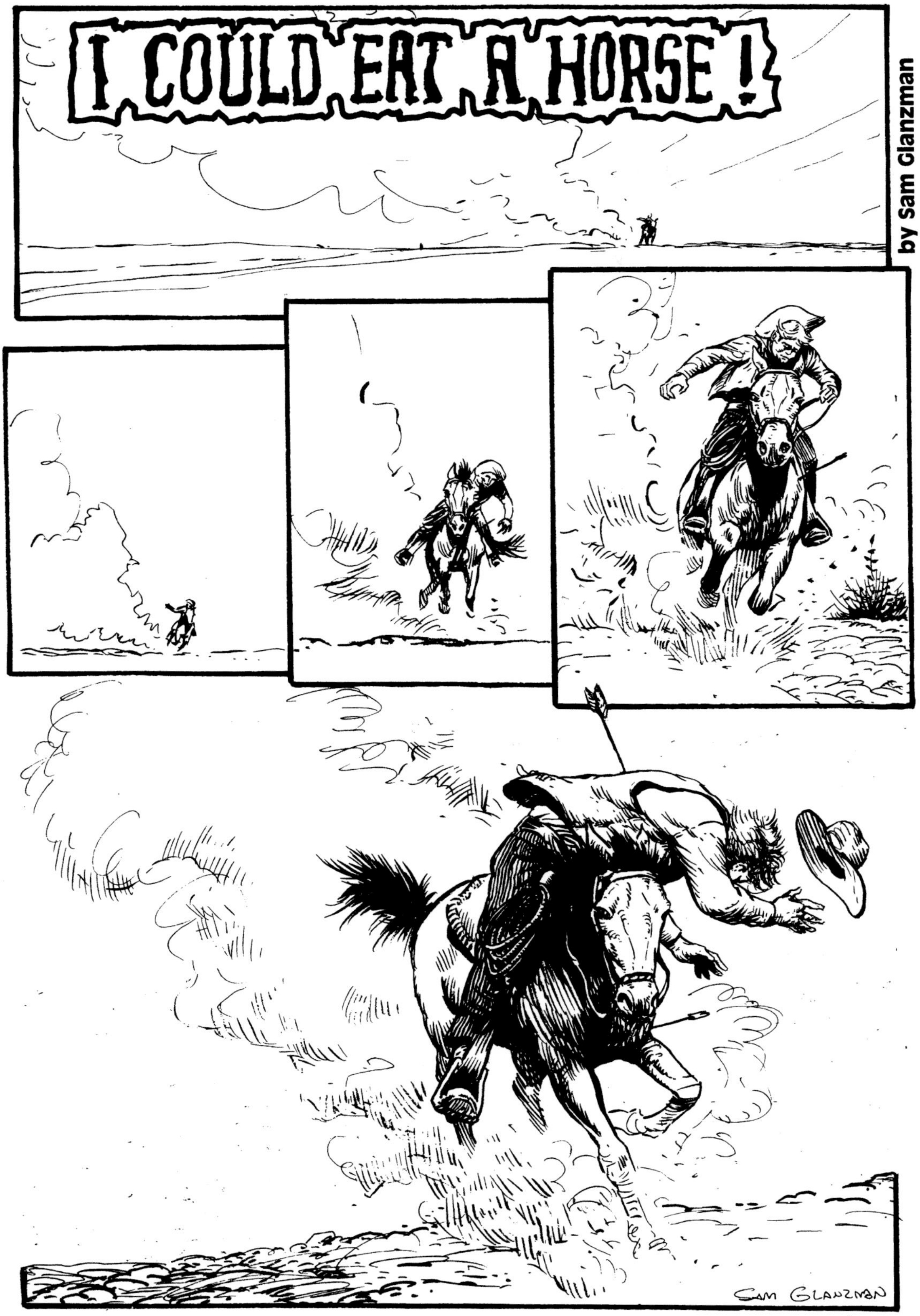
I COULD EAT A HORSE!
SAM GLANZMAN

by Sam Glanzman

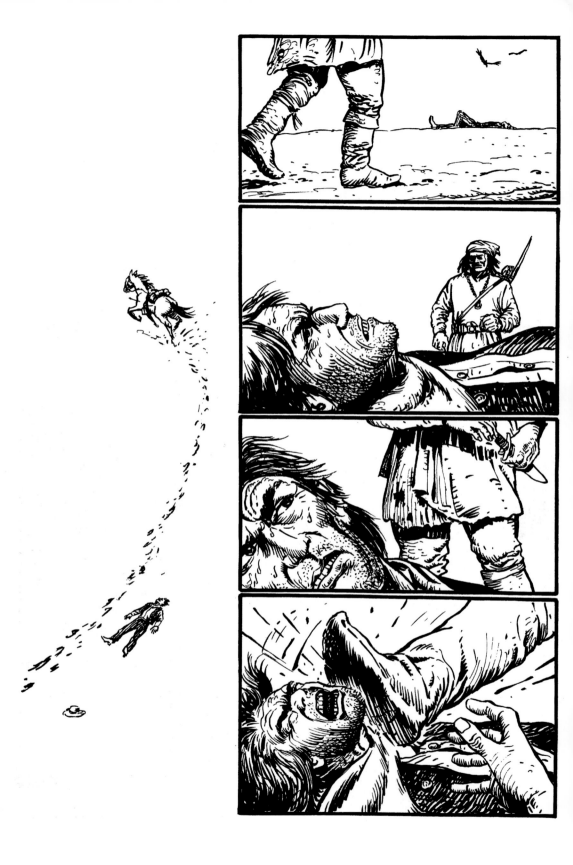

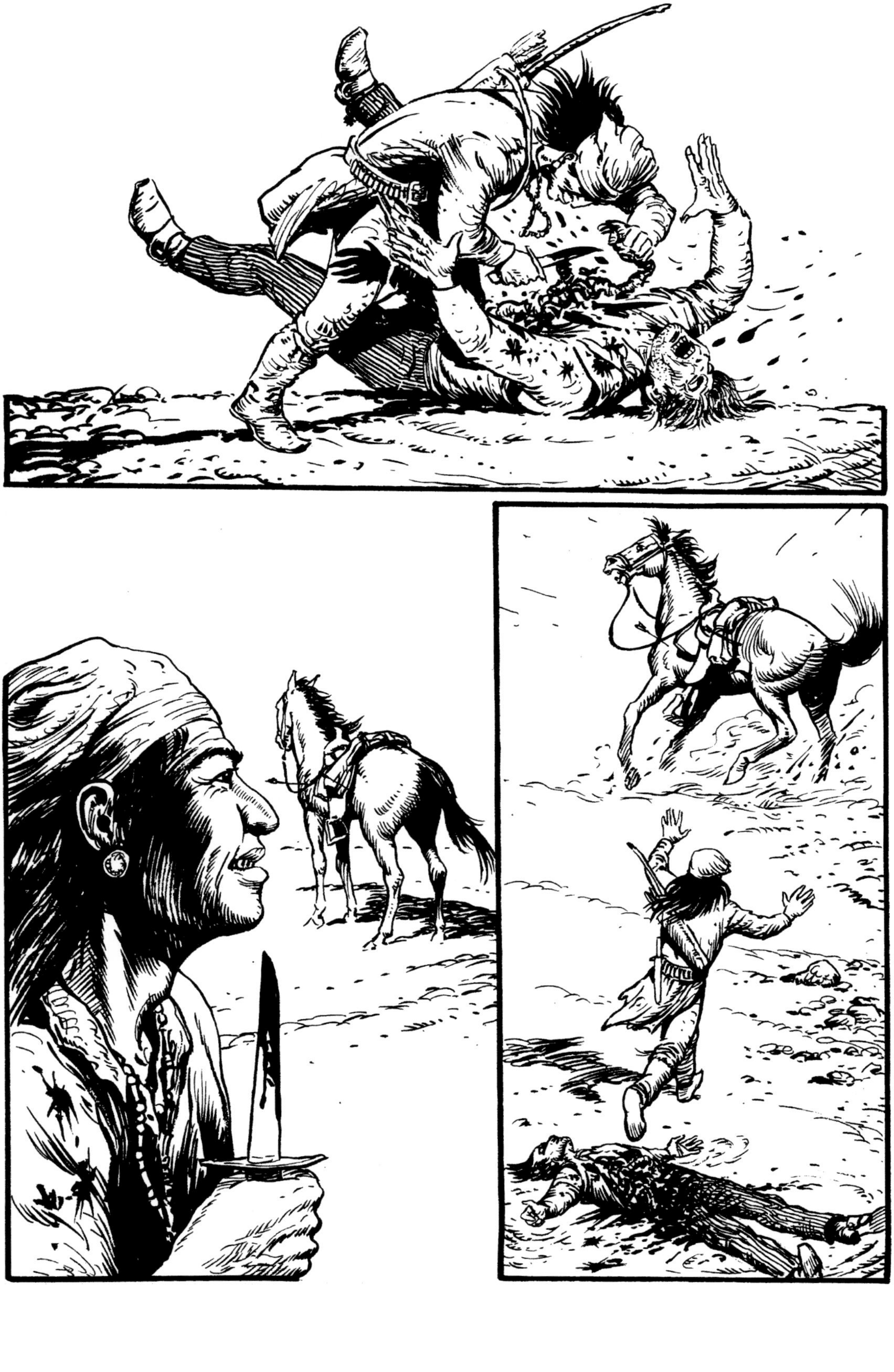

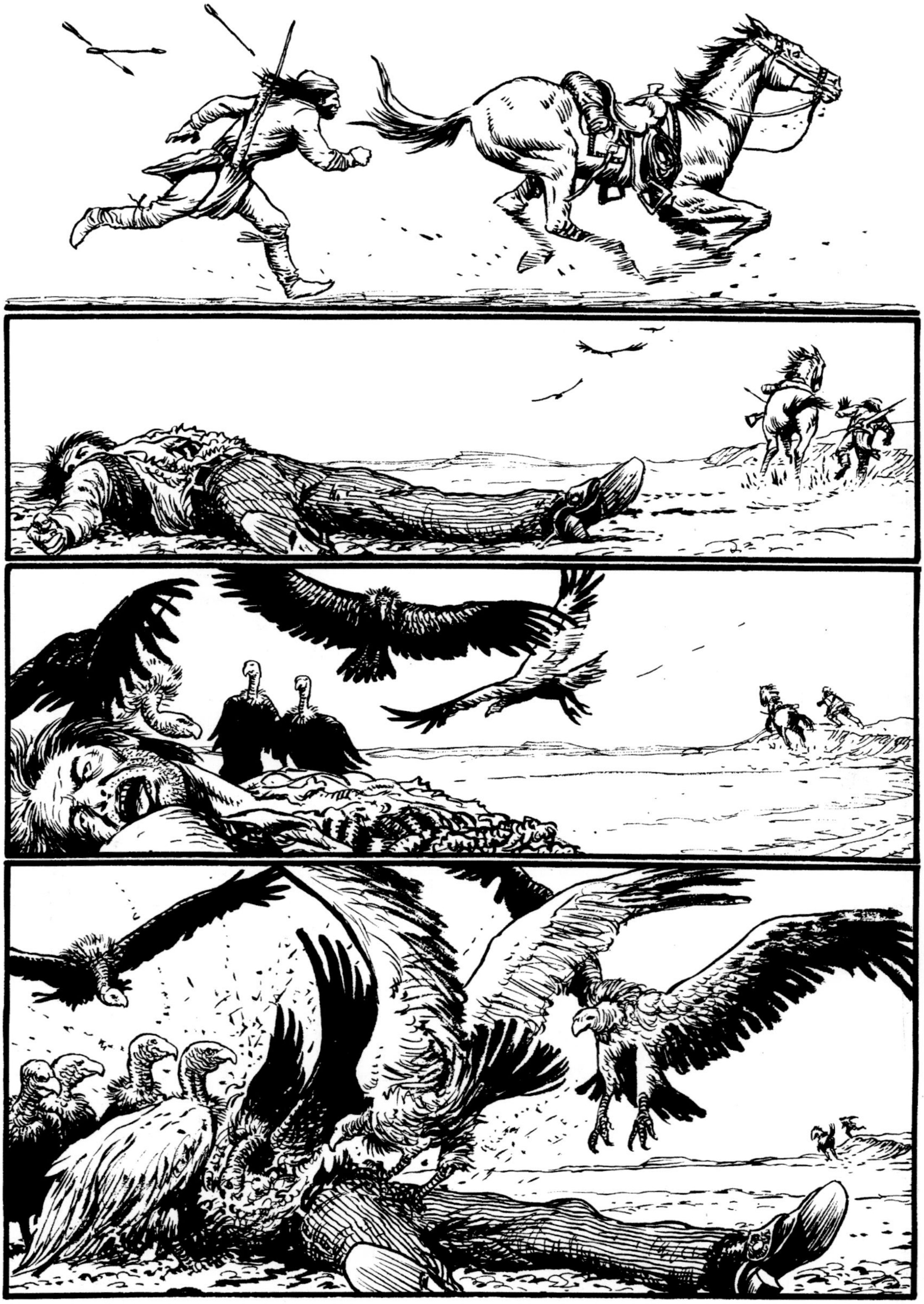

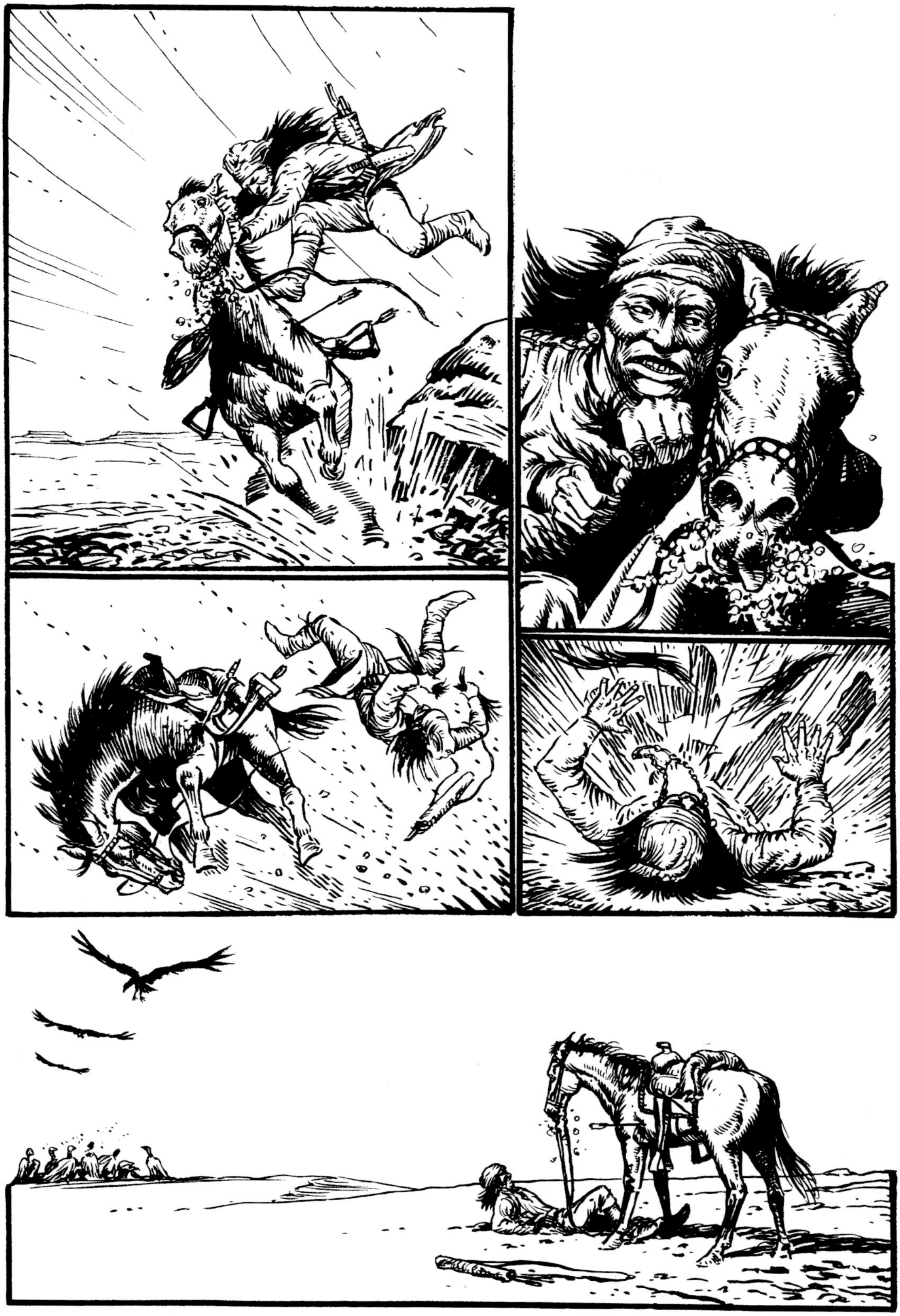

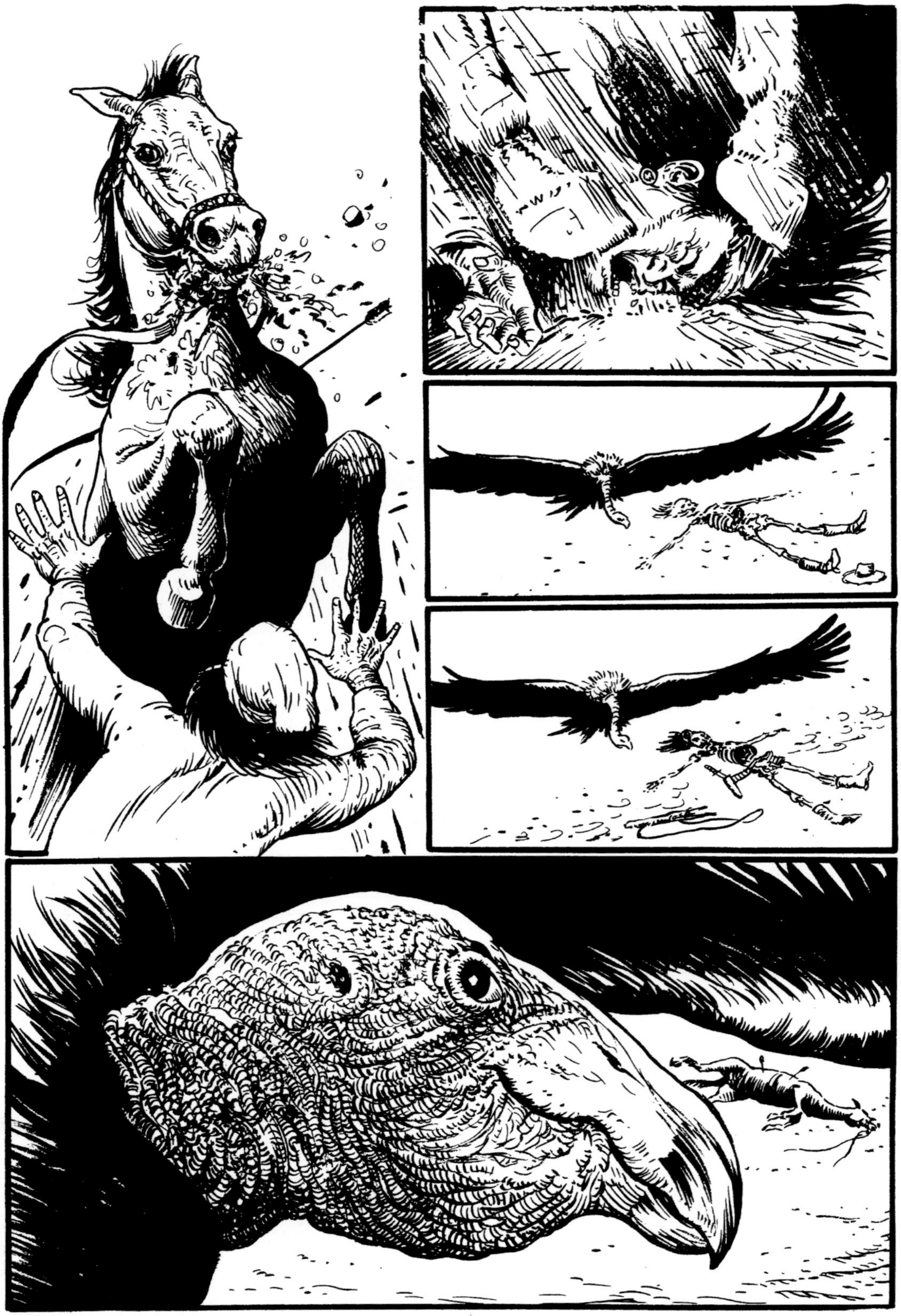

A BRIEF HISTORY OF COWBOYS & DINOSAURS

Pop Culture Cowpokes & Carnosaurs by Stephen R. Bissette

Technically, the whole dinosaurs-in-the-American-Wild-West in literature dates back to the actual Wild West era, or damned near. The nascent science of paleontology and public fascination with fossils and prehistoric life rose as the "Western era" was eclipsed, and fiction authors capitalized on the un- likely crossover potential. Before science-fiction was a defined genre (much less a marketable commodity, which emerged in the pulp era of the 1920s and Hugo Gernsback's pioneer pulp, *Amazing Stories*), story magazines featured the occasional tale of cowboys, militia men, or prospectors facing still-living primordial creatures, though it was most often sailors and castaways who discovered such things far, far from the American West. The wildest and wooliest of these early Western/paleontology tales, to my mind, remains Wardon Allan Curtis's "The Monster of Lake Metrie" (*Pearson's Magazine*, September 1899), set in the remote titular mountain lake in Wyoming, where primordial lifeforms still live, including an Elasmosaurus. In a twist no later Western dino tale ever dared, the story's explorer/scientist transplants the brain of his sickly, dying teenage sidekick

into the plesiosaur's skull! One slice of great northern Yukon territory fiction—well, I'm convinced it's fiction, having tracked down the original English-language publication of the Georges Dupuy story, "The Monster of 'Partridge Creek,'" in *The Strand Magazine* (November 1908, Vol. 36, #214, pp. 383– 389)—has become enshrined as the real thing by certain cryptozoology circles, known as the Partridge Creek Beast or the Partridge Creek Monster.

Right: Illustration from *The Strand Magazine*'s "Stories Strange and True" entry for Nov. 1908, Georges Dupuy's "The Monster of 'Partridge Creek,'" which included the caption, "The beast held in his jaws some- thing which seemed to me to be a caribou." Artist unknown.

Above: Stop-motion animator Willis O'Brien first conceived of a "cowboys vs. dinosaurs" film in the 1940s, though it would take almost three decades and the efforts of protégé Ray Harryhausen to produce *The Valley of Gwangi* (1969). This concept drawing by O'Brien was included in the original pitch for *Gwangi or Valley Where Time Stood Still* (1941).

Cowboys and dinosaurs also tangled in the comic strips at times, in back-up stories in various Golden Age Western comic books (*Tex Taylor #7*, 1949; etc.), and in movies, made and unmade. *King Kong*'s special effects creator Willis O'Brien labored long and hard to bring his pet project *Gwangi* to the screen, in which cowboys wrangled dinosaurs; though preproduction materials have survived, including photos of stop-motion animation model maquettes of the titular Allosaurus Gwangi, *Gwangi* was scuttled. O'Brien's storyboarded sequence, in which cowboys struggled to rope and capture Gwangi, was adapted (and transported to Africa) for the opening stop-motion cowboys-vs.-giant-gorilla Joe Young sequence in *Mighty Joe Young* (1949). A young up-and-coming animator named Ray Harryhausen worked under mentor Willis O'Brien on the Oscar-winning effects for *Mighty Joe Young*, and, two decades later, he resurrected *Gwangi*—sadly after O'Brien's death—to make the 1969 *The Valley of Gwangi*, complete with O'Brien's meticulously planned cowboys-vs-Allosaurus show-stopper. Between the unproduced *Gwangi* and Warner Brothers' release of *The Valley of Gwangi*, O'Brien's proposal for another cowboys-vs-dinosaurs film project was purchased and produced (sans O'Brien's involvement) as the full-color widescreen *The Beast of Hollow Mountain* (1956), combining O'Brien's method of stop-motion animation with producer Edward Nassour's unique "replacement animation" technique (adapted from George Pal's Puppetoons, Nassour and his team created fully sculpted individual Allosaurus models in different stages of movement, replacing one another frame-by-frame to create the illusion of smooth motion). For most Americans, *The Beast of Hollow Mountain* was likely their initial exposure to cowboys and dinosaurs tangling in the same milieu.

Betwixt the official end of the fan-defined Golden Age and rise of the late 1950s' Silver Age, dinosaurs would pop up in the West in comics like *Ken Maynard Western* (see #7, 1951), *Straight Arrow* (see Bob Powell's "The Canyon Beast," #39, October 1954), and others. Joe Simon and Jack Kirby had their Western hero Bulls Eye and companion Yellow Snake facing off with a lively living pterosaur in the story, "Devil Bird!" (*Bulls Eye* #3, December 1954). Western Publishing/Dell Comics introduced Turok, Son of Stone, in 1955 (launching his own title in May 1956), the ultimate pre-Colonial First Nation "lost valley" comic of 'em all. After *Turok*, Western-set dinosaur stories proliferated in comic books. Even National Periodicals/DC Comics' Western-like "Eastern," *Tomahawk*, peppered its pages with living fossils, starting with the cover-featured "The Frontier Dinosaur!" in #58 (September 1958). *Tomahawk* devoted eight covers to the carnivores over its 140 issues.

BULLSEYE in
DEVIL BIRD
IN THE VALLEY OF LOST TRAILS...IN THE HOT COUNTRY OF THE BLOWING GEYSERS, THE FAMOUS SCOUT, BULLSEYE, TRACKS DOWN A TERRIFYING AND UNBELIEVABLE CREATURE...
RED HAWK
NOTHING CAN KILL IT! AND IF I DON'T STOP IT, IT WILL SLAY ALL MY PEOPLE!
IT CAME OUT OF THE DIM DAYS OF EARTH'S YOUTH, IN THE EON-DISTANT DAWN WORLD, MONSTROUS AND TERRIFYING! NO LANCE OR ARROW COULD PIERCE ITS PLATE-ARMOR HIDE, NO WARCLUB COULD DO MORE THAN BOUNCE OFF ITS TOUGH SKIN. THERE SEEMS TO BE NO HOPE AT ALL FOR RED HAWK AND HIS CHEYENNE PEOPLE AS THEY ARE RUTHLESSLY HUNTED DOWN BY—
THE CANYON BEAST
POWELL
THE ELECTRICAL STORM THAT BREAKS ACROSS THE HUNTING LANDS OF THE CHEYENNE IS ELEMENTAL AND DESTRUCTIVE. THUNDER ROLLS WITH THE SOUND OF WARDRUMS AS LIGHTNING RIPS THE SKY. AND ONE JAGGED BOLT CATCHES A RIM OF ANCIENT LAVA ROCK...
SOMETHING WHITE AND OVAL ROLLS FROM THE CRACKED CAVERN THAT HAS SEALED IT HERMETICALLY FOR OVER A MILLION YEARS. THE WARM RAINS WASH IT DOWN...
HAS THE WESTERN HERO AT LAST MET HIS WATERLOO?
HE CAN SWALLOW ME IN ONE GULP!
BUT SORRY, PARD! I DON'T AIM TO FURNISH YOU VITTLES! I HAD TO TIME THIS RIGHT! WHILE YOU CHOMP, I JUMP!
SNAP!

This page: As mentioned by the writer, in American comic books, dinosaurs tangled with cowboys and Native Americans during the days of the Old West, including (clockwise from upper left) Joe Simon and Jack Kirby's *Bulls Eye* #3 [Dec. '54–Jan. '55], artist Bob Powell's Red Hawk story in *Straight Arrow* #39 [Nov.–Dec. '54], and *Ken Maynard Western* #7 [Dec. '51], by unknown artist and writer.

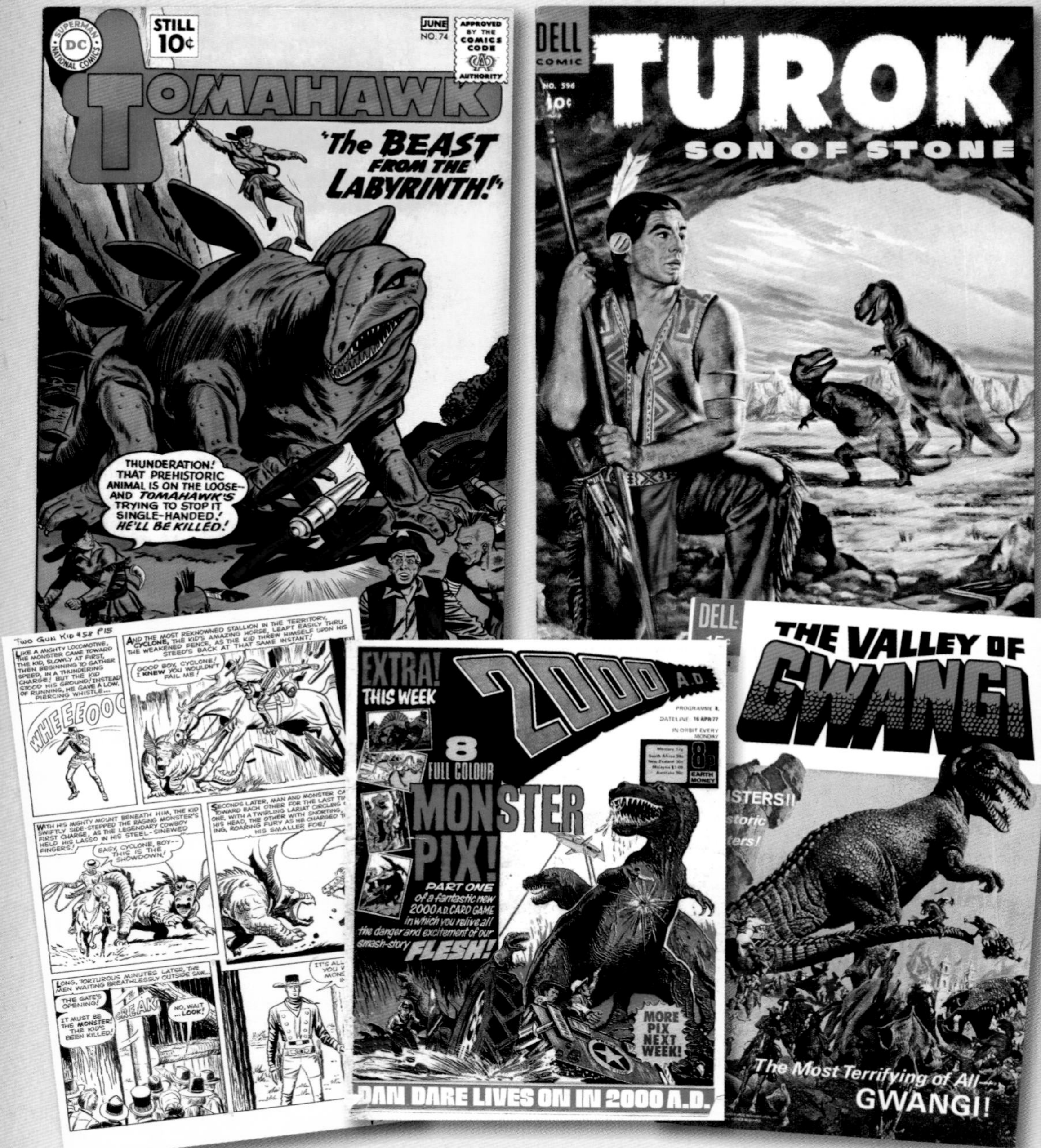

STILL 10¢
SUPERMAN DC NATIONAL COMICS
JUNE NO. 74
APPROVED BY THE COMICS CODE AUTHORITY
TOMAHAWK
'The BEAST FROM THE LABYRINTH!'
THUNDERATION! THAT PREHISTORIC ANIMAL IS ON THE LOOSE-- AND TOMAHAWK'S TRYING TO STOP IT SINGLE-HANDED! HE'LL BE KILLED!
DELL COMIC
NO. 596
10¢
TUROK
SON OF STONE
TWO GUN KID #58 P15
WHEEEOOO
GOOD BOY, CYCLONE! I KNEW YOU WOULDN'T FAIL ME!
EASY, CYCLONE, BOY-- THIS IS THE SHOWDOWN!
CREAK
EXTRA! THIS WEEK
2000 A.D.
8 FULL COLOUR MONSTER PIX!
PART ONE of a fantastic new 2000 A.D. CARD GAME in which you relive all the danger and excitement of our smash-story FLESH!
MORE PIX NEXT WEEK!
DAN DARE LIVES ON IN 2000 A.D.
DELL
THE VALLEY OF GWANGI
The Most Terrifying of All— GWANGI!

This page: A batch of dinosaur comics with Western themes (or is it vice versa?). From top left clockwise, one of eight or so *Tomahawk* covers devoted to the prehistoric monsters, this being #74 [May–June '61], with pencils by Dick Dillin and inks by Sheldon Moldoff; the first appearance of Turok, Son of Stone, in Dell Comics' *Four Color* #596 [Dec. '54], with cover painting by Robert C. Susor; *The Valley of Gwangi* movie was adapted as a Dell one-shot in Dec. 1969, with a cover painting by Frank McCarthy; the British comics weekly *2000 AD* boasted a quasi-Western science-fiction serial replete with dinosaurs bred to be food, in "Flesh," which debuted in the first issue, in 1977, and is still a recurring series in the title (this Joan Boix cover is from #8 [Apr. 16, '77]); and even "giant Atlas creature" practitioners Stan Lee (writer), Jack Kirby (penciler), and Dick Ayers (inker) joined in the cowboy/monster mash-up as seen in this page repro'd from original art, from *Two-Gun Kid* #58 [Feb. '61].

ABOUT THE AUTHORS

Joe R. Lansdale

For East Texas homeboy Joe Richard Lansdale, it all started with Tarzan, a passion for the character and writings of the Ape Man's creator, Edgar Rice Burroughs, which would result in a remarkably versatile career as a writer in an astonishingly wide array of genres in various mediums. Joe began his career in the early '70s, writing a book with his mom about farming, and he soon turned to fiction. "By 1986," Joe told an interviewer, "I was doing my stuff, and it just kept rolling."

That stuff rolled into forty-plus novels, thirty short story collections, scripts for *Batman* cartoons, editing over a dozen short story anthologies, his own TV and film projects, and, at last count, around 75 comic book stories. Joe's long-running Hap and Leonard crime series is currently a television show; his horror-comedy novella "Bubba Ho-Tep" was adapted into a 2002 movie starring Bruce Campbell as Elvis Presley (an instant cult fave); and Joe's novel, *Cold in July*, was made into a 2014 motion picture, a Sundance Grand Jury Prize nominee. His work is deeply ironic, hilariously funny, violent, and ofttimes gruesome as all get out.

In the early '90s, the author first teamed with his *Red Range* collaborator, artist Sam J. Glanzman, in a creative threesome that included penciler Tim Truman, producing a trilogy of *Jonah Hex* graphic novels (originally released as respective mini-series). Hex, appropriately the longtime headliner of *Weird Western Tales*, with its mash-up of Old West gunplay and overtones of the macabre, proved a perfect vehicle for Joe's taste for the weird, by then well-expressed in his "Zombie Western" novel, *Dead in the West* (1986).

Joe, much appreciated for his horror work, is the recipient of ten Bram Stoker Awards, the British Fantasy Award, the Edgar Award, the Grinzani Cavour Prize for Literature, the Herodotus Historical Fiction Award, and an Inkpot Award from Comic-Con International, as well as many other honors (including a Lifetime Achievement Award from his peers at the Horror Writers Association). Today, the scribe is "Writer in Residence" at Stephen F. Austin State University and, as legend would have it, he resides in "Texas' oldest town," Nacogdoches, with his wife, dog, and two cats.

Sam J. Glanzman

Samuel Joseph Glanzman has a career in comics stretching back to the field's Golden Age, when he both wrote and drew "The Fly-Man," in 1941, for Harvey Comics. Born of a talented brood that included renowned magazine illustrator and painter Louis Glanzman, SJG's most formative life experience took place aboard the Navy destroyer *U.S.S. Stevens*. His participation as a seaman in the Pacific Theater during World War II would, decades later, be poignantly recounted in the highly regarded graphic memoirs, *A Sailor's Story* and its *Winds, Dreams, and Dragons* sequel, as well as some 60 vignettes written and drawn for the "Big Two" comics publishers, DC and Marvel.

Prior to his *U.S.S. Stevens* material, Sam was recognized for a number of other comic book features, including the anti-war series, "The Lonely War of Willy Schultz," and the title *Hercules* (both for Charlton), as well as the fondly-recalled *Kona, Monarch of Monster Isle* and the non-fiction series, *Combat* (both for Dell). Also well remembered is his work on Charlton's *Jungle Tales of Tarzan* (an unauthorized series cut short after only four issues upon the threat of litigation). In the '70s and '80s, SJG provided over 2,600 pages of art for an astonishing 225 episodes of "The Haunted Tank" for DC.

While many of his fellow Golden Age comics veterans were winding down and settling into retirement, Sam remained tenaciously active in the comics industry, creating consistently excellent art, often imbued with tremendously effective storytelling. With the support of artist and sometime publisher Tim Truman, SJG produced a pair of graphic novels starring his prehistoric hero, Attu, and teamed with Truman and writer Joe R. Lansdale for a trio of *Jonah Hex* mini-series (that got the crew in some legal hot water for a spell — see Steve Bissette's "(A Sort of) Afterword" herein).

In 1999, Sam received the Inkpot Award for lifetime achievement in the comics field, from San Diego's Comic-Con International. Today, the 92-year-old raconteur resides with his beloved wife, Sue, in the wooded splendor of upstate New York, and the artist, long neglected by the comics world in general, is finally receiving long overdue accolades, particularly in light of the recent reprinting of his *U.S.S. Stevens* material and *Attu* books. No less than the 41st and 44th Presidents of the United States shared their appreciation of Sam in letters published in *U.S.S. Stevens: The Collected Stories* (2016).